Eugenia and Adelaide, A Novel

Frances Sheridan's *Eugenia and Adelaide* is an astonishing first novel of parental tyranny, infidelity, kidnap, blackmail, and violence played out over two volumes against the backdrop of continental Europe. The friendship of Eugenia and Adelaide endures in spite of their separation at the beginning of the novel and remains central to a complex yet coherently drawn web of intriguing tales situated in palatial apartments and remote moss-covered castles. Drawing upon the tragic and comic possibilities of disguise familiar to her from Shakespearean and Restoration drama, and influenced by the romantic entanglements of early prose fiction, Sheridan adopts a sometimes satirical approach to extraordinary events at the same time that she demonstrates a sincere and convincing commitment to the ingenious art of storytelling. Sheridan completed the novel in 1739 when she was just fifteen years old, and *Eugenia and Adelaide* would prove instrumental to the establishing of Sheridan's literary reputation as one of the most successful novelists and dramatists of the mid-eighteenth century. This is the first modern edition of *Eugenia and Adelaide* to be published since the original posthumous publication of 1791 and presents a unique opportunity to explore Sheridan's contribution to our current understandings of the history of women's writing, and of reading tastes and practices in the long eighteenth century.

Anna M. Fitzer, BA (Hons), PhD (Wales), FHEA, is Senior Lecturer in Eighteenth-Century Literature at the University of Hull. She completed her doctorate on eighteenth-century sentimental fiction and the female rake at the University of Wales, and is Fellow of the Higher Education Academy. She has published widely on the work of the Sheridan family, and is editor of the four-volume *Memoirs of Women Writers, Part I* (2012), and of *Strathallan* (2008), the first novel written by Frances Sheridan's granddaughter, Alicia LeFanu. Her co-edited collection, *Editing Women's Writing 1670–1840*, was published by Routledge in 2018.

The Early Modern Englishwoman, 1500–1750: Contemporary Editions

Series Editors: Betty S. Travitsky and Anne Lake Prescott

Designed to complement The Early Modern Englishwoman: A Facsimile Library of Essential Works, Contemporary Editions presents both modernized and old-spelling editions of texts not only by women but also for and about women. Contents of a volume can range from a single text to an anthology depending on the subject and the audience. Introductions to the editions are written with the general reader as well as the specialist in mind. They are designed to provide an introduction not only to the edited text itself but also to the larger historical discourses expressed through the text.

Two Early Modern Marriage Sermons
Henry Smith's *A Preparative to Marriage* (1591) and William Whately's *A Bride-Bush* (1623)
Edited by Robert Matz

The Experience of Domestic Service for Women in Early Modern London
Edited by Paula Humfrey

The Correspondence (c. 1626–1659) of Dorothy Percy Sidney, Countess of Leicester
Edited by Michael G. Brennan, Noel J. Kinnamon and Margaret P. Hannay

Eugenia and Adelaide, A Novel
Frances Sheridan
Edited by Anna M. Fitzer

For more information about this series, please visit: www.routledge.com/The-Early-Modern-Englishwoman-1500-1750-Contemporary-Editions/book-series/ASHSER2055

Eugenia and Adelaide, A Novel

Frances Sheridan

Edited by Anna M. Fitzer

NEW YORK AND LONDON

First published 2019
by Routledge
605 Third Avenue, New York, NY 10017

and by Routledge
2 Park Square, Milton Park, Abingdon, Oxon, OX14 4RN

First issued in paperback 2021

Routledge is an imprint of the Taylor & Francis Group, an informa business

Publisher's Note
The publisher has gone to great lengths to ensure the quality of this reprint but points out that some imperfections in the original copies may be apparent.

Library of Congress Cataloging-in-Publication Data
A catalog record for this book has been requested

ISBN 13: 978-1-03-209223-2 (pbk)
ISBN 13: 978-0-367-15017-4 (hbk)

Typeset in Bembo
by Apex CoVantage, LLC

For Mary and Alan Fitzer
and
In memory of Joshua Andrew Brown
1989–2019

Contents

Acknowledgements

I am grateful to the British Library for the reproduction of its copy of *Eugenia and Adelaide*, and to staff at the following for their help with access to Frances Sheridan's correspondence: King's College Library, Cambridge, the Houghton Library, Harvard University, the Morgan Library & Museum, the Historical Society of Pennsylvania, the Beinecke Rare Book and Manuscript Library, Yale, and the Department of Rare Books and Special Collections, Princeton University Library. As always, the greatest debt is to my family for their continuing support.

Editor's Introduction

I

In the early 1760s Richard Chamberlaine, a former naval surgeon later described as 'a neat little man, of some wit and literary acquirements,' received a letter directed to him at the Grecian Coffee House, Devereux Court, London.[1] In it, his anonymous correspondent encourages him in the belief that, yes, he is 'really mad; not a little, but very mad,' and playfully berates him for the 'Flights and Vagaries' of his own last letter, in which he soars 'too high for me!' and is too 'Sublime for my Earthly capacity!' Chamberlaine's suspicion that he has been previously teased by his correspondent's deliberately disguised handwriting is addressed in this reply: 'I write no particular hand, my Character varies with my Pen.'[2] Such easy familiarity and self-deprecating wit is a trait of Chamberlaine's younger sister, Frances Sheridan (as she was then known), to whom the letter has been attributed, and whose literary celebrity as author of *Memoirs of Miss Sidney Bidulph* (1761) was at that point taking flight. It is owing to the success of *Sidney Bidulph* that some accounts of Sheridan have tended to emphasise her literary credentials within the traditions of the era demarcated 'after Richardson,' a reference to the influence Samuel Richardson's *Pamela* (1740), *Clarissa* (1747/8), and *Sir Charles Grandison* (1753/4) variously exerted on women's writing in particular in the second half of the eighteenth century. However, Sheridan was as 'ingenious' as she was 'unassuming,' as James Boswell put it, and the variety of handwriting styles occasioned by any number of unruly quills also serves as a reminder of her remarkable versatility as a novelist and comic dramatist.[3] The origins of this can be traced to *Eugenia and Adelaide*, a novel completed by the young Frances Chamberlaine in the 1730s and published in the same year as Bowell's *Life of Johnson* in 1791. Part romance, part intrigue, part comic satire, *Eugenia and Adelaide* redraws the chronological scope of its author's contribution to eighteenth-century writing and further inscribes the inventive character of her pen.

Frances Chamberlaine was born in Dublin in 1724, the youngest child of Anastasia and Philip Chamberlaine, whose father, Walter, had settled in Dublin some fifty years earlier upon being appointed Procurator of the Ecclesiastical

Courts. Walter Chamberlaine was a fourth-generation descendant of the Chamberlaines of Kingsclere, who were mentioned in the earliest registers to be created in the Hampshire diocese of Winchester in 1538 and possibly connected to the noble family established after the conquest by John, Comte de Tancarville of Tancarville Castle, Normandy, and later chamberlain to King Henry I.[4] Of her four siblings, Frances's brother Richard Chamberlaine was in his eleventh year when she arrived, and their eldest brother, Walter, was a young man of eighteen and Trinity scholar. He settled with difficulty into clerical life and remained aware of the capricious authority to which his father subjected his youngest sister. Though Philip Chamberlaine had begun his career at Trinity with less opportunities than he was able to afford his son, he had been made prebendary of Rathmichael in 1713. Shortly after Jonathan Swift replaced Laurence Sterne as Dean of St Patrick's, Chamberlaine was appointed Rector of St Nicholas Without, a church which formed part of the north transept of the cathedral and, in 1718, Archdeacon of Glendalough. Philip Chamberlaine was approaching fifty when Frances was born and had a distinguished reputation among the number of Church of Ireland clerics regularly preaching from the pulpits on the importance of piety and morality. The city landscape had significantly altered in the first decades of the eighteenth century with the construction and restoration of church buildings making visible a religious infrastructure working with a civilising movement.[5] This was supportive of the establishment of charitable schools and, as exemplified in such as *The Excellent Daughter, or Rules and Directions for Charity Girls*, an inclusive education for the Protestant poor. The instruction of the respectable daughters of Ireland, however, generally continued to be a private affair, conducted at home and, in the case of Frances Chamberlaine, with caution.

Philip Chamberlaine ruled out his daughter's learning to write, principally on account of his suspicion that it led only to the exchange of frivolous letters with other young women. Female correspondence excited the passions and inevitably occasioned an overly reciprocal and dangerous indulgence in sentiment. His son Walter disagreed. Extending Frances's reading to Latin, he set about a plan of education designed to sharpen her pen and, with the help of their brother Richard, develop her understanding of the natural sciences. This scene is set in Alicia LeFanu's *Memoirs of the Life and Writings of Mrs Frances Sheridan* (1824), which also describes how Frances was inspired to pass on the benefits of her tuition to a young parishioner whom she taught to recite and, in spite of her brothers' amused misgivings, eventually display his understanding of the Creed and the Lord's Prayer. However, as Frances approached adolescence, the Chamberlaine household was gradually emptied of ready witnesses to her precocity. Her brother William was admitted to Lincoln's Inn in 1738, and her sister Ann was increasingly preoccupied with her marriage to the Rev. John Fish, later chaplain of Dublin's Bluecoat hospital and free school. Philip Chamberlaine's surveillance abated with the early signs of mental instability and, although this left Walter and Richard at liberty to escort their prodigy to the theatre, it also meant that Frances had more time at her disposal for solitary reading.

Fictional portraits of literate girls left home alone suggest that the volumes of books which make for her library are the legacy of absent mothers. In Charlotte Lennox's *The Female Quixote* (1752), Arabella is taught to read and write by her father but is unsupervised in her appetite for the store of lengthy French heroic romances in translation which had softened the disagreeable solitude of her late mother. Alicia LeFanu's first novel, *Strathallan* (1816), magnifies the female quixote's misreading of Madeleine de Scudéry and La Calprenède in the character of the motherless Sophia Mountain. For her, these writers, along with authors such as Roger Boyle, afterwards first Earl of Orrery, whose *Parthenissa* adapted the polite heroic tradition, 'had descended, like heirlooms, from one generation to another, 'till bought up with the rest of the fixtures by her father.' When he dies, the twenty-three-year-old Miss Mountain's enthusiasm for fiction dwindles to the 'quaint reveries' of Sidney's 'tedious Arcadian Knight.'[6] In LeFanu's *Memoirs*, however, the possible influence of Anastasia Chamberlaine upon Frances's reading habits and aspirations to authorship is written out of the picture altogether. Contrary to records which suggest that Anastasia survived Philip Chamberlaine's death in 1751 by some three years, LeFanu states that she died soon after the birth of their daughter in 1724.[7]

Spectral traces of Frances Chamberlaine's mother give rise to conjectures equally too airy to confirm, but hint at a possible estrangement which LeFanu, who was Frances's granddaughter, would be expected to avoid. Anastasia Chamberlaine, née Whyte, was descended from a family of some social standing. Her English father had fought in the Battle of the Boyne in 1690 and established an estate in southwest county Wexford. Of the two brothers he sent to serve as pages to Queen Anne before their joining the Guards, Captain Solomon Whyte held office as Governor of Dublin's Bermingham Tower. A much beloved uncle to the young Frances, he later occupied a townhouse opposite her own marital home in Dorset Street. In a will dated 1742, Solomon Whyte names Anastasia, along with Philip Chamberlaine, as beneficiaries of five shillings in recognition of the care extended to him upon the death of his wife.[8] There may have been a hint of grim sarcasm in this bequest; five shillings was a proportionately decent sum of money for the majority of households, but is relatively modest against the £50 Whyte left to his nephew and namesake. To put this in another context, Elizabeth Sheridan, mother of Frances's future husband, received five shillings from her own husband in a will identifying her as his 'unkind wife.'[9] There are of course any number of reasons for LeFanu's omission and apparent mistake. Her principal sources, Frances's own daughters, spent relatively short periods of time in their mother's company and, after her death when the eldest was still quite young, were forbidden to speak of her by their grieving father. They may well have known very little about their maternal grandmother, or their own early trauma perhaps compromised their recollections of childhood conversations.

The fate of Anastasia Chamberlaine presents an intriguing if presently irresolvable context for her daughter's steps toward committing her 'first literary sin,' as LeFanu describes *Eugenia and Adelaide*. The Rev. Chamberlaine was oblivious to its completion on paper he had given to the housekeeper for account keeping, and Frances was blessed either with her indifference to or ignorance of its appropriation 'to the far nobler purpose of writing a romance.'[10] A tale predicated on the friendship of its eponymous heroines, and propelled in parts by the exchange of letters and notes, *Eugenia and Adelaide* would seem a deliberate riposte to a father's uneasiness about girls and their epistolary confidences. But it is more ambivalent in its approach to maternal authority and female conspiracy. Adelaide's mother dies before the action of the story begins and, though Eugenia's is very much present, Madame Burganeze energetically competes with her daughter in a relationship devoid of mutual respect. Madame Deffari does serve as a benign substitute for both parents when Adelaide hears of her father's death, but with the exception of firm allies Clara and Cynthia, to whom Deffari introduces her young charge, *Eugenia and Adelaide* is as interested in fractured relationships between women as it is in their enduring bonds of friendship or kinship.

Prompted by the unreasonable demands of daughterly duty, *Eugenia and Adelaide*'s heroines flirt with some seriously compromising behaviour. However, Eugenia's weakness for clandestine meetings, Adelaide's questionable decision to elope, and Clementina's absolute commitment to the role of runaway, impostor and hostage are absolved in marriages to deserving husbands. In the few pages dedicated in the *Memoirs* to Frances Chamberlaine's own teenage adventures, Alicia LeFanu gives due credit to the inventive range of *Eugenia and Adelaide*, if not a fuller sense of the circumstances of its arrival on the shelves of booksellers in 1791. But she too moves onto the subject of worthy suitors and describes how, after writing two (non-extant) sermons in the spirit of imitating her father and brother, 'Miss Chamberlaine resumed her pen' with 'very different intentions' (17–18). LeFanu specifies a poem and refers to a 'pamphlet' (33) which, despite LeFanu's confusing the cause and date of its composition, was likely Frances's seven-page 'Letter from a Young Lady to Mr Cibber' written in July 1743. In LeFanu's version of events, the pamphlet, like the poem, was an opportunistic venture undertaken as a preliminary to meeting Thomas Sheridan, an actor who had made his Smock-Alley debut in January that year as Richard III. The godson of Swift, Sheridan is said to have been something of an overnight success and had performed regularly for the first five months in a range of leading parts. The verse and pamphlet were contributions to a dispute between Sheridan and the actor Theophilus Cibber, though Frances Chamberlaine's writing in Sheridan's favour—at least according to LeFanu—primarily answered her need to express admiration for him without 'transgressing the bounds of propriety' (27). 'It is needless to inform the reader' (to borrow a phrase used with some irony by the narrator of *Eugenia and Adelaide*), the plan was effective. Frances met Sheridan that year, and they were married in a service conducted by her brother, Walter, in 1747.

LeFanu was a published author of five novels by the time she completed the *Memoirs* and was variously motivated to frame her literal, and respectably literary, foremother in a conservative way. While not discounting this, or the fact that LeFanu was herself an ironist, her take on the pamphlet in particular is misleading. LeFanu underplays its significance to the longer view of Frances Chamberlaine's development as an author which *Eugenia and Adelaide* sets in motion. Having given due credit to Frances's talents in composing a romance 'we may suppose, to her own satisfaction,' LeFanu implies that *Eugenia and Adelaide* was a less ambitious undertaking than her attempts to write the kind of sermons in which her family were well practised (17). As Frances's literary ambition increases, so its objectives are more and more grounded within the context of her identity as a daughter, sister, and wife: her early writings repurposed only as acts of rebellion against a father, emulation of a brother, and interest in a potential lover.

The 'Letter' may well have been indicative of Frances's impressive initiative in private matters of the heart, but as an intervention in Thomas Sheridan's very public fall out with Cibber, which influenced the fortunes of the Smock-Alley theatre, it marks her further determination to engage in Dublin's print culture. Reflecting a progressively inquisitive and versatile approach to literary composition, the 'Letter' displays a tendency to explore the boundaries and possibilities of literary form which is, from *Eugenia and Adelaide* to *The History of Nourjahad*, the oriental tale published posthumously in 1767, a distinctive feature of Frances Chamberlaine Sheridan's work.

The present edition's refocusing of attention on *Eugenia and Adelaide* as a first composition is a timely opportunity to acknowledge those publications which pre-date the mid-century writing for which its author is best known. Frances Chamberlaine's 'Letter' takes on Cibber, who was an established actor by the time of the dispute and admired for his comic performances. Like many of his London-based contemporaries, he had migrated across the water to reap the rewards of a Dublin summer season. Frances had been out of the city in the suburbs of Loughlinstown for most of July but, upon her return, spent a day reviewing nearly two weeks' worth of printed copy on the so-called Cato affair, and entered the fray when the abrasive tone of the dispute was intensifying. Advertisements and poetry on the subject had been posted around the city, letters sent to the press, and blows exchanged between rival supporters. Her 'Letter' offered a direct and witty rebuke to Cibber's latest missive in which he had described Thomas Sheridan's public address on the matter as an act of scurrilous libel.

The conflict had originated with Thomas Sheridan's discovering, as he was about to take to the stage as the eponymous hero of Joseph Addison's *Cato*, that the robe he normally wore for the part was missing.[11] This was not simply inconvenient; it also fed Sheridan's anxieties. He suspected that the robe, to which he had attached symbolic significance, had been deliberately removed by the theatre's then manager, Thomas Phillips. Sheridan precipitately decided to cancel the entire evening's entertainment, which included his self-penned afterpiece, *The Brave Irishman.* Backstage, Cibber, who had been cast in the supporting role of Syphax, announced he would proceed regardless and play the part of Cato in addition to his own. He promptly walked in front of the audience beside Sheridan, who was as rapidly losing his voice as he was control of the situation, and made his magnanimous offer. That evening, a rather farcical performance of Addison's tragedy went ahead without Dublin's rising star.

Frances is scornful of Cibber's pretensions to good breeding and systematically refutes his criticism of Sheridan from her perspective as a fellow Dublin citizen; defending Thomas Sheridan against the actor in his capacity as a 'Gentleman' player reduced 'by the Narrowness of his Fortune' to 'the sad Necessity of being Company for the Gentry of the Stage.' She accuses Cibber of gamesmanship in choosing 'the Fatigue of playing two Characters (a Thing perhaps not so new to you) where that little, obstinate, perverse Chit, SHERIDAN, wouldn't [. . .] play one.—Kind, indeed, but, between you and I, I suspect you in this plausible Intention.' A page short of her conclusion, she adds, 'I am almost tired of you, but I will go on.'[12] The young woman's assured sense of authority and superiority elicited a swift and unflinching response from the pen of the pseudonymous 'Mrs Slammekin,' who first claims to know that the anonymous author of the 'Letter' cut a laughably 'uncouth Figure' amongst other women during her time in the country. 'Slammekin' addresses the author of the 'Letter' as 'Miss Tabitha Tammy.' This is later abbreviated to 'Tam' and, in a concluding scatological turn, to 'you filthy *Hoyden*'; names given to the disenfranchised younger sibling of John Vanbrugh's *The Relapse* (1697) and his vigorous country wife.[13] Frances, however, might be considered to have had the last word by way of 'Verses address'd to Mr. Sheridan, on his late Affair in the Theatre,' her poetic fable in which Thomas Sheridan's celebrated 'Merit' and 'worth' is vainly pursued by 'Envy.'[14] First published in the *Dublin News Letter* in August 1743, 'Verses' was included with the 'Letter' to complete, bar an epilogue and back matter, the collection of papers on this theatrical squabble which comprised that year's *Cibber and Sheridan: or, The Dublin Miscellany*.

II

From its completion to its eventual publication, *Eugenia and Adelaide* is, like its fugitive and shape-shifting heroine Donna Clementina, tantalising elusive. It next appears in 1756, by which time Frances Sheridan (to use her married name) was on politely friendly terms with Samuel Richardson. Sheridan had first met Richardson soon after having joined her husband at his lodgings near London's Covent Garden Theatre, less than half a mile from Richardson's premises at Salisbury Court. Thomas Sheridan had begun acting with the company in October 1754 after a series of controversies at Smock-Alley (where he had achieved the role of manager) had forced his resignation and contradicted his depiction in 'Verses address'd to Mr. Sheridan' as the fabled '*Phoebus*, Source of Light and Heat' forever destined to 'Rise and Shine.' That year had been an especially difficult one for Frances, who was by then the mother of three young children: Charles, at that time aged four, and Richard Brinsley and Alicia, who were three years and eighteen months old, respectively. The early part of 1754 had seen the death of her infant son, Sackville, likely that of her mother and, in July, of her beloved brother Walter. During the course of the following year Frances had travelled to London accompanied solely by Charles, whose 'domestic and sedentary turn' she thought 'best suited to a home education.'[15] By February 1756 her self-styled 'first-born,' *Eugenia and Adelaide* had been introduced to Richardson.[16]

Richardson was by this time well known as the author of *Pamela* and *Clarissa* though had more recently antagonised a proportion of his Irish readership in an attempt to prevent the circulation in Dublin of pirated copies of *The History of Sir Charles Grandison.* Catherine Talbot, a tireless reader of early drafts of that seven-volume novel, was one friend and correspondent drawn from a circle of women writers which comprised, as Sheridan herself put it, Richardson's 'favourite and patronized part of the creation.'[17] Sheridan's friendship with the author Sarah Fielding, author of *The Adventures of David Simple* (1744) and sister to the creator of *Tom Jones*, was fostered in Richardson's company and he had printed Charlotte Lennox's second novel, *The Female Quixote.* The bookseller Andrew Millar was another friend of Richardson's and, in little over ten years after he had achieved success with Lennox's work, he would be presenting Frances Sheridan with £100 generated from rapid sales of her third comedy *The Dupe.* Her follow-up to the acclaimed *The Discovery* (1763), *The Dupe* fared dismally upon its first and only performance at Drury Lane in December 1763 but proved exceptionally popular in print. Shifts in the reading preferences of a mid-century audience were very much in Sheridan's mind when in 1756 she confided in Richardson her doubts as to *Eugenia and Adelaide*'s appeal 'to the present tast[e].' These were alleviated by Richardson's favourable opinion and, writing to him on 5 February that year, Sheridan expressed confidence in a judgement she considered he had exercised independently of any personal bias: 'I think vanity under a shew of modesty is of all the lights it can appear in the most contemptible, how ridiculous then would it be in me to say, I don't think the novel worth printing, after it has had your approbation?'[18]

Sheridan's letter sees her looking over the novel again herself, and concluding that, as 'the efforts of a very young girl' and one 'who doesn't now look upon herself as the same person,' *Eugenia and Adelaide* 'wants a great deal of polishing.' Venturing an 'improper request' that Richardson's daughter, Patty, 'would be so good as to file it a little for me,' Sheridan appears not to send it to him for that purpose for another eight months.[19] In an unpublished letter dated 3 October 1756, just days before report of her return to Dublin with Thomas, Sheridan writes to Richardson, 'in hast[e] & in the dark':

> I commit my eldest offspring to your hands, Dear Sir, don't think me an unnatural Parent when I tell you I am indifferent about its fate, if your Humanity preserves it, I shall think it an undeserved Honour, if your

> Judgement condemns it, I shall be satisfied with your Justice. [. . .] do just what you please with [. . .] the Novel—I will add no more, my Heart is filled with Gratitude and reverence for you.[20]

Sheridan's respect for and friendship with Richardson and his family had certainly intensified during those intervening spring and summer months of 1756, and their company provided a welcome distraction from the relative solitude of living for several weeks as sole parent to Charles. Thomas Sheridan had embarked on a visit to Dublin in May and though Frances envisaged that he would be preoccupied for two weeks, his reappointment within that time as manager of Smock-Alley likely delayed his return to London until August. Certainly, by midsummer, Frances was gently berating Richardson for having also 'deserted' London, probably for Parson's Green, his country house in Kensington. In an unpublished letter, dated 21 June 1756, Sheridan declares herself 'prouder' of Richardson's 'good Opinion [. . .] than I should be of anybody's in England,' so much so, that she ought not 'descend to anything which could lessen me with you.' And yet, she adds, 'behold what poor Creatures we women are when we are left to ourselves!' Sheridan's ironic gesture of feminine weakness is offered by way of an excuse for her complaining of low spirits and a scarcity of female acquaintance.[21] She thought to remedy this by asking that Richardson spare her the company of the poet, Elizabeth Pennington, or 'Penny,' whom she had previously met at Richardson's house along with John Duncombe. In his verse tribute to British female poets, *The Feminiad* (1754), Duncombe had created another 'Eugenia' by means of which character he applauded the literary talents of his soon-to-be wife, Susannah Highmore, also a regular visitor to Parson's Green. Frances and her son were duly invited there that summer where they instilled in all its inhabitants an oft-expressed love and esteem.

Following the Sheridans' joint return to Dublin in late 1756, neither the custodian of *Eugenia and Adelaide* nor its 'unnatural parent' were in any position to discuss its progress. For Frances, the prestige of sailing to Ireland on the vice-regal yacht offered no forward protection against discovering the distresses of her younger children's ill health or the oppressive air of the apartments next to Smock-Alley in which they all lodged. Dublin's social scene was relatively quiet, the biannual pattern of each parliamentary session—and there was none that winter—exerting its effect. Within a month, Sheridan was preparing her own retreat two miles away to Glasnevin where, in the vicinity of the villa occupied by the Dean of Down, Patrick Delany, and his wife, Mary, she might at least 'breathe more freely.'[22] As it turned out, the frosts of late December prevailed for much of January, and brought with them 'the sharp clear air' Sheridan thought most 'likely to bring on my old complaint of a rheumatism in my head.'[23] In England, rheumatic disorders also dominated Parson's Green. Richardson's wife, and two other friends whose illnesses would later prove incurable, made up his 'family of nurses and nurselings': 'We have been so much indisposed,' he wrote to Sheridan on 19

December 1756, 'and I have been so busy that I have not had time to give your pretty little novel any further attention as yet.'[24]

It would be another fifteen months before the fate of *Eugenia and Adelaide* was confirmed by Richardson in a letter of 9 April 1758. During this time Thomas Sheridan had variously, and unsuccessfully, petitioned for parliamentary intervention in the establishment of a new theatre in Dublin's Crow Street, which would rival the already struggling fortunes of Smock-Alley. Heavily indebted to his creditors, Thomas Sheridan would again resign his position and be joined in London by Frances in the summer of 1758. In his letter, Richardson was sympathetic to Thomas Sheridan's struggles and optimistic about his plans for improving education, elocution, and oratory. He requested that love be passed on to 'dear' Charles, upon whom his wife and daughters doted, and Richardson also asked that Frances herself might write to update him on the couple's more deserved 'Successes' and 'Victories': 'Be pleased to tell her,' he had added, 'that her MS is safe. I mentioned it once to Mr Dodsley; but he seemed to think the demand for Writings of Entertainment and Fancy, was over.'[25] Upon receipt of such warm reassurance and disappointment, the latter rendered with potentially devastating matter-of-factness, Frances Sheridan promptly replied. In the final paragraph of a short letter of 11 April given over to her husband's affairs she thanked Richardson 'for mentioning my child, my two children, I should say; but as for my first-born, which you have in your hands, I am so unnatural a parent that I never think of it, and don't care if I never see it.'[26]

Frances Sheridan's response reflects the 'calm sense and good humour' Sarah Fielding found so appealing in her friend.[27] But her repeated references to *Eugenia and Adelaide* in terms of the relationship between parent and child is complex. The easy assimilation of real-life and figurative children sits alongside a very definitive dismissal of literary progeny which, nonetheless, retains the privileged status of 'first-born.' Richardson's confirmation that *Eugenia and Adelaide* was safe but far from likely to thrive comes eighteenth months after she entrusted it to his care. Upon being confronted with the fact that *Eugenia and Adelaide*'s fate ultimately resided with a bookseller, and not with her mentor, Sheridan's claim to being unnatural in her concern is perhaps bravado. As the nineteen-year-old author of the 'Letter' to Cibber, she had dismissed Cibber's claim to have secured on his side the favourable opinion of George Faulkner, the bookseller once described by Swift as 'the Prince of Dublin Printers.'[28] 'A *Printer's Opinion!*—Why, Man,' she had asserted, 'poor *Faulkner* is an honest Fellow, but for God's sake don't talk of his *Opinion*!'[29]

Just over five years after receiving Richardson's news that the shelf life of *Eugenia and Adelaide* was over before it had even begun, Sheridan returned to the 'disagreeable task' of defending 'one's own writing,' and did so with renewed claims to being its 'natural parent.'[30] Then living in the French town of Blois, where Thomas Sheridan sought respite from his creditors, Frances had seen her first novel *Sidney Bidulph* run to two editions within its first two months and prosper in the country of her birth as a novel 'more read and admired' than any other.[31] *The Discovery* and *The Dupe* had been, in turn, critically acclaimed and financially lucrative. Emboldened by this success, she defends the script of her new play, *A Journey to Bath*, against David Garrick's negative judgement: 'I think it a maternal duty to exculpate my child, as far as it is in my power, from so many complicated faults, more especially as these vices have not been acquired by evil communications, but were born with it, and consequently take their rise originally from myself.'[32] Despite Sheridan's telling Richardson in 1756 that she did not look upon herself as 'the same person' as 'the very young girl' who wrote *Eugenia and Adelaide*, her repeated use of the parent-child motif suggests an enduring sense of responsibility for her work, irrespective of its perceived flaws.[33] Arguably, it was the legitimacy of authorship which entitled Sheridan to a voice in debates about literary value—a voice which previously, a mixture of inexperience and shrewd ambition, rather than indifference, had seen fit to silence.

III

When *Eugenia and Adelaide* was published anonymously in 1791, its author was long since deceased. Sheridan had died after being taken ill in France in August 1766. The novel appeared with or without Patty Richardson's possible mid-century changes, and included a short Preface (as it appears in this current edition) exonerating its merits 'above the extravagant fictions which are daily served up under the title of Genuine History and Adventures.' Its content differentiates it from the most likely lost 'little advertisement by way of Preface' which had been written by Thomas Sheridan and enclosed by Frances with the manuscript of *Eugenia and Adelaide* sent to Richardson in October 1756.[34] On one hand, it is not beyond the realms of possibility that the existing Preface was written by Frances Chamberlaine herself and part of her original project. Posing as pseudo-editor of a work 'written some years back by an original hand' affords it a gravity which, as is implied, is sadly lacking in contemporary culture. On the other, the Preface as convincingly bears the hallmarks of a late-eighteenth century 'Editor' preparing it for a new readership.

The initiative to bring *Eugenia and Adelaide* to print was likely a collaboration between Elizabeth LeFanu and Alicia LeFanu. Not to be confused with Alicia LeFanu, author of the *Memoirs*, who was born in the year of the novel's publication, this Mrs Alicia LeFanu was Frances Sheridan's eldest daughter. In 1781 she had married Joseph LeFanu, son of William—often begrudgingly referred to as 'the old Gentleman'—who had managed Thomas Sheridan's finances and been stubbornly sceptical about those of his future daughter-in-law. Alicia's sister, and the youngest of the Sheridan siblings, Elizabeth, married Joseph's brother, Henry, in 1789. Mrs Alicia LeFanu is credited in the *Memoirs* with having at some point adapted *Eugenia and Adelaide* for the stage and her interest in her mother's novel looks to have begun by the summer of 1779, when she was working on at least two comedies. Of these, a two-act farce, entitled *The Ambiguous Lover* premiered at Dublin's Crow Street Theatre on 5 March 1781 as an afterpiece to *Every Man in his Humour.* It was staged again on 9 March after *The School for Scandal* by Alicia's brother, Richard Brinsley Sheridan. Although it 'was favourably received and from the repeated and involuntary bursts of applause bestowed upon it throughout' was poised to be, 'according to the theatrical phrase, a living piece,' *The Ambiguous Lover* appears not to have been performed again, or printed.[35] However, in comparisons drawn with Elizabeth Inchbald's *The Widow's Vow* (1786), itself an adaptation of Joseph Parat's *l'Heureuse erreur* (1783), *The Ambiguous Lover* exploited the very confusions consequent upon female masquerade which are integral to *Eugenia and Adelaide.* In 1796 the theatre historian, Walley Chamberlain Oulton, thought the subject 'very ill calculated for a lady's pen,' but the audiences of the early 1780s were decidedly more appreciative:

> Probability may very allowably be violated in an after-piece, but such a violation ever in a degree takes from its value. The Ambiguous Lover is as strictly in nature as any of our severest comedies. Add to this, that the dialogue has all the smartness and wit which distinguishes the best English dramas from those of any other language, yet is simple and easy to such a degree as at first view to appear but mere conversation. This is a rare union; and persons of taste in the art of dramatic writing well know the astonishing difficulty of it. The success of this piece, we hope, will encourage the young lady to exert her talents for the public entertainment.[36]

Alicia did continue to write for the stage, although it would be another thirty-one years before she achieved public recognition with *Prejudice; or Modern Sentiment,* a five-act comedy first performed on 11 April 1812 by the Drury Lane company at London's Lyceum Theatre. The intervening years saw her establish a reputation in Dublin circles as the hostess of and participant in private theatricals, an interest she shared with her husband. Also a keen playwright, Joseph LeFanu had encouraged Alicia's writing throughout their ardent and troubled courtship, not least of all in the sanguine hope that commercial success might alleviate their mutually straitened circumstances. A widower, LeFanu had worked at the Irish Customs Office since 1764 and had seen only one of his pieces professionally staged to an abysmal reception at Covent Garden in 1775. In the summer of 1779 he had asked if Alicia would condescend to live on a modest income with a man ten years her senior. Her answer was unequivocal, but ongoing personal and domestic struggles, and the erosion of confidence in an ability to earn by her own pen, perhaps made the prospect of giving *Eugenia and Adelaide* long-overdue recognition both just and potentially profitable.

Alicia's unwitting participation in the well-documented ebb and flow of relations between her father and his two sons played its part in this decision.

In 1779 Alicia's own relationship with Thomas Sheridan was one of mutual disappointment. She doubted his inclination, let alone capacity, to offer her material support. Thomas had informed Joseph LeFanu he approved of his moral character but not his limited income, and was resolute he could ill afford to increase Alicia's allowance at least until such time as he could be sure her elder brother Charles's future was adequately secured. The worsened state of Thomas's own finances at this time owed something to an unprofitable season at Drury Lane, in which he had a nominal stake in the running of business ultimately under the management of his younger son, Richard. Their perpetually testy relationship was already under strain on account of the collapse of an uneasy coalition between Drury Lane and its rival Covent Garden—a crisis which also served as a backdrop to Thomas's flare-up with another long-term adversary, the manager of the Haymarket Theatre (and Joseph LeFanu's sometime mentor), George Colman, the elder.

Such obstructions looked set to be overcome by profitable sales of Thomas Sheridan's *General Dictionary of the English Language* in February 1780, but Alicia was rightly apprehensive of her irritable father's intransigence. He confided in Charles his disappointment in both of his daughters. Despite possible efforts to recruit Alicia to the instruction of young gentlemen in reading, reciting and grammar at an Academy Thomas Sheridan had intended to open in Bath when she was seventeen, she, and the sister she had made 'good for nothing' by her example, remained 'utterly unqualified to do anything for themselves.' They were 'a burden on their old father' and the situation, he grumbled, 'entirely their own fault.' Charles was a sympathetic ear, he being typically more antagonist than ally when it came to the affairs of his younger siblings, but Thomas needed little encouragement in seeing himself a selfless, grieving widower whose happiness was at the mercy of Alicia's 'temper and utter dissipation.'[37]

Part of the problem potentially lay with Alicia's interest in writing as opposed to more gainful employment. In November 1782, Alicia ventured to her father that she might try her hand at translating French works into English and, at the same time, outlined for him a play she had been encouraged to complete by Richard's wife, Eliza Sheridan, née Linley. Thomas Sheridan offered to scout for a text for her to translate (on the basis that 'booksellers are not the proper judges') but greeted her play with cautious pessimism. Eliza had joked that Alicia could provide a service to Drury Lane were she to send 'us a grand comedy' which might compete with the slew of tragedies 'passed in from all quarters, on all subjects,' in the wake of the near hysterical reaction which had greeted the actress Sarah Siddons's triumphant return to the London stage.[38] In contrast, it seemed that Thomas saw in Alicia's efforts an opportunity to score a point against his son: 'if you send it to me I will do the best I can with it. If it gets into your brother [Richard's] hands, you may rely on it it will be put on the shelf.' He did, though, offer some additional advice: 'I wish you could light upon some good story, upon which you might form a substantial plot. When the ground work is right it is easy to give it a colouring.'[39] This clumsy if well-meaning affront to Alicia's own creative abilities could have refocused her attention on *Eugenia and Adelaide* as the source material for the *Ambiguous Lover* and basis of her only literary success.

Eugenia and Adelaide also signified for Alicia as a timely connection to her mother. Like Frances before her, whose eldest child Thomas died in infancy, Alicia suffered the loss of her first-born, a daughter, in the summer of 1783. A son was born in January 1784, but recurrent bouts of the debilitating rheumatic pain which had affected her mother, as well as marital tensions, marked the years leading to the arrival of a third child in May 1787. The early 1780s also saw a complete and disorientating realignment of Thomas Sheridan's paternal sympathies. In the spring of 1783 he concluded that Charles, who had taken office as under-secretary of state in the Irish parliament, had discarded his old father in the selfish pursuit of worldly ambition. By the end of 1784, Thomas was contrasting the ingratitude of both Charles and Richard with the duty and affection shown him by his daughters, both of whom he was convinced could remedy his heartfelt anguish. Alicia, it seemed, was finding favour by default at a time when she was facing her own tumultuous experiences as a parent. That it was frustrating is evident from later reflections, prompted by the death of her brother Richard in 1816. Recollecting their being schooled together in Dublin while their parents lived in England, Alicia claimed 'neither he or I were very happy, we were strongly attached to each other. We had no one else to love.' Of her father's partiality for their siblings, she wrote, 'Had my mother lived our fate would have been different, for she had a spirit of justice that would have prevented her from showing favour to any of her children but as they might deserve it.'[40]

It is probably no coincidence that *Eugenia and Adelaide*'s deserving moment came after Thomas Sheridan's death in August 1788. Given her father's initial reluctance to allow discussion of her mother—which, given his morose tendencies he likely continued—any predetermined scheme Alicia had to resurrect *Eugenia and Adelaide* may have been deferred. Upon his death, her sister Elizabeth, who had been for much of the 1780s Thomas Sheridan's sole companion, was herself poised to leave behind 'the life of uniform vexation and disappointment' she had 'led for years' and in which she was 'perpetually kept between dependence and unkindness.'[41] This 'painful' existence had originated with the hostility she had experienced at the hands of her brother Charles, with whom she had lived for a time after Alicia's marriage in 1781. In 1788 he looked set to perpetuate Elizabeth's misery, withholding funds owing to her—as joint beneficiary with Alicia—from their father's estate, at the same time as judging Elizabeth's intention to marry Henry LeFanu as financially imprudent. Elizabeth, who was facing additional opposition from her future father-in-law, was determined to draw upon other resources which were exclusive to herself and Alicia. In June 1789 she arranged with the publisher Charles Dilly to receive profits from sales of their father's *General Dictionary*. 'So you see,' she told her sister, 'I am endeavouring to counteract Charles's kind wish to cross my future plans.'[42]

Richard Brinsley Sheridan's own role as *Eugenia and Adelaide*'s most likely advocate might be presumed because of, or perhaps in spite of, his tendency to borrow from his mother's writings in the shaping of his own. However, he makes no mention of the draft or print version of *Eugenia and Adelaide* in his undated autograph manuscript outlining his mother's life and works, and the timing of the novel's publication coincided with an intensification of his political commitments. June 1789 had seen the start of the trial of Warren Hastings, governor general of Bengal, and Richard was involved in the first session for the prosecution which did not close until May 1791. His political preoccupations more generally and, as his sister Elizabeth put it, 'the hurry he lives in, [which] makes him often unconscious of the length of time that passes between his promise and performance,' possibly inclined her not to rely upon him to execute any plan in which 'one's support is at stake.'[43] Charles Dilly was a highly respected and long-established bookseller. His premises in the Poultry, located in what is now the City of London and principal district of business and finance, served in the 1760s as 'an important nexus for social, political, and literary figures,' including Frances Sheridan's acquaintances, Boswell, and Samuel Johnson.[44] The Sheridan sisters were well placed to exploit these connections. In the words of the Preface, 'to say more might be looked upon as impertinent; and it would not be acting as a friend to the Work and the memory of the Author to say less.'

IV

Eugenia and Adelaide is set far from eighteenth-century Dublin in locations across the Iberian peninsula during the reign of the real-life monarch, Philip III of Spain (1598-1621). Suggesting its young author's passing acquaintance with the region's landmarks and some aspects of its seventeenth-century history, the novel also incorporates the extraordinary incidents of masquerade, kidnap and piracy more typical of fiction. By way of 'a hermit and a wood, a battle and a shipwreck,' *Eugenia and Adelaide* certainly assembles elements which Samuel Johnson, in his *Rambler* essay of 1750, deemed essential to 'almost all the fictions of the last age.'[45] Dispensing with the supernatural dimensions of medieval chivalric romance and its early modern incarnations, *Eugenia and Adelaide* adopts a framework more familiar to seventeenth-century French romance, in which the principal narrative accommodates other aristocratic heroines' tales of love's intrigues, triumphs, and disappointments.[46] However, by means of this, it also stages the kind of parallel action and movement towards resolution developed in a five-act play, and its devices are characteristically dramatic: garden trysts, flits at midnight, intercepted letters, and reliably disloyal servants.

At the centre of this shifting landscape are *Eugenia and Adelaide*'s eponymous heroines who, known to each other since childhood, enter into the ordinary terms of friendship—its confidences, encouragements, occasionally tactless attempts at advice, and ultimate endurance. Their resilience in the face of injustice is shared by Donna Clementina, Cynthia, and Clara, all of whom encounter, in the duplicitous stratagems of other seemingly trustworthy and respectable women, a different kind of female enterprise. Eugenia's mother, Madame Burganeze; Adelaide's cousin, Faustina; and Clara's rival in love, Violante, turn in compelling performances of lasciviousness which are by turns desperate, conniving and consummately professional. All of this is choreographed in a sequence of interpolated first-person accounts, at the close of which order is restored and the perfidious consigned to oblivion or, in Faustina's case, a watery grave.

As a contribution to the picture of fiction written in the early decades of the eighteenth century, *Eugenia and Adelaide* allows for further scrutiny of the very critical paradigms, as well as commercial imperatives, which authorised its initial suppression, eventual selection and more recent obscurity. The usefulness of 1740 as a literary threshold beyond which Richardson and Henry Fielding put into practice their 'new species of writing' has long since been disputed. William B. Warner describes as unstable the 'vantage point' from which they attempted to give the novel 'a higher cultural calling' than the works of writers active in the six decades prior to the arrival of *Pamela*, and Ros Ballaster's early treatment of Aphra Behn, Delarivier Manley and Eliza Haywood, demonstrated how 'the perception of women's different, and frequently disruptive use of fictional forms is precisely *instrumental* in the novel's formation.'[47] Although suppressed until its emergence at the end of the century, *Eugenia and Adelaide* is intriguing as a novel clearly forged in defiance of rules as to what kind of early fictional forms were fit or not for a daughter's consumption. Frances Chamberlaine was a secretive and, to an extent, indiscriminate reader, and *Eugenia and Adelaide* bears the traces of material its author could get her hands on, or contrive to see performed on stage. While the novel is influenced by prior texts, it dares with the fearlessness of adolescence to pastiche and expose their complications, over-simplifications, and improbabilities.

Frances Sheridan's grown-up addiction to reading 'old romances,' as her biographer LeFanu puts it, might have originated with the habits of her youth (210). Since the 1600s Elizabethan revivals of chivalric romance had circulated in the chapbook versions accessible to children, including *Don Bellianis of Greece*, by the Catalan Jerónimo Fernández, and Richard Johnson's *Seven Champions of Christendom*, first published in two parts in 1596 and 1597. James Grantham Turner points out that the bookseller and author Francis Kirkman, who wrote a continuation of *Don Bellianis* in the early 1670s, singled out 'the educational effect of chivalric romance in Ireland, for which purpose he [. . .] "fitted" his new *Bellianis* with Irish episodes.'[48] A young Samuel Johnson is reputed to have indulged a similar dependency to Sheridan, notably reading in folio the Spanish Melchor de Ortega's *Felixmarte of Hircania*. Published in 1556, it was identified in *Don Quixote* as amongst similar 'senseless rhapsodies of falsehoods and folly' which are no less than 'the chimeras and fictions of idle and luxuriant wits.'[49] The writer and anthologist Thomas Percy 'heard [Johnson] attribute to these extravagant fictions that unsettled turn of mind which prevented his ever fixing in any profession,'[50] a consideration which recalls a further point made in Cervantes: namely that 'wits' write romances 'for the same reason' that readers read them: 'because they had nothing else to do.'[51]

By 1705 Delarivier Manley was announcing the obsolescence of French romances in her preface to *The Secret History of Queen Zarah and the Zarazians.* The 'Fury' with which they were once read had been finally confounded by the 'Humour of the English, who have naturally no Taste for long-winded Performances, for they have no sooner begun a Book but they desire to see the End of it.'[52] For Dubliners, the city's booksellers certainly presented opportunities for at least a passing acquaintance with more recent publications and current news. Arrival at the older part of town, where the Aungier Street and Smock-Alley theatres were located, would have brought Frances to her brother Walter's stomping ground within the vicinity of Trinity. Skinner's Row was an area located at the eastern end of Christchurch, and it was here as well as in nearby College Green and Dame Street in particular that Dublin's book trade flourished. Ireland's exemption from the restrictions on printing introduced by the Copyright Act of 1710 encouraged the circulation of pirated versions of London editions, but by the 1720s Dublin booksellers readily supplied original copies and subscription titles alongside re-printings of works first published across the Irish Sea. In around 1737, the city established its first circulating library.[53]

Elizabeth Singer Rowe's didactic *Friendship in Death*, and *Letters Moral and Entertaining*, both printed in Dublin in 1735, could be had from Edward Exshaw, who was also one of the city's leading suppliers of London periodicals, but Dublin editions of popular fictions of intrigue supplied a growing demand. These included a 1739 edition of Aphra Behn's *Love Letters between a Nobleman and his Sister*, Manley's *The Power of Love: in Seven Novels* (1720), and Mary Davys's *The Reforme'd Coquet* (1724; Dublin, 1735), in which the heroines' adoption of male disguise is central. Eliza Haywood's *The Injur'd Husband* (1723; Dublin, 1724) and *The Perplex'd Dutchess* (1727) had followed her *Love in Excess*, rivalled only by *Robinson Crusoe* as the best-selling novel of 1719. It is to the lesser known fictions of continental adventure, however, that Frances Chamberlaine's Eugenia, finds her namesake. *Love Victorious: or, The Adventures of Oronces and Eugenia, A novel*, translated from the French of Alexandre de la Roberdière, was published in 1684. Its Eugenia is a heroine forbidden by her mother to marry Oronces, the son of a French state governor, who also opposes the match. Eugenia refuses another suitor and wilfully accepts her punitive removal to a convent where she tries to forget her lover. However, Oronces disguises himself as a nun, gains admission to the cloister and, referred to from this point only as 'Aurelia,' or 'she,' conceals his true identity from all but his beloved. Eventually, Eugenia and 'Aurelia' contrive to escape through a secluded section of the garden, board a ship bound for Genoa in male guise, and survive capture by pirates and threatened enslavement before escaping to marry, happily.

Anticipating the readers' incredulity at Oronces's disguise, the narrator of *Love Victorious* argues that in life we are daily surprised by the adventures that befall us: 'and if, in a Comedy, a Player, whom we have already seen, becomes afterwards unknown, by the change of his Part and Garments, why should it be difficult, to believe the success of a Stratagem, perfectly contrived, and executed with a marvellous audacity?'[54] It is an ironic question. Despite his striking good looks, Oronces's scheme is utterly audacious and unconvincing, to the reader at least. The nuns who welcome him to their cloister are of a quite different opinion, and the central conceit of female impersonation on which this slight tale turns is the occasion of some particularly salacious scenes. Admired by all, 'Aurelia' inspires in one particular nun, Pamphilia, a love which, though far from 'impure,' is one she hopes to express in their shared room at night: 'knowing by experience' it to be 'more proper than the Day for a thousand amorous declarations and an infinity of engaging wantonnesses.'[55] 'Aurelia' complies, apparently to avoid suspicion, though an indignant Eugenia is prompted by jealousy to take advantage of nightfall too and, in a bid to ensure her lover's fidelity, at one point secretly substitutes herself for 'Aurelia' in the amorous nun's caresses.

In its own take on the triumph of ingenuity over the abuses of parental authority, *Eugenia and Adelaide* ultimately avoids Roberdière's use of disguise as a license for titillating, pseudo-erotic scenes of same-sex attraction. It does, however, incorporate the confusions and more audacious elements of earlier sexual comedy. The plot involving Clementina, who assumes in the interests of self-preservation the identity of her twin brother, Don Clement, leads to the kind of excruciating encounters with would be-lovers familiar from *Twelfth Night.* As the principal comic casualty of Clementina's deception, Eugenia's mother, Madame Burganeze (who is in her forty-fifth year) appears to recall the humiliation of the duped dowager Lady Wishfort, whose misplaced vanity and comical infatuation with the wrong man is exploited in William Congreve's *The Way of the World* (1700). Wishfort's attempts to control her niece's fortune is punished in a blackmail plot which sees her labour to greet the arrival of her supposed lover (a disguised servant) in an attitude of studied negligence, the key attraction of which will be her foot, 'a little dangling off' her couch and 'jogging in a thoughtful way.'[56] Burganeze invites to her room the man she thinks is the same Don Clement who first spiked her interest, when this was in fact Clementina in male disguise. Burganeze's visitor is genuinely Clementina's brother, whom she prepares to greet lying on her couch in elegant dishabille: 'a loose gown of silver brocade was wrapped carelessly around her' and her hair is newly coloured and extravagantly coiffed. Eugenia is in fact the first to discover her mother in this state of 'unexpected metamorphosis' and has 'opportunity of surveying this enamoured dame, as she lay in a reverie, something between slumber and the most agreeable contemplation' (1 48). The ensuing 'farce,' as an exasperated Don Clement puts it, nods toward *The Country Wife's* (1675) well-known china scene in which a locked door necessitating the arrival of the expectant lover 'the back way' (1 52) plays upon a bawdy distortion of the symbolic association between porcelain china (and its fragility) and female chastity. In Wycherley's play, Lady Fidget's quest for her lover's best piece of china is a euphemism for sex. When Madame Burganeze is rejected by Don Clement, she brings crashing to the floor a display of china and vows to avenge his 'unparalleled villainy' (1 53).

Unlike other deluded comical dames, however, this so-called 'old lady' (1 50; 55) resists dismissal as a pathetic victim of male exploitation. Driven by a mixture of pent-up frustration and fury, she is understandably as well as entertainingly angry, and not straightforwardly ridiculous. She is only as misled by Don Clement's parallel, Clementina, as everyone else. In volume two, when Clementina lends her own first-person perspective to the adventures previously described in volume one, the reader is also made fully aware of the 'violent passion' she feigned for Burganeze, along with a 'great deal' else 'to strengthen what I asserted' (2 9). Such dedication to the role of ardent lover on Clementina's part reminds any reader quick to judge as foolish Burganeze's reciprocal desire, that there is much in this novel which is not quite as it seems. A theatre goer is typically witness to all the action in whatever sequence it unfolds, but *Eugenia and Adelaide*'s non-linear approach to cause and effect sometimes leaves its reader in as much suspense as its protagonists. This demands the narrator's occasional intervention. In the case of Don Clement's ill-fated visit to Burganeze, which he describes to Eugenia and her uncle, the Marquis, in advance of Clementina's retrospective tale, the narrator combines the promise of exposition with an ironic understatement of the plot's complications: 'I believe my reader is by this time as much surprised at Don Clement's behaviour as the Marquis and the two ladies were; and think him a very audacious and lying Spaniard: but we shall see presently how he came out of this whimsical situation' (1 55).

Eugenia and Adelaide appears to delight in such ambivalence, engaging in the faint mockery of conventional plot trajectories at the same time as contemplating the significance of female liberty to which they give rise. The denouement of the Don Clement/Clementina plot, for example, which sees the sister rescued from Don Gabriel—another so-called 'treacherous Spaniard'—by her brother and the Marquis of Pescara, seems a parody (2 22). When Pescara is informed that the first 'Don Clement' to whom he was himself attracted is in fact Clementina, he earnestly declares himself ready to 'die with impatience to see my ever-loved creature, and free her from the insolent ravisher' (2 3). However, when he and the real Don Clement arrive at the suitably moss-covered castle on the outskirts of Madrid where Clementina is held, they indulge in a kind of literary tourism, first finding something 'so romantic and charming in the situation' that they hang about 'to contemplate the awful solitude' (2 3). By means of a kind of dramatic tableau, and the heroes' self-conscious posturing, immediate action to effect the crucial release of a damsel in distress is deferred.

The displacement of the heroine's importance to her own story continues as the gallants enter Don Gabriel's fortress. Upon surprising his sister, who has been held captive for several weeks, Don Clement asks that she overcome her embarrassed confusion at their arrival, prove him right that her 'innocence never gave [it] cause,' and show more gratitude (2 5). This he claims she owes especially to Pescara, in whom she has already, in her guise as 'Don Clement,' excited feelings for which Pescara was 'at a loss to find a name' (2 2). The freedom that a recently orphaned Clementina has gained from the obligations expected of a daughter, and physical liberation from the tyranny of Don Gabriel as her father's chosen suitor, coincides with her brother's prompt assumption of paternal authority. But the romantic arc of this novel demands that Clementina embrace her lover, especially given that Pescara, who later kills Don Gabriel in an ambush, will be conveniently (if audaciously) cleared of responsibility by no less an authority than the King of Spain himself.

Clementina's acceptance of Pescara as if it were a foregone conclusion essentially repeats Eugenia's experience. When the genuine Don Clement had announced himself to her as a replacement for the lover Eugenia thought she had in the disguised Clementina, she responds 'with an obliging look' (2 2). Speaking for her, Eugenia's uncle, Pescara, had agreed that it was a matter of straightforwardly transferring her affections from the pretending sister to the genuine brother, a logic with which the narrator had ironically concurred: 'Indeed the resemblance was so perfect' between these beautiful twins 'that it could hardly be called a change in Eugenia's heart, which now felt the same sentiments for the true Don Clement that it had at first conceived for the supposed one' (2 2).

However, *Eugenia and Adelaide*'s apparent obfuscation of the complexities of attraction caused by Clementina's 'ramble about in masquerade,' as her captor sneeringly puts it (2 12), works on another level to bring more sharply into focus the heroine's agency. Clementina is still wearing her male costume when her brother and Pescara find her, albeit only because the choice of an alternative was conditional upon her surrender to Don Gabriel's demand that she be his wife. Pescara, insisting that he has a right to that place in her heart he knew he had secured in that of the disguised 'Don Clement,' reasons with Clementina that a change of habit should not make 'you change your mind; and if I thought it would have that effect, I would rather for ever see you in this dress than endure the loss of your affection' (2 6). Although a fine expression of how the integrity of their existing bond is more important than the outward significations of heterosexual love, this arguably belies Pescara's anxiety about female constancy and the determination to achieve compliance at any cost.

As Clementina's retrospective first-person account of her experience reveals, Pescara perhaps ought to be more apprehensive of her ingenuity. Relating all that has happened prior to her rescue, and details of a scheme of disguise which was, from its inception, executed 'so cunningly' (2 1),

Clementina explains how she had already single-handedly resisted Don Gabriel's claim to be 'absolute master of [her] destiny' (2 12). Clementina boasts the ease with which she was, as 'Don Clement,' assimilated into society of the 'first quality,' and emphatically reminds Pescara of how 'your ignorance of my sex gave me the liberty of discoursing with you without reserve!' (2 7). Kidnapped by Don Gabriel, she nevertheless defies his attempts to exploit her vulnerability and combats his 'insolent menace' with mounting contempt (2 12). Even when he brings her news of the death of her father, she drew 'consolation from it' (2 13), her torment at the hands of her present captor owing much to her father's previous 'cruel resolution in his favour' (2 12). Though at first frightened when an enraged and increasingly desperate Don Gabriel threatens to kill her, Clementina realises that his fury is more tiresome than terrifying, and determines upon a strategy 'to treat him with so much scorn and aversion, that he must at length [. . .] abandon me to my fate. This reflection made me pass the day with some little tranquillity' (2 14). Throughout an ordeal which sees her endure long periods of solitude, Clementina is sustained by a sense of her own innocence in a focused quest for what she repeatedly identifies as her liberty.

At this point the narrator of *Eugenia and Adelaide* returns to the real-time of Clementina's rescue, stating, 'I believe it is needless to inform the reader that the passion she had conceived for that accomplished gentleman [Pescara] had governed all her actions, and had enabled her so strenuously to resist Don Gabriel's violence' (2 16). Such acknowledgement of the reader's quick comprehension is double-voiced. The narrator flatters the reader's reliable familiarity with patterns of female action, in so far as it goes without saying that in addition to her stated motivations, the captive Clementina is also in thrall to love. At the same time, the narrator invites another reader to share an ironic joke: it is unnecessary to point this out because Clementina's testimony has betrayed little to suggest that this is strictly true. Such interruptions, and asides to the reader, work alongside a clever positioning of past and present action, which seems designed to subvert the conventions within which the story is otherwise working. In this, *Eugenia and Adelaide* perhaps sees its young author practising the sophisticated 'handling of time' which Margaret Anne Doody, with reference to *Sidney Bidulph* and *Nourjahad*, describes as Frances Sheridan's 'really significantly new' contribution to fiction.[57]

Upon *Eugenia and Adelaide*'s publication in January 1791, its ambivalence of perspective was interpreted rather differently by contemporary reviewers who observed that the novel amounted to neither one thing nor the other. *The Town and Country Magazine* was succinct in its judgement of 'a performance perfectly mediocre: it has no great beauties, nor any glaring defects,' and seemed to strike a chord with the *Critical Review*'s claim that although this novel 'is disgraced by no considerable faults, it is distinguished by few excellencies.' A suspicion that the reviewers were reading one another as much as they were the many 'compositions of love and the vicissitudes of its success' which crossed their desks has some basis in the *Monthly*'s observation. The distinctions between these works are so slight as to 'prevent us from discriminating the merits of one from another; so that they might be bundled up by the dozen, under a general description.' As for *Eugenia and Adelaide*, 'all that the present instance demands, is an acknowledgement that it is not one of the worst.'[58] Despite focussing on individual liberty and duty as a concern central to the debates of the 1790s, the increasing popularity of romance novels was underwhelming critical opinion. Had Sheridan lived to see her novel in print, she might have treated its dismissal with the poise that marked her reaction to Garrick's opinion of her play, *A Journey to Bath*. Expressing thanks for Garrick's delivering 'his sentiments so frankly,' she thought 'it shows, at least, that he has some opinion of my philosophy, though he has none of my genius.'[59]

In 1790, a year before *Eugenia and Adelaide* appeared in print, a fourteen-year-old Jane Austen wrote *Love and Freindship*, first published (with the original spelling) in 1922. In her foreword to the Hesperus edition of the work, Fay Weldon argues that 'juvenilia' is a misleading term for such fiction, particularly as written by an author whose lifespan was severely curtailed (Austen died aged forty-one) and who demonstrated in it that 'lively use of language,' and 'sense of the keen, desperate intelligence' found in *Pride and Prejudice*.[60] Recognition of *Eugenia and Adelaide* as more than an adventure which, as LeFanu puts it, 'may be said to breathe the freshness of fifteen—the happy period at which [it] was written' (15–16)—is similarly poised to enrich understandings of its author's developing aesthetic. Sheridan's literary reputation has been established on the basis of a relatively brief publishing career which spanned 1761 to 1767. A keener sense of Sheridan's much earlier engagement with print culture, and *Eugenia and Adelaide*'s publication in the last decade of the eighteenth century might encourage further discussion of her work beyond that of her immediate mid-century contemporaries.

For a long time, women writers of the eighteenth century existed in Austen's shadow, including her acknowledged influences, Frances Burney and Maria Edgeworth. But revising the co-ordinates of a writer's career can create an almost kaleidoscopic pattern of literary relationships. The coincidence of Austen and Sheridan as writers sharpening their pens at the ages of fourteen and fifteen brings into focus other affinities. *Eugenia and Adelaide* was written in Ireland by a Dublin-born young woman whose paternal ancestors hailed from Austen's Hampshire. As well as being precocious, both women were prolific in the limited space of careers cut short, in each case, by death in their early forties. Overcoming financial insecurities to achieve professional success is as much a part of Sheridan's story as it is Austen's, and while this is in itself not exclusive to them, it further closes the gap created between generations of writers because of a perceived antagonism. After all, Austen's mock-epistolary *Love and Friendship* burlesques the novels of sentiment with which Sheridan is principally associated. But Sheridan's complex response to Richardson in *Sidney Bidulph* can be seen to anticipate Austen's inclination to interrogate her literary past. Looked at this way, lines of connection redouble and turn upon themselves. Richard Brinsley Sheridan admired Austen, who appreciated the satire at play in *The Rivals* (1775), which owes a debt to his mother's *A Journey to Bath*. He followed *The Rivals* with another collaboration, this time with his wife and other musically accomplished members of the Linley family. A comic opera described as 'rooted in a lengthy stage tradition of "Spanish honour" dramas' with their absconding daughters and precariously compromising instances of mistaken identity 'on nocturnal streets,' *The Duenna* perhaps glimpses at a source closer to home.[61] Frances Sheridan is a writer whose significance newly extends from the 1730s to the 1790s on account of a novel in which, as one reader put it, we might look in vain for 'the colouring of the passions, or the sober shades of the moral pencil; but if he delights in the sudden shifted-scene, in striking situation, and in all the complicated intrigue of Spanish romance, his desire will be gratified.'[62]

Notes

1. [Anon.], *The Gentleman's Magazine: and Historical Chronicle* (September 1827): 199.
2. Frances Sheridan to Richard Chamberlaine, 23 August [1760?]. King's College, Library, Cambridge, LEF/PP/2/29.
3. James Boswell, *The Life of Samuel Johnson*, vol. 1 (London: Henry Baldwin for Charles Dilly, 1791), 210.
4. See Patrick W. Montague-Smith, 'Sheridan's Maternal Ancestors, The Chamberlaines of Kingsclere,' *The Genealogists' Magazine* 15, no. 9 (1967): 319–30.
5. Raymond Gillespie, 'Religion and Urban Society: The Case of Early Modern Dublin,' *Proceedings of the British Academy* 107 (2001): esp. 231.
6. Alicia LeFanu, *Strathallan*, ed. Anna M. Fitzer (London: Pickering & Chatto, 2008), 52.
7. There is a record of the burial of Anastasia Chamberlin in the parish of St Nicholas Within on 6 April 1754. Esther K. Sheldon notes that the *Dublin Journal* of April 2–6 records 'the death "after a lingering Illness" of a Mrs. Anne "Chamberlain," relict of the late Rev. Dr. Philip "Chamberlain".' See *Thomas Sheridan of Smock-Alley* (Princeton, NJ: Princeton University Press, 1967), 207 n. 57.
8. Montague-Smith, 'Sheridan's Maternal Ancestors,' 326.
9. Sheldon, *Thomas Sheridan*, 19.
10. Alicia LeFanu, *Memoirs of the Life and Writings of Mrs. Frances Sheridan*, ed. Anna M. Fitzer, *Memoirs of Women Writers*, vol. 1 (London: Pickering & Chatto, 2012), 17, 15. All subsequent references to this edition will be incorporated in the text.
11. For a fuller account of the incident to which my own is indebted see Sheldon, *Thomas Sheridan*, esp. 40–7. Sheldon notes that LeFanu mistakenly connects Frances's poem in Sheridan's defence (detailed below) with the later so-called Kelly riot of 1747. Clarification as to the attribution of authorship, and date of the 'Letter' is given in Norma H. Russell, 'Some Uncollected Authors XXXVIII: Frances Sheridan, 1724–1766', *The Book Collector* 13 (1964): 204–205.
12. 'A Letter from a Young Lady to Mr. Cibber,' in *Cibber and Sheridan: or, The Dublin Miscellany* (Dublin: Printed for Peter Wilson, 1743), 57, 60.
13. 'An Answer to the Young Lady; or, a Letter from Mrs. Slammekin to Miss Tabitha Tammy,' in *Cibber and Sheridan*, 62, 69.

14. 'Verses address'd to Mr. Sheridan, on his late Affair in the Theatre,' in *Cibber and Sheridan*, 70. In her *Memoirs* LeFanu prefixes this title, with the exception of 'Verses', with 'The Owls: a Fable'.
15. Frances Sheridan to Samuel Whyte, 25 February 1762, in Samuel Whyte and Edward-Athenry Whyte, *A Miscellany* (Dublin: Robert Marchbank, 1799), 105.
16. The phrase is used in a letter: Frances Sheridan to Samuel Richardson, 11 April 1758, in *The Correspondence of Samuel Richardson*, ed. Anna Laetitia Barbauld, vol. 4 (New York: AMS, 1966), 176.
17. Frances Sheridan to Samuel Richardson, 5 February 1756. Robert H. Taylor Collection of English and American Literature (RTC01); Manuscripts Division, Department of Rare Books and Special Collections, Princeton University Library.
18. Frances Sheridan to Samuel Richardson, 5 February 1756. This is reproduced in *The Correspondence of Samuel Richardson* and incorporates the note written on it in another hand which incorrectly identifies 'the novel' to which Sheridan refers as *Sidney Bidulph*. Barbauld includes a similar note to this effect in her version of the letter of 11 April, above.
19. Frances Sheridan to Samuel Richardson, 5 February 1756.
20. Frances Sheridan to Samuel Richardson, 3 October 1756. The James Marshall and Marie-Louise Osborn Collection, Beinecke Rare Book and Manuscript Library, Yale University.
21. 21 June 1756. MS Eng 1473 (Sheridan, Frances Chamberlaine letter to Samuel Richardson), Houghton Library, Harvard University.
22. Frances Sheridan to Samuel Richardson, 20 November 1756, in *Correspondence*, 148.
23. Frances Sheridan to Samuel Richardson, 8 February 1757, in *Correspondence*, 154.
24. Samuel Richardson to Frances Sheridan, 19 December 1756. The Historical Society of Pennsylvania.
25. Samuel Richardson to Thomas Sheridan, 9 April 1758. The Morgan Library & Museum. MA 1024.8.
26. Frances Sheridan to Samuel Richardson, 11 April 1758, in *Correspondence*, 176.
27. Samuel Richardson to Frances Sheridan, 19 December 1756.
28. James E. Tierney, 'Faulkner, George (1703?–1775), printer and bookseller,' *Oxford Dictionary of National Biography*. https://doi.org/10.1093/ref:odnb/9205.
29. 'Letter', 55–6.
30. Frances Sheridan to Mrs Victor, 16 November 17[63], in *The Private Correspondence of David Garrick*, vol.1, ed. James Boaden (London: Henry Colburn and Richard Bentley, 1831), 16.
31. John O' Keeffe, *Recollections of the Life of John O' Keeffe*, vol. 1 (London: Henry Colburn, 1826), 86.
32. Frances Sheridan to Mrs Victor, 16 November 17[63], in *Correspondence of David Garrick*, 17.
33. Frances Sheridan to Samuel Richardson, 5 February 1756.
34. Frances Sheridan to Samuel Richardson, 3 October 1756.
35. Quoted in John C. Greene, *Theatre in Dublin 1745–1820: A Calendar of Performances*, vol. 3 (Bethlehem: Lehigh University Press, 2011), 1955.
36. Walley Chamberlain Oulton, *The History of the Theatres of London*, vol. 1 (London: Martin and Bain; T. Egerton; W. Miller; J. Bell; T. Boosey, 1796), p. 152; 'Irish Theatrical Intelligence,' *The London Courant, and Westminster Chronicle*, 16 March 1781 [n.p.].
37. Quoted in W. Fraser Rae, 'Sheridan's Sisters,' *Temple Bar* 118, no. 466 (September 1899): 46.
38. Thomas Sheridan to Alicia LeFanu, 25 November 1782, LEF/PP/2/35; Elizabeth Sheridan to Alicia LeFanu, n.d. [1782/83]. LEF/PP/2/14.

39. Thomas Sheridan to Alicia LeFanu, 25 November 1782, LEF/PP/2/35.
40. Alicia LeFanu to Hester Sheridan, 9 November 1816, LEF/PP/2/9.
41. 1 April 1789, in *Betsy Sheridan's Journal: Letters from Sheridan's Sister*, ed. William LeFanu (Oxford and New York: Oxford University Press, 1986), 154.
42. 9 June 1789, *Betsy Sheridan's Journal*, 167.
43. 9 December 1789 and 9 June 1789, *Betsy Sheridan's Journal*, 189, 165.
44. James J. Caudle, 'Dilly, Charles (1739–1807), bookseller,' *Oxford Dictionary of National Biography.* https://doi.org/10.1093/ref:odnb/7671.
45. Samuel Johnson, *The Rambler*, no. 4 (31 March 1750): 28.
46. For an extended treatment of French Romance in England see Thomas Philip Haviland, *The* Roman de Longue Haleine *on English Soil* (Philadelphia, PA: University of Pennsylvania, 1931).
47. William B. Warner, 'The Elevation of the Novel in England: Hegemony and Literary History,' *ELH* 59, no. 3 (Autumn 1992): 582, 577; Ros Ballaster, *Seductive Forms: Women's Amatory Fiction from 1684 to 1740* (Oxford: Clarendon Press, 1992), 14.
48. James Grantham Turner, '"Romance" and the Novel in Restoration England,' *Review of English Studies* 63, no. 258 (2011): 63.
49. Cervantes, *Don Quixote* (Ware: Wordsworth, 1993), 227, 228.
50. From, James Boswell *The Life of Samuel Johnson*, quoted in Norma Clarke, *Dr Johnson's Women* (London: Pimlico, 2005), 99. Robert DeMaria Jr suggests that Johnson probably learned to read with *Don Bellianis of Greece* and *Seven Champions of Christendom* which were 'more trivial' than other versions of romance which served as moral allegories. See *Samuel Johnson and the Life of Reading* (Baltimore, MD: Johns Hopkins University Press, 2009), 187.
51. Cervantes, *Don Quixote*, 228.
52. [Delarivier Manley], *The Secret History of Queen Zarah and the Zarazians* (London: [n.pub.], 1705), [n.p.].
53. Patrick Fagan, *The Second City: Portrait of Dublin 1700–1760* (Dublin: Branar, 1986), esp. 172; David Dickson, *Dublin: The Making of a Capital City* (London: Profile, 2015), 149.
54. Alexandre de La Roberdière, *Love Victorious: or The Adventures of Oronces and Eugenia, A novel*, trans. by J. E. (London: Printed for R. Bentley and S. Magnes, 1684), 63.
55. La Roberdière, *Love Victorious*, 68.
56. William Congreve, *The Way of the World*, ed. Brian Gibbons (London: A & C Black, 1993), IV i ll 21–2.
57. Margaret Anne Doody, 'Frances Sheridan: Morality and Annihilated Time,' in *Fetter'd or Free: British Women Novelists, 1670–1815*, ed. Mary Anne Schofield and Cecilia Macheski (Athens, OH, and London: Ohio University Press, 1987), 355, 353.
58. *The Town and Country Magazine*, issue 23 (May 1791): 216; *Critical Review*, vol. 1 (April 1791): 469; *Monthly Review*, vol. 8 (July 1792): 341.
59. Frances Sheridan to Mrs Victor, 16 November 17[63], in *The Private Correspondence of David Garrick*, 16.
60. Fay Weldon, 'Foreword,' in Jane Austen, *Love and Friendship* (London: Hesperus, 2004), x.
61. Michael Cordner, 'Introduction,' in Richard Brinsley Sheridan, *'The School for Scandal' and Other Plays*, ed. Michael Cordner (Oxford and New York: Oxford University Press, 1998), xviii.
62. *English Review of Literature, Science, Discoveries, Inventions and Practical Controversies and Contests*, vol. 17 (April 1791): 310.

Select Bibliography and Further Reading

[Anon.] 'An Answer to the Young Lady; or, a Letter from Mrs. Slammekin to Miss Tabitha Tammy.' In *Cibber and Sheridan: or, The Dublin Miscellany*: 62–70. Dublin: Printed for Peter Wilson, 1743.

[Anon.] *Critical Review*, vol. 1 (April 1791): 469.

[Anon.] *English Review of Literature, Science, Discoveries, Inventions and Practical Controversies and Contests*, vol. 17 (April 1791): 310.

[Anon.] *The Gentleman's Magazine: And Historical Chronicle*, September 1827: 199–200.

[Anon.] *Monthly Review*, vol. 8 (July 1792): 341.

[Anon.] 'Irish Theatrical Intelligence.' *The London Courant, and Westminster Chronicle*, 16 March 1781 [n.p.].

[Anon.] *The Town and Country Magazine*, issue 23 (May 1791): 216.

Aulnoy, Madame d'. *The Ingenious and Diverting Letters of a Lady's Travels into Spain. Describing the Devotions, Nunneries, Humour, Customs, Laws, Militia, Trade, Diet, and Recreations of that People. Intermixt with Great Variety of Modern Adventures, and Surprising Accidents: Being the Truest and Best Remarks Extant on that Court and Country*. 5th edn. London: Printed for Samuel Crouch, 1703.

Austen, Jane. *Love and Friendship*. Foreword by Fay Weldon. London: Hesperus, 2004.

Ballaster, Ros. *Seductive Forms: Women's Amatory Fiction from 1684 to 1740*. Oxford: Clarendon Press, 1992.

Barbauld, Anna Laetitia, ed. *The Correspondence of Samuel Richardson*, vol. 4. New York: AMS, 1966.

Boaden, James, ed. *The Private Correspondence of David Garrick*, vol. 1. London: Henry Colburn and Richard Bentley, 1831.

Boswell, James, *The Life of Samuel Johnson*, vol. 1. London: Henry Baldwin for Charles Dilly, 1791.

Caudle, James J. 'Dilly, Charles (1739–1807), bookseller.' *Oxford Dictionary of National Biography*. https://doi.org/10.1093/ref:odnb/7671

Cervantes, *Don Quixote*. Ware: Wordsworth, 1993.

[Chamberlaine, Frances]. 'A Letter from a Young Lady to Mr. Cibber.' In *Cibber and Sheridan: or, The Dublin Miscellany*: 55–61. Dublin: Printed for Peter Wilson, 1743.

[Chamberlaine, Frances]. 'Verses address'd to Mr. Sheridan, on his late Affair in the Theatre.' In *Cibber and Sheridan: or, The Dublin Miscellany*: 70–1. Dublin: Peter Wilson, 1743.

Clarke, Norma. *Dr Johnson's Women*. London: Pimlico, 2005.

Congreve, William. *The Way of the World*. Edited by Brian Gibbons. London: A & C Black, 1993.

DeMaria Jr, Robert. *Samuel Johnson and the Life of Reading*. Baltimore, MD: Johns Hopkins University Press, 2009.

Dickson, David. *Dublin: The Making of a Capital City*. London: Profile, 2015.

Doody, Margaret Anne. 'Frances Sheridan: Morality and Annihilated Time.' In *Fetter'd or Free: British Women Novelists, 1670–1815*, ed. Mary Anne Schofield and Cecilia Macheski, 324–58. Athens, OH and London: Ohio University Press, 1987.

Fagan, Patrick. *The Second City: Portrait of Dublin 1700–1760*. Dublin: Branar, 1986.

Gillespie, Raymond. 'Religion and Urban Society: The Case of Early Modern Dublin.' *Proceedings of the British Academy* 107 (2001): 223–38.

Greene, John C. *Theatre in Dublin 1745–1820: A Calendar of Performances*, vol. 3. Bethlehem: Lehigh University Press, 2011.

Haviland, Thomas Philip. *The* Roman de Longue Haleine *on English Soil*. Philadelphia, PA: University of Pennsylvania, 1931.

Johnson, Samuel. *The Rambler*, no. 4 (31 March 1750), 28–36.

La Roberdière, Alexandre de. *Love Victorious: or The Adventures of Oronces and Eugenia, A novel*. Translated by J. E. London: Printed for R. Bentley and S. Magnes, 1684.

LeFanu, Alicia. *Memoirs of the Life and Writings of Mrs. Frances Sheridan*. Edited by Anna M. Fitzer, *Memoirs of Women Writers*, vol. 1. London: Pickering & Chatto, 2012.

LeFanu, Alicia. *Strathallan*. Edited by Anna M. Fitzer. London: Pickering & Chatto, 2008.

[Manley, Delarivier]. *The Secret History of Queen Zarah and the Zarazians*. London, 1705.

Montague-Smith, Patrick W. 'Sheridan's Maternal Ancestors, The Chamberlaines of Kingsclere.' *The Genealogists' Magazine* 15, no. 9 (1967): 319–30.

O'Keeffe, John. *Recollections of the Life of John O'Keeffe*, vol. 1. London: Henry Colburn, 1826.

Rae, W. Fraser. 'Sheridan's Sisters.' *Temple Bar* 118, no. 466 (September 1899): 45–63.

Russell, Norma H. 'Some Uncollected Authors XXXVIII: Frances Sheridan, 1724–1766.' *The Book Collector* 13 (1964): 196–205.

Sheldon, Esther K. *Thomas Sheridan of Smock-Alley*. Princeton, NJ: Princeton University Press, 1967.

Sheridan, Elizabeth. *Betsy Sheridan's Journal: Letters from Sheridan's Sister*. Edited by William LeFanu. Oxford and New York: Oxford University Press, 1986.

Sheridan, Frances. 'The History of Nourjahad.' In *Oriental Tales*, ed. Robert L. Mack. London and New York: Oxford University Press, 1992.

Sheridan, Frances. *Memoirs of Miss Sidney Bidulph*. Edited by Patricia Köster and Jean Coates Cleary. London and New York: Oxford University Press, 1995.

Sheridan, Frances. *The Plays of Frances Sheridan*. Edited by Robert Hogan and Jerry C. Beasley. Cranbury, NJ, London and Mississauga, ON: Associated University Presses, 1984.

Sheridan, Richard Brinsley. *'The School for Scandal' and Other Plays*. Edited by Michael Cordner. Oxford and New York: Oxford University Press, 1998.

Tierney, James E. 'Faulkner, George (1703?–1775), printer and bookseller.' *Oxford Dictionary of National Biography*. https://doi.org/10.1093/ref:odnb/9205.

Turner, James Grantham. '"Romance" and the Novel in Restoration England.' *Review of English Studies* 63, no. 258 (2011): 58–85.

Warner, William B. 'The Elevation of the Novel in England: Hegemony and Literary History.' *ELH* 59, no. 3 (Autumn 1992): 577–96.

Whyte, Samuel, and Whyte, Edward-Athenry. *A Miscellany*. Dublin: Robert Marchbank, 1799.

Wycherley, William. *The Country Wife*. Edited by James Ogden. London: A & C Black, 1997.

Note on the Text

This text reproduces the first edition of *Eugenia and Adelaide, A Novel* published by Charles Dilly in 1791. In preparation of this volume, the long 's' has been modernised and the convention of placing quotation marks at the beginning of each new paragraph of long narration eliminated. The use of single and double quotation marks to indicate alternate speakers is revised and all such marks made single. The text is faithful to the original's omission of quotation marks for dialogue within interpolated first-person narratives, where the syntax is sufficient to indicate shifts from one speaker to another, though some inconsistencies and complexities of the original are addressed. The original's use of parenthetical reminders of speaker orientation within long first-person narratives is applied sparingly in other cases where the original quotation mark(s) are disruptive. Spellings in use in the eighteenth century have been retained. There are few inconsistencies though instances where the same word appears in its older form and in acceptable alternative or modern spelling have not been corrected. Other original punctuation has been retained. Obvious errors or misprints have been silently corrected.

Preface

THE following Work was written some years back by an original hand, now cold, whose manner will probably be traced and relished by those Readers who are inclined to rank nature and truth above the extravagant fictions which are daily served up under the title of Genuine History and Adventures.

The Editor trusts the Reader will find incident, interest, and character in the story now before him:—To say more might be looked upon as impertinent; and it would not be acting as a friend to the Work and the memory of the Author to say less.

Volume I

Eugenia and Adelaide

Adelaide and Eugenia were both natives of Salerno, in the kingdom of Naples;[1] the one, daughter of the Baron St. Seberina;[2] the other, to Signior Lorenzo Burganeze, of the illustrious house of Sulmona.[3]

These two young persons had contracted a friendship almost in their infancy, which the intimacy subsisting between their parents served to strengthen as they grew up. Adelaide was never easy without her dear Eugenia; nor could that lady be happy in any company but that of her charming friend.

The years of childhood stole away insensibly, in the enjoyment of a tender and mutual friendship, their pleasures were the same, and their pains (if they had any) were so too. In short, there was so perfect a union between them, that they appeared to be informed by one mind. But the time was now arrived when they must part, and each experience different fortunes and cares, unfelt before.

Signior Burganeze died, and left his widow and daughter in such moderate circumstances, as obliged them all at once to retrench their expences. Madame Burganeze, mortified at this sudden change in her condition, determined to leave Salerno and retire to a monastery, since she could no longer appear there with her usual splendour. She was already preparing to depart, when she received a very obliging letter from her brother the Marquis of Pescara,[4] who at that time resided at Milan, where he had a considerable post.

This nobleman, on receiving an account of the death of Signior Burganeze, wrote to his sister in the warmest terms, inviting her and her daughter to accept of his house for their future abode, assuring them they should meet with a reception answerable to the love he bore them.

Madame Burganeze did not hesitate to accept of so kind an offer: she bid her daughter prepare for their journey; and, having their equipage considerably diminished, they were soon in readiness to leave Salerno.

Whatever pleasure Eugenia felt on the prospect of so agreeable a change in her fortune, she could not think of being separated from her beloved companion without a lively sorrow; but when the day of her departure came, on which she was to bid adieu to Adelaide, tears and embraces were on this occasion employed to supply the place of words; and Eugenia, unable to speak, broke from the arms of her friend; and, throwing herself into a chariot (in which her mother was already placed at the door) they set out directly for Milan.

We will here for a while take leave of the disconsolate Adelaide, and accompany Madame Burganeze and her daughter, who by easy journeys arrived in ten days at Milan; and were received by the Marquis of Pescara with the highest marks of affection.

This nobleman was many years younger than Madame Burganeze, being her brother only by the father's side. He was handsome, accomplished, and magnificent; which, joined to one of the gayest tempers in the world, made his house the rendezvous of all the youth of quality in Milan: but notwithstanding the merits of the Marquis had rendered him the distinguished favourite of the fair, he had as yet preserved his heart; and, whilst many in secret sighed for him, he behaved towards all with equal appearance of gallantry, though he felt nothing but real indifference.

After the arrival of Madame Burganeze and Eugenia, numbers of ladies had come to visit them, who had no pretence for appearing at the house of the Marquis before, but were now glad of this opportunity of seeing and conversing with him. In short, the concourse of nobility, of both sexes, who flocked daily to the palace of Pescara, formed it into a kind of little court.

Madame Burganeze was in her forty-fifth year; personal vanity her reigning foible; a passion for admiration was of course the result of such a turn of mind: but during the life-time of Signior Burganeze, she had been obliged, as much as possible, to hide this disposition, as he was not of a temper to allow for it, in the smallest degree. She had never loved him; and was but moderately afflicted at his death. Her daughter she considered rather as a rival than a friend; but concealed those sentiments as carefully, and those that more immediately concerned herself. Her freedom recovered, and her brother's invitation to what she knew must be a scene of gaiety, had roused those latent sparks of vanity that time had nearly subdued; and she went to Milan with the strongest hopes of finding every wish of her heart gratified. She had now for almost a year been a partaker with her daughter in those pleasures which reigned, and perpetually succeeded each other, at the house of the Marquis; but alas, she was more and more convinced she was no longer able to charm! cold respect was all she met with from the men; and from the younger part of her own sex a sort of insipid kindness, that showed her how little formidable she appeared to them. This observation at first sensibly afflicted her; when, reflecting that if she should continue with the Marquis, she should only expose herself to new mortifications every day, she resolved at once to abjure those pleasures which (to her) had now lost their chief relish. Thus determined, she took an opportunity one day (after having expressed the warmest acknowledgments for her brother's tenderness) to inform him, that it was now high time for her to think of bidding adieu to the vain enjoyments of this life, and of dedicating the remainder of her days to devotion. She told him, the Prioress of St. Bridget's, who was her relation, had invited her to her house on the death of Signior Burganeze, and she was about to accept of her offer when she received the kind and generous tender of his service; that it was chiefly on Eugenia's account she had declined the invitation made her by the prioress, whom she acknowledged she would not think of secluding from the world but with the greatest reluctance; yet, finding herself now disposed to reassume her first intentions, she was inclined to take her daughter with her; beauty and innocence being all her portion, she dreaded leaving her exposed to the many temptations which youth and want of experience might lead her into, and with which, she said, the house of the Marquis was surrounded: 'perhaps,' said she, 'my daughter may marry below her quality, or have her charms blasted by some envious tongue. Oh, brother, I tremble at the thought! and would sooner bury Eugenia in a nunnery, than'—The Marquis interrupted his sister here, and conjured her to banish such thoughts; telling her, if ever she loved, or confided in him, she would not scruple to trust Eugenia to his care. 'I will be as tender of her happiness,' added he, 'as you yourself would be; and as I mean to give her a fortune equal to her birth, I have even cast my eyes on a husband for her, in whose possession (if he has your approbation, and I find his estate suitable to his other endowments) I should think my niece happy. Let me therefore, dear sister, beg of you to talk no more of a cloister, since there are much more desirable prospects for your daughter.' The Marquis added many arguments to dissuade Madame Burganeze from her intentions of retiring; but she assured him, her resolution with regard to herself was fixed:—'I yield Eugenia however to you,' said she, 'and transfer all my right in her to your fraternal goodness: take her, brother, dispose of her; for I am sure your prudence will make no choice but such as I shall approve of; and as I should be glad to see her under the protection of a husband before I go to my retreat, tell me who the person is you have thoughts of bestowing her on?'—'He is a Spaniard of high quality,' answered the Marquis: 'his name is Don Clement Pimenteles, and he is descended from the House of Telbes,[5] one of the most ancient in Castile.[6] He was introduced to me a few days ago by the Prince of Bassiniano,[7] with whom he came into Italy. The Prince has a particular esteem for him: and indeed he is so very amiable, that I think it is impossible to see him without loving him.'—'I see, brother,' said Madame Burganeze, 'that you are already charmed, and will make my daughter so too, if you paint him in such fine colours.'—'As for that,' replied the Marquis, 'you shall neither of you be left to judge by my description of him; for he is to dine with me to-day, and you will then see whether I have done him justice.'

Eugenia entered the room just as the Marquis said these words: 'We are speaking of a person,' said he, addressing himself to his niece, 'whom Madame Burganeze already prophecies you will fall in love with: for my part, I own, were I a woman, I should prefer him to all the men I have ever yet seen; and if I could find one of your sex every way so charming as Don Clement Pimenteles, I should no longer have that liberty to boast of which I have hitherto preserved. In a word, this young cavalier is so very agreeable, that I was struck with him at first sight. The Prince tells me his wit is as engaging as his person; and indeed, by what I could judge from the short conversation I had with him, he is perfectly accomplished. Such a conquest therefore, Eugenia,' proceeded he, smiling, 'would do no small honour to your beauty.'

Though Eugenia had but little occasion for the help of art to set off one of the finest persons that ever nature formed, she was not free from the little vanity of her sex: she omitted nothing in her dress that day which could add to her charms. The Marquis was rallying her on the great pains she had taken to adorn herself, when a page came to inform him that Don Clement was come.

The Marquis went to receive him, and soon returned with him into Madame Burganeze's apartment; where presenting him to that lady and Eugenia, one after the other, 'You see, Signior,' said he, 'that I am more devoted to the fair than people imagine: these ladies live with me; and I think myself the happiest man in the world in their society. My sister indeed has formed an unkind purpose of leaving me, in order to retire into a convent: perhaps if you join with me, we may yet dissuade her from it, though I have been so unhappy as not to succeed in my endeavours towards it: nay, it was with some difficulty that I could prevail to have Eugenia left with me.'

'Madame Burganeze,' answered Don Clement, 'has more justice than to rob the world at once of two such ornaments. But you, my Lord, I must say, are too selfish in desiring to engross so much merit and so many charms, and to deprive the convent of the share it has a right to by the pious choice the lady, your sister, has made.' It was easy to perceive which part of this compliment was addressed to Madame Burganeze; and though it seemed rather to encourage her in her resolution than dissuade her from it, yet it did not displease her; every thing which Don Clement said was accompanied with a gracefulness that could not fail of charming. The most delicate praises from one who is disagreeable to us may be uttered without the least effect; but the slightest compliment pronounced by a beautiful mouth, is sure to make an impression. This observation Madame Burganeze already found verified in herself, and that her years and piety were too feeble a guard against youth and irresistible charms; for such Don Clement was possessed of: no wonder then if the breast of Eugenia, defenceless as it was, was warmed as soon as that of Madame Burganeze.

Don Clement discovered so much wit and delicacy in his conversation, that his company was as acceptable to the two ladies as it was to the Marquis:—he staid till it was late; and the Marquis would not suffer him to retire, without first making him promise to pass the next day at his house.

When Eugenia was alone she had time to reflect on the person and behaviour of this stranger: she thought her uncle's menaces were not without foundation, and that she ought to have secured her heart against charms that she already began to find too powerful. In short, she perceived a change in it which alarmed her; she passed the night unquietly, and no sooner saw daylight than she arose and called her woman to dress her.

She waited impatiently for the hour which was to bring Pimenteles to her sight:—at length he appeared; and Eugenia thought him a thousand times handsomer than before. This second day's interview entirely subdued her heart. With what joy then did she hear the Marquis (who was highly charmed with Don Clement) insist on his living at his hotel during his stay at Venice! The young Spaniard accepted his invitation with pleasure; of which Eugenia flattered herself she might be the occasion.

He was now become their guest: she saw and conversed with him every day; and every day became more and more enamoured. She was not ignorant of her uncle's designs; and longed to know how Don Clement's heart was affected towards her, when an opportunity offered to satisfy her impatience.

She was alone walking in the garden, her thoughts full of Pimenteles, when she saw him enter with the Marquis; to whose discourse he seemed listening attentively. Eugenia did not care to interrupt them by her presence; and had just time to slip behind an alabaster statue when they passed her by, and turned down a close walk that was almost darkened by a thick row of orange trees, which shaded it on each side.

Eugenia heard her uncle pronounce her name as he walked by her; when, seized with a lover's curiosity on finding herself the subject of their conversation, she stole softly into a little alley, which ran parallel to the walk in which the Marquis and Don Clement were engaged in discourse. The former spoke so loud, that Eugenia could easily hear him say, 'and yet I could not prevail on my sister till I assured her I had other views for Eugenia; and that, as I could give her a fortune equal almost to any lady in Milan, I intended to look out for a match for her suitable to her rank. If Madame Burganeze persists in her design of going into a convent, I must be the more speedy in disposing of my niece; for my house, without a mother's care, may not be a sanctuary for one so young and handsome.'—'Your prudence, my Lord, is highly to be commended,' answered Don Clement; and turned the conversation with an indifference that touched Eugenia to the quick: she had not lost a word of what her uncle had said, and listened greedily to what Don Clement would reply to so broad a hint; but the coldness of his answer filled her with a good deal of confusion.—'What can be the meaning of this!' said she; 'Don Clement is very young, and, if I have any judgment, far from being insensible; I am not disagreeable, and have some advantages which might recommend me: perhaps he is in love elsewhere, or has discovered my weakness for him; or—I know not what to think. Cruel Pimenteles! how easy are you in that indifference which is so tormenting to me!' Here some tears stole down her cheeks, which a consciousness of her own worth made her so ashamed of, that she quickly wiped them off. It is a sufficient mortification for a woman's pride to find her heart in the possession of a man who never asked her for it; but to find that man even cold and negligent, is a circumstance that few know how to support:—such was Eugenia's situation; and she now began to experience all those vicissitudes of hopes, fears, and jealousies, of which before she had but an imperfect idea.

Now it was she wanted a faithful friend to complain to: a thousand times did she wish for Adelaide; but those wishes were fruitless, and she continued in a kind of languor, which with all her endeavours she could scarcely hide. At length she resolved to write to her friend, and hoped for some consolation. Her letter was as follows:—'Though since we parted I have perpetually regretted your absence, yet I now feel the loss of you more sensibly than ever. I wish you were with me; but alas, I can no more entertain you as I used to do: Eugenia is no longer the same! You will doubtless ask the occasion of this change, and I will confess it to you:—Don Clement Pimenteles, whom I mentioned to you in my last, has worked this strange metamorphosis; and, from the most cheerful person in the world, has made me the most melancholy: in short, I shall ever love him. Dear Adelaide, if you were to see him!—and yet, would you believe it, he is as cold as marble! and I could kill myself for having the least tenderness for him. Oh that my sighs would bear me to happy Salerno, the scene of all my past innocent pleasures! where I first tasted the sweets of friendship, when unacquainted with the pains of love! Why did I leave you? or why did Don Clement leave Castile? Adieu, my Adelaide: advise and pity me.'

Eugenia had but just dispatched this letter to her friend, and was passing along a gallery which led to her apartment, when she met the Marquis and Don Clement; the latter of whom saluting her, stepped back, and hastily threw a little note at her feet, and, without speaking, immediately joined the Marquis.

Eugenia ran, or rather flew, to her chamber, to see what this unexpected billet contained: she was ready to tear it, so great was her impatience to get it open. These were the contents:—'I have long wished for an opportunity to reveal the secrets of my heart to you; but my wishes have always been disappointed: it is in your power to deliver me from the greatest anxiety of my soul. Suffer me then, fair Eugenia, to throw myself at your feet this night, in your own apartment, where I may, without witnesses, make an explanation to you—on which the happiness of my life depends.'

The pleasure that Eugenia felt on reading these words is not to be conceived by any but those who have been in the like circumstances. She, who the moment before had abandoned herself to sorrow, was now transported with joy: what was past appeared like a dream to her; and she persuaded herself that she was as dear to Don Clement as he was to her. The satisfaction she took in this reflection was nevertheless not unmixed with some alloy of doubt: she could not account for the reserve of Don Clement's behaviour on the Marquis's conference with him in the garden; nor had she in his whole conduct towards herself ever remarked any symptoms of love. However, as we find it an easy matter to persuade ourselves to believe what we wish, so Eugenia, satisfied that Pimenteles loved her with a flame equal to her own, entirely gave way to the agreeable reflection. 'No doubt,' said she, 'he has prudent reasons for having hitherto concealed his love, which he now means to lay open to me in this interview.—Yes, Don Clement,' said she, 'I will see you to-night, and deliver both you and myself from the pain of a cruel suspense.'

She saw Don Clement at supper; he watched her eyes; and they did not fail to give a favourable answer to his note. She retired early to her apartment, and, dismissing her woman, shut herself into her dressing-room: she took a book in her hand to beguile the tedious minutes till Pimenteles should arrive. Her eyes indeed were fixed on the paper, and she strove to attend to what she was reading; but her thoughts were too much agitated for such an employment, from which she was not released so speedily as she wished; for the clock struck twelve before Don Clement approached. At length she heard him rap softly at the door which opened from her dressing-room to the back-stairs: she arose, trembling, to let him in; he entered, and seemed to be in as much confusion as herself. He excused his stay, by telling her the Marquis had engaged him till that minute; and added, 'How much am I obliged to you, amiable Eugenia, for this piece of condescension! and how miserable would a denial of my request have made me!'

'I cannot tell you, Signior,' said Eugenia, 'how I can answer it to discretion, to admit a visit from a young cavalier so unseasonably; and, I assure you, you are indebted entirely to my curiosity for this compliance.'—'I bless the motive, let it be what it will,' answered Don Clement, 'that has procured me such a favour. But I dare not proceed, without being first assured of your forgiveness; which, thus suppliant, I entreat.'—Saying this, he bent one knee to the ground, and, taking Eugenia's hand with a respect mixed with tenderness, 'Do you promise to pardon me, Madam,' said he, 'if I declare myself freely? Oh tell me,—for you are all my hope—excellent Eugenia, may I speak!'—'You may,' answered Eugenia, in a broken voice (her confusion almost depriving her of speech) 'you may speak; but don't take advantage of this liberty, by saying more than I ought to hear.'

Don Clement, after a short pause, was going to reply, when Madame Burganeze (whose apartment joined close to those of her daughter) hearing two persons talk in that lady's chamber, rose out of bed, and, with her night-gown only thrown loose about her, entered the room with some precipitation.

The consternation they were both in is not to be described. Eugenia remained with her face covered with blushes; her eyes fixed on the ground, not once so much as daring to lift them up towards her mother. Don Clement, who had started from his knees, was almost in the same condition with herself; and, not having the courage to speak, gave Madame Burganeze an opportunity of looking at them both by turns, with eyes inflamed with anger, as if doubtful which should first feel the effects of her rage. At length she turned it all on poor Eugenia; she gave a shriek before she could get her words out (for she was almost choaked with passion) and then flying at her daughter with the utmost fury, she would certainly have done her some mischief, if Don Clement (who was by this time recovered from his surprise) had not interposed. 'I beseech you, Madam,' said he, 'be pacified; or turn all your anger upon me, who alone deserve it: Eugenia is not to blame.'—'Who then is to blame, traitor?' replied she, turning fiercely towards him. 'Ask yourself, Madam,' said he, assuming a languishing air; 'accuse your own charms, which have been the cause of this intrusion.'—'How!' said Madame Burganeze, 'Was it the influence of my charms that brought you to my daughter's chamber at midnight? Ah Don Clement! that is a weak pretence to screen your own baseness and Eugenia's folly.'—'Alas,' replied Don Clement, 'if you will but hear me, you will be satisfied of the injustice you do both your daughter and me.'—'Well, let me hear what you have to say,' cried Madame Burganeze, who began to grow a little calm. 'Know then, Madam,' replied Don Clement, 'that I have adored you from the first moment I beheld you; but the fear of offending you, always obliged me to conceal my presumptuous flame. My Lord Marquis informed me of your resolution of retiring to a convent:—a resolution that, while it added to my love, heightened my despair. At the same time he encouraged me to raise my wishes to the fair Eugenia. To any other person this would have been a happiness to be received with transport: but, prepossessed as I was with another passion, I could only look upon the honour he intended me as a fresh obstacle to my desires. Thus embarrassed, I knew no way to extricate myself, but by disclosing the secret of my love to the generous Eugenia, and imploring her interest and assistance in so delicate an affair.' Here Don Clement ceased; and cast his eyes on the ground, as if waiting for a favourable answer.

Madame Burganeze remained some time in suspense what to answer. At length, with a look half-smiling and half-reserved, 'Methinks, Don Clement,' said she, 'you have not acted altogether very discreetly: you had near made me very angry with my daughter. But I can forgive you, since it was owing to an excess of modesty:—Modesty is commendable in a young man. But go; I will hear no more at present, 'tis late: so I beg you may retire.—Eugenia, go to bed, child:—I am sorry for what has passed; but you must forget it: you see I am pacified.' With these words she left the room, and locked the door on her daughter, having first made Don Clement withdraw; who had but just time to give Eugenia to understand, by a sign, the part he intended to act.

If Eugenia, on the one hand, was rejoiced that she had escaped her mother's resentment, she was however not a little mortified at being disappointed of the pleasure she proposed to herself in hearing Don Clement breathe out his vows at her feet. She was in pain to think how he would extricate himself out of the difficulty into which he had been brought by this contrivance; for she saw but too plainly with what pleasure her mother had received the declaration he had made; and was terribly afraid of the consequences.

She spent the remainder of the night in those uneasy reflections. Don Clement, on his part, was not without his cares:—and Madame Burganeze was as restless as either of them: but her thoughts were employed in the gayest manner imaginable. She had conceived an affection for Don Clement from the first moment she saw him: nay, and flattered herself with the hopes of a return: but the great reserve of that young Spaniard had almost tired her expectations.—How agreeably then was she surprised, when he told her that he loved her! and that at a time too, when her jealous fears persuaded her that he was paying his court to her daughter!

She did not indeed sleep the whole night; but the thoughts of this new amour was so pleasing to her, that it took place of every other consideration:—the convent was no longer remembered; and her whole study was now bent on rendering herself agreeable in her lover's eyes.

Accordingly she was no sooner risen than she seated herself at her toilet:—jewels were now to be placed advantageously in her hair; a vanity which she had lately affected to have an utter abhorrence to. The weather was grown too sultry for a veil; so that was thrown aside, to display the diamonds in her ears: and her woman was of a sudden become so very unhandy, that she was obliged to dress and undress her lady several times, before she could get her clothes to sit with any tolerable grace.

At length Madame Burganeze, adorned as gay and as splendidly as she was on her wedding-day, stood before her glass, to contemplate herself; and remembering Pimenteles had expressed his fear of offending her by a discovery of his love, —'La Pointz,'[8] said she, 'have I any thing forbidding in my looks? I always thought I had rather an air of too much complaisance.'—'Madam,' answered the cunning La Pointz (who knew her lady's failing) 'you have without doubt a most affable countenance; but then you have a certain air of majesty in your eyes that must infallibly strike an awe into every beholder.'—'Answer me another question,' cried Madame Burganeze, 'and answer me sincerely; How old do I appear to be?'—'Why, Madam,' said La Pointz, 'only that I know, from the time that I have been in your Ladyship's family, that you can't be much under forty, I should think that you had hardly seen three-and-thirty.'—'Impossible!' cried Madame Burganeze: 'You flatter: you certainly flatter! I am sure if I should own to six-and-thirty no one would disbelieve me.'—'Indeed but they would,' replied the woman, laughing (who knew she might have added several years to the account): 'I don't believe any one that looked at you would be persuaded of that.'

The infatuated Burganeze, who was a coquette in addition to her other follies, did not perceive that her woman was ridiculing her vanity: and, beginning to reassume her former ideas, she now looked upon herself as irresistible; and made no doubt of her being able to secure Don Clement's heart. But, notwithstanding the good opinion she had revived of her own charms, she was not without some fears on account of the youth and beauty of her daughter: and, as jealous eyes are more penetrating than others, she for a long time had observed that Eugenia did not look upon Don Clement with indifference; and she saw that the Marquis, her brother, was well disposed to favour an union between them. These two circumstances, therefore, made her resolve to be as watchful over her daughter's conduct as possible: for this purpose she placed an old waiting-maid about her (that she had known and confided in for many years) with strict orders to lie in her chamber, and attend her where-ever she went.

This unusual restraint soon became intolerable to Eugenia; and the more so, as she saw it gave Don Clement the greatest uneasiness; for she had it not in her power to speak to him, but in her mother's presence, ever since he had declared himself that lady's lover.

However, she flattered herself that he would, by some means or other, find an opportunity of conversing with her. Nor was she deceived; for, sitting one evening in an arbour in the garden, she saw her mother enter, leaning on Don Clement's arm. Eugenia rose up, out of respect to the former (to whom she thought her presence would not be very acceptable) and withdrew, to leave her the more at liberty.

Don Clement was vexed at her retiring so hastily, as he had prepared a little billet, which he resolved at all hazards to convey to her; but her sudden absenting herself disappointed him in his design. He inwardly cursed Madame Burganeze, while she was leading him to a seat, singing an amorous air. He was forced, however, to affect an appearance of satisfaction; and, placing himself by her side, he observed a book lying on one of the seats, which Eugenia had by accident left behind her: he immediately thought of slipping his letter between the leaves of it; and by that means to convey it into Eugenia's own hands, without her mother's suspecting any thing of the matter: wherefore, taking up the book, after some discourse with Madame Burganeze, he proposed taking a turn or two more in the garden; and, rising up, he gave that lady his hand, and led her towards that quarter of the garden to which he had seen Eugenia direct her steps: he soon perceived her sitting at the end of a long terrace: but Madame Burganeze no sooner spied her daughter than she cried, 'Fye, Don Clement, what makes you chuse this walk? It is the most unpleasant of the whole garden.'—'I am of your opinion, Madam,' replied Don Clement; 'and I know not how I came to wander hither: but, since we are here, suffer me to restore this book to your daughter, which, I suppose, was her entertainment when we frighted her out of the arbour.'—'Let me see it first,' cried Madame Burganeze; and immediately taking it out of Don Clement's hand, the leaves, without mercy, opened directly at the place where the note was concealed:—'What have we got here?' said she, and straight unfolded it; for it was but doubled carelessly, without being sealed. I leave my reader to judge what a situation Don Clement was in at this unexpected misfortune:—he cursed Madame Burganeze, the letter, and his own indiscretion; and expected every minute that she would upbraid him with his falsehood: but happy was it for him that his mistress's sight was so impaired (owing to a heavy illness she had had); she could not read a word without the help of her glasses, which she thought would be a disgrace to make use of in the presence of her lover: however, she affected to examine the paper; when, returning it to Don Clement, 'Prithee, read this,' said she; 'for, I protest, my eyes have been so weak ever since the death of my husband, that I can scarce distinguish a letter.' Don Clement was rejoiced at this unexpected turn of good luck: 'It is only a song, Madam,' said he; and, pretending to read it, he repeated the first lines that came into his head, which Madame

Burganeze was mightily pleased with, and suffered him to restore the book and the song to her daughter.

Eugenia no sooner found herself alone than she perused her lover's letter, which contained these words:—'The constraint I am under towards you, and the complaisance I am obliged to shew your mother, are equally painful to me; but the time is not yet come for me to undeceive her. You see the difficulty of my situation; and yet you do not know the half of what I suffer. Dear Eugenia; if you have any pity for me, permit me once more to talk to you without reserve. If you will walk this evening, about seven o'clock, in the great wood adjoining the park, I will find means to converse with you.—When you see a person covered with a white veil, know that for your obliged

PIMENTELES.'

The reading this note revived Eugenia's hopes again: she returned into the house, with her thoughts more agreeably employed than they had been for some days past. She was told that Don Clement was just going to Lodi,[9] in order to see a friend; and, making no doubt but that he feigned this journey, on purpose that he might have the better opportunity of meeting her at the expected rendezvous, she longed for the appointed hour.

On account of Don Clement's absence she the more easily obtained leave of Madame Burganeze to go abroad. Wherefore, setting out, attended by the old woman, she quickly crossed the park which joined the Marquis's gardens; and, having reached the wood, she was not long before she discovered Don Clement in the disguise he had mentioned in his letter.

He was covered with a white silk veil striped with silver; which, reaching from head to foot, concealed him so entirely, that neither his shape nor clothes could be discovered; and, had not Eugenia been apprized of his design, she could never have suspected him for any other than what he appeared to be.

Don Clement was at some little distance; but, having spied Eugenia as soon as she did him, and altering his voice, he called out to her; at the same time advancing to meet her.—Eugenia, affecting surprise, ran towards him:—'Is it possible,' said she, 'that this is Donna Aurora?[10] Who would have dreamt of meeting you at Milan? How charmed will my mother be to see you!'—'I have so short a time to stay,' answered the counterfeit Donna, 'that I can't wait on Madame Burganeze; therefore I beg you will not let her know of having seen me.' Saying this, he took Eugenia under the arm; and speaking in a tone not to be heard by her attendant, 'Thus far,' said he, 'we have succeeded happily; but your troublesome guardian pursues us so closely that I am as much to seek as ever; for she will certainly suspect something if we whisper too long.'—'I know no way to get rid of her,' answered Eugenia, 'but to tire her so heartily that she will be glad to sit down to rest, and we may then saunter out of her hearing.' Don Clement could not help laughing at this contrivance; and, much approving of it, they both walked as fast as possible, resolving to lead the old duenna[11] such a dance as would make her glad to sit down, and leave them at liberty.

Ursina[12] (that was the attendant's name) trotted after them as fast as she was able, when, being unused to so much walking, she called to them, conjuring them, for God's sake, not to walk at such a rate, as she found it impossible to keep up with them; and assured them she was ready to faint with weariness. This was just what they wanted. Eugenia slackened her pace, and told Ursina, she might sit down in the shade, whilst she and her companion continued their walk. The duenna begged they wouldn't go out of sight: which Eugenia faithfully promising, the old woman flung herself on the grass, and, being much fatigued, soon fell asleep.

Now it was that the lovers found themselves in possession of a few undisturbed minutes, which they had so ardently wished for: but they could not enjoy this happiness long enough to enter into an explanation, which would have spared each of them many sighs.

They were got into a part of the wood which was by the side of a by-road, and was separated from it only by a shallow brook: the sun was almost set, and Don Clement, fearing to lose more time, prayed Eugenia to sit down on the brink of the water, which they found very refreshing. Eugenia would have made choice of a place still more retired; but, fearing to alarm Ursina, lest she should chance to awake and miss them, she consented to remain where they were; when, seating herself on the brink of the rivulet, Don Clement placed himself by her.

He had drawn the veil from his face, as well for coolness as to be able to speak with the greater freedom, and was just entering into a conversation equally desired both by him and Eugenia, when they were alarmed by the appearance of two horsemen, well mounted and in Spanish habits, who came in a brisk trot towards them.

As they had rode out from a cross path, Eugenia and her lover were not aware of them, till they were so near as to have their faces and dress distinguished at once.

Don Clement no sooner saw them than he endeavoured, with great precipitation, to cover his face with the veil, when, through the most unlucky accident imaginable, it had got fast on a bush which hung just over his head: the haste he made to disengage it, together with the confusion he was in, served only to entangle it the more; so that, making a violent effort to tear it from the bush that held it, he dragged it quite off him; and at once made a discovery of what he so vainly endeavoured to conceal.

The two cavaliers, who had made a full stop from the first moment they observed him, now alighted from their horses, which they gave into the hands of a servant, who was leading an empty calash[13] after them; and one of them, crying out in a tone of the greatest exultation, 'Ha! art thou found at last, vile fugitive?' he leapt over the brook, and seized hold of Don Clement's shoulder.

Eugenia, in her first emotion of fear and surprise, fled to some little distance from the place where she had been sitting; but, her love overcoming her terror, she turned back, resolving to partake with her dear Pimenteles in the danger which she apprehended threatened him; but great was her astonishment and grief at seeing him surrounded by three men. She could perceive that one of them wrested a poniard out of his hand; whilst the other two, who had come to the assistance of the first, took him under each arm, and, notwithstanding his resistance, forced him into the calash; the eldest of the two cavaliers getting into it with him, whilst the other mounted his horse again; and all drove off like lightning.

Eugenia during this transaction was almost senseless; when the cries of the old duenna, who was by this time awake, roused her from her lethargy. Ursina ran to her charge:—'And are you safe?' said she: 'Are you, Eugenia? What is become of the lady? and who are those men that drove away just now?'—'I can answer none of your questions,' replied Eugenia; 'for I am frightened to death.'—'Oh! so I have you safe, it is no matter,' said Ursina. 'Let us make haste home. Madam, your mother will chide me for letting you stay so long.'

Eugenia was so overwhelmed with grief that she made her no reply; but, casting her eyes towards the fatal spot where Don Clement had been forced away, she saw his poniard lying on the ground, which had been dropped in the scuffle: the handle was gold; on which his name was decyphered in small diamonds. She snatched it up, and hid it under her gown, without being observed by her duenna.

As they were returning back, Ursina asked her several questions about the supposed lady who had met her in the wood; and Eugenia, finding by her inquiries that she had not discovered it to be Don Clement (for she did not awake till the strangers were driving away) she resolved not to let her into the truth of an adventure in which she had so near and tender an interest.

'That young lady,' said Eugenia, 'is called Donna Aurora de Silvio: she is a particular friend of mine; and I should be much concerned if I thought any misfortune had befallen her. She has indeed been just now taken away by two cavaliers; but I am inclined to believe it is with her own consent; for, you know, she desired me not to acquaint my mother with her being at Milan; and, at the same time, told me that she was not to remain here long: therefore I charge you, Ursina, not to mention the least word of any thing you have seen; for, if Donna Aurora's relations come to hear of it, it may bring both you and me into trouble.' Ursina, who was none of the cunningest of her sex, promised to be silent.

Eugenia returned home; but with a heart much heavier than when she left it. Her mother was indisposed, and the Marquis was abroad; so she saw neither of them that night: but the next day produced a dismal hurricane in the family of the Marquis.

Don Clement had promised faithfully to return next morning; when the impatient Burganeze, not finding him as good as his word, dispatched one of the servants to Lodi, to inquire the occasion of his delay. The messenger went to the house where he expected to find Don Clement; but returned with word that he had not been there at all.

Madame Burganeze, alarmed to the last degree at neither seeing nor hearing from him all that day, had now lost all patience: when the night and the succeeding day passed over without bringing any news of him, she stamped and raved like a mad woman; beat her maids, broke her china, and tore her hair. The Marquis, who till now was an utter stranger to her extravagant passion for Don Clement, was amazed at her behaviour. 'What then, Madam,' said he, 'and did you really love Pimenteles?'—'Yes,' cried she, furiously; 'and was beloved again.'—'I am surprised,' answered the Marquis, with an indignant smile, 'that he should so cruelly desert you, if you were the mistress of his heart.'—'Oh traitor!' said Madame Burganeze, 'are you then at the bottom of this contrivance, to rob me of my love? Be assured, if I find it out, I will make you an example to all perfidious brothers.' She pronounced this in a resolute tone, staring all the while at the Marquis as if she were possessed. 'For shame, sister!' said he, calmly: 'moderate this excessive frenzy, or you will oblige me to abate of that respect I should chuse to treat you with; which as I should be sorry to do, I will leave you to your cooler thoughts.' Saying this, he made her a low bow, and left her to vent her fury by herself.

Whilst many fruitless inquiries were making after Don Clement, Ursina, who began to entertain some suspicions about the adventure in the wood, addressed Eugenia thus:—'Here is a mighty work,' said she, 'to know what is become of Signior Pimenteles! Why, I'll be burnt if it was not he who carried away your friend Donna Aurora. It must be so. What other reason can he have for absenting himself? If you should find this to be the case, I hope you will allow me to be a woman of penetration.'

Eugenia, pleased to find her in such an error, said she was certainly in the right:—'How stupid was I,' said she, 'not to think of this! Aye, I make no doubt that Don Clement was the traitor; for,' added she, 'the fright I was in would not suffer me to make any particular observations on the ravishers. But you remember we are not supposed to know any thing of this matter; I beg therefore you may continue to keep the discreet silence you have hitherto observed.' Ursina could hardly be prevailed upon to lose the merit of this discovery: however she at last promised to hold her tongue.

Eugenia, who saw that the Marquis was equally surprised and grieved at the strange and abrupt manner of Don Clement's disappearing, resolved to keep him no longer in the dark; but to confess the truth of this mysterious adventure. She knew that her uncle loved her, and was discreet. She therefore, with the greatest candour, related the whole story, from the beginning to the end, without disguising the least circumstance, not even the passion she had conceived for Don Clement; and concluded her narration with conjuring the Marquis to forgive her for having made a secret to him of an affair in which her heart was so nearly concerned; assuring him, at the same time, she meant to conceal it no longer than till Don Clement had made the explanation he had promised; and which, she was inclined to believe, would unfold a mystery that had given her great uneasiness.

The Marquis heard her attentively, and with evident marks of surprize:—'You were in the wrong,' said he, 'in not trusting me with this secret; and, had you ventured to make me your confidant, it would have saved us all some trouble. But Don Clement's strange conduct astonishes me. If he really loved you, he had reason to believe that he had my approbation: for, to tell you the truth, Eugenia, I even gave him to understand so much in terms, which at once shewed my esteem for him and the high opinion I had of his desert. He indeed received the overture with all the appearance of gratitude and respect; and made use of words, to testify his acknowledgements, so passionate and expressive, that I thought his heart was sensibly affected. He thanked me for the honour I intended him; and, with his face covered with blushes, told me, he would endeavour to deserve it.

I could not help smiling at his bashfulness, at the same time that I thought it very amiable; but not caring to increase his confusion, I for that time dropped the subject. I imagined that Don Clement would, in politeness, have been the first who would have reassumed it; but quite otherwise;—I found he ever after avoided mentioning any thing that could introduce a theme which, I supposed, would have been most agreeable to him. He even grew melancholy, and sighed whenever you appeared! I took occasion from this to rally him a little on his shyness; he fell again into the same confusion that he had discovered the first time I mentioned you to him. He told me that he was afraid he was not capable of touching your heart; and added, that he had a certain delicacy in his sentiments that made him miserable; for, said he, the person who is to make me happy, must love me with a tenderness equal to that with which my soul is filled; and, alas! I dare not flatter myself that I shall meet with that person in the beautiful Eugenia.

I must own (proceeded the Marquis) that I was much surprised at what Don Clement said. I answered, gravely, I don't know, Signior, how my niece is affected toward you; I suppose she can't be blind to your merit; and I have even heard her express the good opinion she has of you; but for those tender sentiments which you require, you are only to expect a discovery of them from Eugenia's own mouth, and that as a reward of your love and constancy; but, since you are not inclined to make the experiment, we will drop a subject which may not be altogether agreeable to either of us.

I pronounced these last words in a tone so serious, and, at the same time, with some mixture of resentment, that I perceived Don Clement was almost ready to sink with grief and shame. Oh my Lord, said he, in a broken voice, you do me the greatest injustice! Why will you entertain a thought so injurious to the respect I have always entertained for you? Ah, if you knew my heart, added he (laying hold, fearfully, of one of my hands) you would be convinced of the love, the gratitude, and the reverence which I bear you; yes, my Lord, continued he (pressing my hand with a more assured air) it is nothing but a diffidence of my own worth which has prevented me from improving the favourable disposition that you have towards me; for, notwithstanding the flattering prospect which you have permitted me to entertain, I have remarked a coldness and reserve in the fair Eugenia, which have damped all my hopes.

Don Clement spoke this (proceeded the Marquis) in so dejected a tone, that I could not forbear pitying him; and, altering my countenance all at once, I told him, laughing, that he had too much modesty for a cavalier so young and handsome as he was; and that however necessary a certain degree of it might be to make one agreeable, yet an excess served only to render those who possessed it miserable, by making them timorous, and filling their heads with vain doubts and apprehensions. You don't know your own strength, added I; I believe my niece's heart is not pre-engaged; she is a woman, and I suppose, not more obdurate than the rest of her sex; and I think you have as much to recommend you as any of ours. Don Clement answered this with a bow; but, at the same time, told me there was another obstacle to his wishes which gave him new torment: Madame Burganeze, proceeded he, seems averse from my desires, and keeps so strict a watch over her daughter, that I find it impossible to speak to her but in her mother's presence.

I had (continued the Marquis) made the same observation myself; but, little suspecting the real motive of her conduct, I only fancied your mother had conceived some secret dislike to Don Clement; into the cause of which I had resolved to enquire at a proper opportunity. In the mean while I told Don Clement that I would be an advocate for him, both with you and my sister; and that, after having sounded your inclinations, which I promised myself were favourable enough towards him, I was in hopes that Madame Burganeze would not oppose a union which she would find acceptable to me and my niece. Be therefore contented, added I, for I will not rest till I have disposed Eugenia's heart to make you all the kind returns you can wish.

This conversation (continued the Marquis) passed between Don Clement and me the morning of that day on which he appointed you to meet him in the wood. What his design was in this assignation, I am strangely at a loss to conjecture; but certain I am, that Don Clement was guided throughout his whole conduct by so mysterious a principle, that the more I reflect on it the more I am puzzled.'

'I am as much at a loss as you are, my Lord,' replied Eugenia; 'but I am satisfied Don Clement had something important to reveal to me, which probably would have cleared up a behaviour that now appears so unaccountable; and, had he not been pursued by the most whimsical destiny, two minutes would have disclosed what may now, perhaps, keep me to the end of my life in suspense.'

'Time,' answered the Marquis, 'may yet bring this mystery to light; till then I will suspend my judgment, and endeavour to think favourably of a man whom I could wish to find deserving of the most warm esteem I had for him.'

While Madame Burganeze continued to make bitter lamentations for the absence of her lover, poor Eugenia was a thousand times more tortured on the same account; for, not daring to let her mother be a witness of her tears, she was obliged to live under the most painful constraint.

She hourly regretted the loss of Don Clement; and some weeks having passed over without her hearing any news of him, she begged her mother would permit her to revisit her native Salerno, in order, once more, to see her old and dear friend Adelaide.

Madame Burganeze, to whom every thing was now become indifferent, easily consented to let her daughter take this journey. Eugenia was quickly ready, little preparation serving for the time she was allowed to stay; and she set out for the kingdom of Naples, with her governante,[14] and a retinue, more suitable to her quality than that with which she had left it.

Eugenia had not given Adelaide notice of her arrival in Salerno; but impatient to embrace that dear friend, and having a mind to surprise her with the suddenness of her appearance, she alighted at the Baron St. Seberina's house, and, with her accustomed freedom, ran up into Adelaide's apartment.

She found that Lady in her closet, seated at her bureau, where she had just done writing a letter;—she had her pen in one hand, and with the other held her handkerchief before her eyes. Eugenia waited some minutes, to try if her friend would quit this melancholy posture; but finding her still continue in it, she ran to her, and embracing her tenderly, 'what ails my dear Adelaide?' said she; 'you had not this sorrowful air when I last saw you: I came to Salerno on purpose to receive some comfort from your sweet society; but I find you in a way which tells me you have yourself need of consolation.' 'And who is more capable of consoling me than you?' answered Adelaide, returning her friend's caresses; 'if I may yet hope for any happiness, it is in the friendship of my Eugenia. Tell me,' added she, 'are Madame Burganeze and the Marquis, your uncle, well? But above all, say, is Don Clement still coldly ceremonious, or am I to congratulate you on being happy?'

'Oh no! far from it,' answered Eugenia, with a sigh; 'I am more wretched than ever; I have lost Don Clement; had him torn from me when hope began to flatter me! and may perhaps never see him again!' Here she related to her friend the particulars of all that had passed; some part of which she had communicated to her by letter.

'How much am I affected with your story!' said Adelaide; 'there is a purity in our misfortunes that touches me strangely, and if I loved you less, would force me to sympathize with you.'—'How!' cried Eugenia: 'is love then the occasion of this sad alteration which I perceive in you? Is it to love you owe that dejection in your eyes, that faded colour in your cheeks, and that disordered air about your whole person?' 'To that self same passion,' answered Adelaide, assuming a little gaiety, to hide the confusion her friend's words had thrown her into; 'I shall tell you the whole secret,' added she; 'and I had even disclosed it to you in a letter which I just concluded when you entered the closet. But come, it is now dinner-time, and you have not yet seen my father.' Saying this, she led her friend to the old Baron, who was highly pleased at seeing her again; and, after mutual civilities, they sat down to table.

Eugenia was so impatient to be alone with her friend, that dinner was no sooner over than, making a sign to Adelaide, that lady immediately arose from her seat, and, telling the Baron, with a smile, that Eugenia and she had many things to talk of, they retired to Adelaide's apartment; where, having locked themselves in, Eugenia claimed her friend's promise.

'You may remember,' said Adelaide, 'at your departure from Salerno, in how much grief you left me; and indeed, my sorrow at losing you was so great, that my health was visibly impaired by it: my father, with the greatest concern, saw my melancholy, but told me he would not suffer me to indulge it. He assured me I should see you again, though he were himself to undertake a journey with me to Milan for that purpose;—mean time, said he, I will find a companion for you, who, though not perhaps so beloved by you as your Eugenia is, yet may make you some amends for her absence. I am now going to pay a visit to my kinsman, Signior Carassa,[15] whom I have not seen for some time; and I will ask leave for his daughter to come and bear you company.

I thanked my father for his tenderness; and assuring him I would be very glad to have my cousin with me, he went to wait on her father, who very readily granted his request; and Faustina[16] (that was my cousin's name) came to me the same day.

My father was so pleased with the hopes of diverting my melancholy, that I could not help seeming highly satisfied with her company. She was mistress of a great deal of wit, and did not want for good-nature; but her carriage was a little too shy and reserved to make her a very agreeable companion: and, in reality, I did not think myself over and above happy in her conversation.

She had now been some weeks with us, when, one morning, going to hear mass (as was our custom) we had but just kneeled down when Faustina whispered in my ear,—Look, Adelaide, at that cavalier, who stands next the altar, in mourning, and tell me if you ever saw any thing so handsome?—I cast my eyes where she directed me, and saw the gentleman whom she described. He seemed to be an agreeable genteel person, though something past his bloom. I told her I thought he had nothing remarkable in him: and the place we were then in not being proper for observation of this kind, I turned my face away, and opened my breviary.[17]

When mass was over, I observed Faustina under some uneasiness; for the stranger (who had employed her thoughts and her eyes when she should have been minding her devotion) had suddenly stepped out among the crowd. She made all possible haste to get out of church: I followed her; and we had but just got without the gate when we saw our cavalier talking very familiarly to an Abbé of our acquaintance—the latter bowed to us as we came towards him; and immediately the stranger whispered him, which I judged was to enquire who we were for I immediately heard my name pronounced, and the cavalier say,—She is very handsome! Faustina heard those last words; but not knowing to which of us they were directed, she flattered herself they were meant for her.

When we got into our coach, Now, cousin, said she to me, tell me your opinion of that stranger: for my part, I think I never beheld any thing so beautiful.—I could not help smiling at so fantastical a taste; which Faustina observing,—I see, said she, he has not the good fortune to have pleased you; but, as I think you have some skill in beauty, I should be glad you would tell me what he wants to make him completely amiable?—He wants every thing, replied I, laughing out-right; and, if you will hear me patiently, I will describe him in his true colours, for I examined him with a less partial eye than you did—Come then, answered Faustina, peevishly, let me hear.

In the first place then, said I, his stature is too low.—Why I grant you, said she, interrupting me, that it would be better if he was a little taller; but, to make amends for this deficiency, he is perfectly genteel.—I will allow, answered I, that he has a tolerable air, that at first sight strikes, but when you come to examine him, he wants shape; I could almost say proportion: then for his face, since you take me for a judge of beauty, indeed, cousin, I think he has neither features nor complexion; and if I be not much deceived, he could almost be your father.

Though I still kept up my rallying manner, I found that Faustina had lost all patience.—Oh heavens! said she, that I should fancy you have any taste! I suppose you admire the coarse look of a peasant, that lyes down and rises with the sun. The cavalier has a delicacy of complexion that may indeed proceed from a weakly constitution; but his features are the most elegant I have seen: and for his age, which you have advanced so much, I can, for my part, see no disparity between it and my own.

My cousin, who was naturally a little passionate, spoke this with so much earnestness, that I did not care to contradict her any further; and was glad that our conversation was broke off by the carriage stopping at our own door.

From what I have said, you may judge what kind of a person this was. The next morning the Abbé, whom I mentioned to you, came to breakfast with us:—you may be sure Faustina did not forget to enquire particularly after her favourite. The Abbé informed us that his name was Signior Ambrosia de Castellane; that he was a native of the island of Sardinia,[18] and came to Salerno in order to take possession of a small estate that fell to him by the death of an aunt. To these he added some other particulars, which naturally fell in his way (or at least were thrown there by my cousin); such as, that he was unmarried; that he lodged in the college with a student, his relation; and that he intended to stay some months in Salerno.

I know not whether it was by design or accident that Castellane, the next day, passed by our house. Faustina was leaning against the window of my dressing-room, which looked into the street; I was sitting at my toilet. Come hither quickly, Adelaide, said she, in a voice of transport: see the charming stranger!—I rose off my chair, and, stepping to the window, saw Signior Ambrosia, who, remarking us, gazed for a minute, with a look more of curiosity than politeness. How handsome he is! said Faustina, with an air of surprise and pleasure: what would I give (added she, after a short pause) that his quality and fortune were such as would entitle him to ask me of my father!—but what am I thinking of? he does not know me at all; much less does he know that I am charmed with him. We must inform him then, said she (looking at me, with an absent air); and teach him to raise his wishes and his hopes. With this she darted suddenly to my closet, and shut herself in.

I waited, with some impatience, to see what would be the result of her contemplations; little dreaming how she was employed.

In about half an hour she came out to me, with an air of much satisfaction in her face. She had a paper, wrote, in her hand.—I have something to shew you, said she; but you must first promise you will not make any objections; for I tell you, before hand, I have taken a resolution which nothing can make me alter.—Then be assured, said I, that I shall not make any attempts which, I am persuaded, would be fruitless.—You are in the right, replied Faustina; and at the same time gave me the paper, which she had held back whilst she was speaking to me. The words it contained were as follows:—"My tenderness forces me to discover what my pride would, in vain, persuade me to conceal. I love you, Don Ambrosia; and, if you know your own worth, this confession will not surprise you, though I add to it that it comes from a woman of the first quality in Salerno. I shall be at the ball which the Prince gives to-night in hopes of seeing you there; for I propose no other pleasure in going. I shall be in white and gold; and I shall wear a remarkable diamond in my breast, which will be enough to distinguish me: but, should chance alone direct your eyes to mine, they will be sufficient to discover her who admires you above all mankind."

I read this astonishing letter twice (pursued Adelaide) before I could believe my eyes; when, returning it to Faustina, I asked her, gravely, what she meant to do with it?—To dispatch it off hand, replied she, to Castellane: I know where he lives, and my woman can be trusted.—With this she was leaving the room, when I cried out to her, For heaven's sake, cousin, reflect one minute on what you are going to do: you, indeed, forbid me to contradict you, but I am too much your friend to obey you—Spare yourself the trouble of arguments, interrupted Faustina; I believe you love me; and on any other occasion I would be guided wholly by your prudence; but in the interests of the heart, we ourselves are our best counsellors. I knew every thing you would say continued she: you would tell me that I am rash; that I forget what is due to my sex and my quality; in a word, that I break in on the rules of modesty and discretion. Ah, let it be so:—I know this is what you would say, and I even think I deserve it; but, conscious as I am of my own weakness, I have not power to oppose it. See then, Adelaide, if I can be reasoned out of a prepossession which all my own efforts have not been able to conquer: but don't think I yield without reluctance; for, alas, I must yield, and you must assist me with your friendship.—With this she embraced me; and I was so softened by her words, that I found myself more inclined to pity than condemn her.

She saw the temper she had wrought me into; and, leaving me in a moment, she took that opportunity to dispatch her letter, flattering herself that, though I did not approve of her conduct, I would at least not reproach her with it.

The messenger whom she employed acquitted herself very well; for, not finding Don Castellane at home, she gave the letter to his footman; and telling him it was of consequence, charged him to find out his master directly, and deliver it to him.

Faustina, having her head now filled with a thousand pleasing ideas, prepared for the ball. She was genteel, and, though not a beauty, might yet stand amongst the foremost rank of the agreeable. I never saw her take so much pains to dress herself as she did that evening; and, having put on the clothes she described in her note, she added the jewel which, as a propitious star, was to direct her lover. This she made serve as a kind of clasp to fasten a bouquet of flowers in her bosom.

As I had been invited to the ball as well as Faustina, I went with her; and we had but just taken our seats when we saw our little cavalier enter, dressed as richly as any body there. He happened to place himself just opposite to us: but never did I see any one in such perplexity as he seemed to be: there was a splendid appearance of ladies on all sides of us; and, as we happened not to sit in the most conspicuous part of the room, he seemed utterly at a loss where to fix; and, I believe, had almost tired himself with looking for the lady to whom he was so much obliged. When the ball opened, the Prince doing me the honour to dance with me, the company on this occasion stood up; and Don Ambrosia, more intent on finding out his mistress than on observing the dancers, at last discovered her; but whether by the bright signal on her breast, or the more expressive language of her eyes, I never yet could be certain.

He gave her to understand he had found her out by a most profound bow; which salute I just saw her returning, with looks full of more than complaisance. When I was led back to my seat, I observed that Castellane began to give himself more airs than he had done before; and his eyes were seldom off my cousin or me during the whole entertainment.

Faustina wished often to see him dance; but he did not give her that pleasure. However, when the company broke up (which was not till near morning) we saw him pressing through the crowd to get to us, in order, as I supposed, to lead us to our coach; when two gentlemen, who had waited on us to the ball, taking my cousin's hand and mine, took that office upon themselves; which Faustina, for her part, had much rather have bestowed on Don Ambrosia. She therefore was obliged to content herself with casting a look at him; which shewed with what reluctance she gave her hand to another. He returned this with a low bow; and immediately went out with a crowd of other gentlemen.

If Faustina was charmed with him before, this last interview rivetted her chains. She talked of nothing else;—What do you think he will do, said she, now that he knows by whom he is beloved? Do you believe the discovery was agreeable to him?—You need not doubt, replied I, that he will pursue a conquest which does him so much honour. Nor was I out in my supposition: Castellane was too proud of it not to use it to his advantage. He soon found means, by the help of Faustina's woman, to get a letter conveyed to his mistress. I happen to have it still in my possession. You will be a judge of it.' With this Adelaide went to her cabinet, and taking the letter from thence gave it to her friend to read. 'Too sure I am (said the letter) that I have not merit enough to deserve the happiness you flatter me with; or you would certainly make me the vainest of mortals. If it be indeed possible that the sentiments you profess for me are real, I shall endeavour to render myself worthy of them: if feigned only to divert yourself, I can easily forgive such an agreeable deceit: and, either way, I beg you will afford me an opportunity personally to thank you for the honour you have done me.'—Eugenia having read this epistle, returned it to Adelaide, and begged her to pursue her story.

'Though my cousin (continued that lady) was pleased with the gallantry of Signior Ambrosia, relative to his request of seeing her; though it was no more than what she might have expected; she well knew that, as he was not upon a footing with her, either in point of fortune or quality, she must never hope to have him admitted as a lover, either by her father or by mine. Whatever, therefore, was to be done, it must be entirely without the knowledge of either of them.

She had recourse to me in this emergency; and begged my advice and assistance. She told me she was resolved to see Castellane; but did not know in what manner to contrive an interview with him. I was sorry to see her embarked in an affair that I foresaw might end unhappily: but I knew her temper too well to hope for any thing by opposing her; especially where her heart was so nearly concerned. All I could expect then was, that she would conduct herself with as much caution and secresy as so delicate a point required.

I told her I was satisfied she ought to comply with Don Castellane's request of allowing him to see and talk to her, as there was no retreating handsomely, after the advances she had made. Yet I recommended it to her not to be too hasty in granting him a meeting, till we had concerted measures for our mutual safety.

She saw the reasonableness of this advice; and, readily agreeing to it, she answered Don Ambrosia's letter in a few lines, telling him she would consider of the means to gratify him in the desire he expressed to thank her for the favourable sentiments she had for him; the sincerity of which she assured him of, in a manner that left him no more doubt of her being in earnest.

I shall not trouble you with a repetition of all the letters that passed on both sides, and the contrivances that were formed, in order to effect the meeting between the two lovers, before any expedient was fixed upon. At last an opportunity offered that determined Faustina in a desire she had before entertained, of receiving him here; which she was afraid to venture on before, lest my father should discover it: but as he was now obliged, on urgent business, to be absent from home for a few days, my cousin was resolved not to let slip so favourable a juncture. She communicated her design to me:—I thought it feasible, and much less liable to censure than to indulge him in an assignation in any other place. She thanked me for my concurrence; and wrote a little note to Don Ambrosia, appointing the manner and hour of his visit, which was to be that evening.

He did not fail to come agreeably to his instructions; and was conducted by my cousin's woman into a parlour remote from the rest of the apartments. Faustina beseeched me to entertain him for a few minutes, till she had recollected her spirits, which were indeed much agitated at the thoughts of her being so near the object of her love. I went down into the parlour, where I found Castellane in a musing posture, with his eyes fixed on the ground. He started up on my entering the room; and I observed he changed colour as he saluted me. I was in some confusion myself: however I prayed him to sit down. He seemed embarrassed; which increased the disorder that the circumstance of this whimsical adventure had thrown me into. We were both silent. I was very glad when Faustina came in to put an end to this aukward scene.

Her presence seemed to inspire him with more boldness; when, on the contrary, I supposed it would have rather added to his timidity. He thanked her in the politest manner for the honour she had done him; and testified his gratitude in the most obliging terms; but it appeared to me he expressed himself with an ease and freedom that favoured more of the courtier than the lover:—his language wanted that warmth and energy which springs from the heart; the emotions of which are indeed more easily counterfeited than disguised. In a word, I thought I penetrated into his breast, and did not find there so deep a sense of the favours my cousin had vouchsafed him as I could have wished.

After the first compliments were over (which threw Faustina into fresh agitation) Don Ambrosia artfully, and not ungracefully, turned the conversation; which, on becoming more general, I bore an equal part in. I found the Sardinian did not want wit; he was entertaining and sprightly; had an agreeable voice, and a certain vivacity in his manner which rendered his company pleasing enough. This was all I could ever bring myself to think of him, though Faustina discovered some new charms in him every time she saw him.

Before he left us, he obtained his mistress's permission to wait on her again the next evening. He came; and my cousin thought the hours she spent with him too happy not to wish for a long continuance of them. In short, though my father was to return the following day, and Faustina knew it was of the utmost importance to conceal her amour from him, yet, so blinded was she by her passion for Don Castellane, that she engaged him to renew his visits on certain days which she promised to appoint, with this caution only, that he should always come at an early hour, when my father was engaged in his private devotions; which took a large portion of his time every evening.

Having thus concerted measures for their future meetings, Faustina had frequent opportunities of seeing her lover, without any danger of being surprized. It happened one evening that, just as Castellane had been admitted, Faustina received a letter from her mother on some business which required an immediate answer: she begged I would go to him and make her excuses. While she wrote, the messenger waited for her letter, which I knew would employ her for some time. I went into the parlour, and, making an apology to Don Ambrosia for Faustina's absence, I told him she would hasten hither with all the dispatch she could make.—In the mean time, said he (rising off his seat, and advancing towards me with an assured air) we will make ourselves as happy as if she were here.—Saying this, he sat down by me.—Would you be angry with me now, said he, if I should tell you that I love you better than I do your cousin?—As I was far from imagining him serious, I only answered with a careless smile, as a mark of the little stress I laid upon what he said. But, instead of understanding it in this light, he, I suppose, looked upon it as a proof of approbation, which encouraged him to go on.

Believe me, my charming Adelaide, said he, I have adored you from the first moment I saw you; and have a thousand times cursed my fate that did not give me your heart instead of Faustina's.—He concluded this impertinent speech with snatching one of my hands and pressing it eagerly to his lips. A behaviour so unexpected quite confounded me. I pulled back my hand with indignation, and was going to speak, when he prevented me by pursuing his speech with saying, Will you suffer me to tell you the power you have over me,—the joy your presence brings,—and the pain I feel at your absence: that you are the object of my wishes,—the delight of my soul; and, in short, that my existence hangs upon you?—Hold, Signior, said I, scornfully; you carry the jest a little too far!—Oh heavens! said he, do you think I jest? Cruel creature! hear me but swear—Fye, fye, Don Ambrosia! said I, interrupting him: What would Faustina say, if she thought you capable of so much treachery? Reflect but on what you owe her, and you must blush for your ingratitude.—Why, I own, replied Castellane, I owe obligations to that lady, and am sorry I can't make her the return she deserves: but, added he, with a sigh (half-real and half-affected) one can't bestow their heart where they please.—I say the sigh was half-affected, because Ambrosia was not a man that would die for love: and I believe that he even repented of having declared himself so freely to me, when he found in what manner I received his addresses. Be that as it will, I forbade him to say any more on that subject: and, in reality, I conceived such a despicable opinion of him at that moment, that it remained ever after.

Faustina, who had by this time dismissed her mother's messenger, flew to us with her usual impatience; and but just gave Don Ambrosia (who heard her coming) time to return to the chair he had quitted at the beginning of our conversation.

He ran to meet her; and even complained of her being absent so long: but, whether Faustina had remarked any disorder in my countenance, or whether, as she was naturally jealous and had more penetration than I, she might have discovered some symptoms of his inclination for me, 'tis certain she received him with more coldness than she was used to do: she spoke but little; and put Don Castellane in mind of retiring much sooner than he was accustomed to do. When he was gone, I asked her, in the kindest manner, what it was that made her so thoughtful in the presence of one who used to banish every uneasy reflection from her mind?—I was not, answered she, in a humour that would suffer me to be a very agreeable companion to Don Ambrosia; but you, I hope, made amends for my unsociableness. How, added she, fixing her eyes on me, did you entertain him before I came to you? No doubt he was strangely impatient at my long delay: but was there no pretty obliging things passed between you, to make the time appear less tedious?—Indeed, cousin, answered I (a little confused at the ironical air with which she spoke) our conversation was on matters merely indifferent. I don't know what trifles they were we were talking of; but I believe you were partly the subject of our discourse.—Don't be insincere, replied Faustina, gravely:—Do you know that it is possible for a woman to die of curiosity? Tell me therefore ingenuously, does not Don Castellane make love to you?—So home[19] a question made me blush extremely. I remained for some moments silent; notwithstanding which, my cousin as if I had already answered her in the affirmative, cried, Aye, I know it; the ungrateful wretch!—who would have expected this from him?—Here she was silent for some time; and walked to and fro in the chamber, with a very disturbed air. I did not interrupt her; but was considering with myself in what manner I should lay open Don Ambrosia's falsehood, without too much shocking her tenderness; or leaving her room to suspect I had given any encouragement to the ridiculous declarations he had made me.

If, on the one hand, I was grieved to wound her heart with the knowledge of his perfidy; I was, on the other, highly pleased to think that so flagrant a proof of it would at once cure her of a blind passion, which she had so unhappily conceived.—This last reflection made me resolve what part to take immediately. Therefore, addressing Faustina:—That Castellane has made some foolish professions of love to me I will not deny; but, if you think that I either heard him with pleasure, or am inclined to make him the least return, you do me the greatest injustice. On the contrary, I most heartily despise him; and could wish to see him meet with the punishment which he deserves:—I mean that of your banishing him from your thoughts, and forbidding him appearing before you again.—Ah dissembler! cried Faustina, this artifice is too gross! Is it thus then you would have me punish Castellane? You would have me banish him my sight, that you may for ever keep him in yours. Yes; you would engage me to cast away my happiness, in order to secure your own. No, Adelaide; no; 'tis you who must banish him your presence. Alas! I don't wonder that you love him: but, if you love me, and would have me believe you innocent, you must never see Castellane again.

I was strangely surprised to hear Faustina talk thus. I imagined that, whatever share of her resentment I was to feel, that which she would conceive against Don Ambrosia must produce the effects I wished; and that nothing less than an utter contempt of him must have followed the discovery of his crime; but, by the most whimsical caprice imaginable, my cousin accused me of having a passion for Ambrosia, whilst she overlooked a fault in him, which is the last a woman can pardon in a lover.

I could easily forgive the first part of her error, as it is natural for us, when we are prepossessed with too favourable an opinion of another, to believe every one else possessed with the same sentiments. However, I quickly undeceived Faustina as to this particular, by assuring her that Castellane was so very indifferent to me, that, if she desired no other proof of it than my never seeing him again, I should consent to it with a peculiar satisfaction; which, however, would be doubled if she would join me in the same resolution: and I protested to her, that I urged it from no other motive but a consciousness of Ambrosia's ingratitude, and a desire to see her heart freed from engagements so unworthy of it.—I shall, replied Faustina, require no other testimony of your regard for me than that which I have already mentioned: for the rest, leave it to myself.

I again repeated it to her, that I would never see Ambrosia more; and was as good as my word. But, at the same time, it gave me real concern to find, that the light I had given her into this insincere man's character had made an impression on her so contrary to my hopes; and that, altogether neglecting my counsel, she obliged me to abandon her to her own inclinations. And indeed, so far was she from breaking with Castellane, that she permitted him to visit her a few days after; and, I found by her behaviour, this cunning stranger had the art to turn every thing which passed between him and me into ridicule. Faustina had no doubt accused him; and I soon perceived that he had justified himself at my expence; for my cousin told me, after her first conversation with him, that I had been a little too hasty in giving credit to the professions of love which Don Ambrosia had amused me with, purely out of gallantry, and to pass away half an hour that hung heavily on his hands; but that he was far from supposing I could be so childish as to believe him serious, much less to repeat what he had said to his mistress.

I did not attempt to disabuse her;—and indeed it would have been in vain: for, notwithstanding that it was her own suspicion which had given rise to the discovery of Ambrosia's falsehood, and that she was at first persuaded of the certainty of it; yet, so inconsistent was her judgment, and so great was the ascendant Castellane had over her, that he found it an easy matter to persuade her to believe what she wished to be true. In a word, her passion became so extravagant, that I began to dread the effect of it; and was resolved to advise her mother to recall her home; when an accident happened which prevented my design.

There was a property in the neighbourhood of Salerno which had for some years been in dispute between my father and a lawyer, named Osorio[20]:—a suit had been depending on this occasion for a long time: both parties were obstinate in the defence of it; and the cause was pursued so warmly, that it cost both my father and the lawyer almost the worth of the estate, without either of them being the nearer gaining their point; when, tired at length with the delays they met with, they, by mutual consent, let the affair drop.—Things remained in this posture near two years, when a certain nobleman, who had set his heart on this domain (intending to dedicate it to some religious use) applied to the lawyer, in order to purchase it. This revived the controversy. My father insisted on its being his property (as it really was); and Osorio was as obstinate in maintaining that the right lay solely in him; and was determined to dispose of it, as soon as ever he could get possession. My father, on the other hand, determined not to part with it out of his family, if he recovered his hereditary right to it.

This last circumstance inclined the nobleman, who had a mind to be the purchaser, to use all his interest in favour of Osorio. In short, by the artificial management of the lawyer and his patron, my father was upon the point of seeing himself cast, when he resolved to apply to the Viceroy of Naples,[21] to whom he had the honour of being personally known.—Accordingly, our whole family removed to that city: for my father, not caring to leave me behind him, begged of Faustina to accompany me: and, having before obtained leave of Signior Carassa, she could not refuse to go. I the rather pressed her to this journey, as I believed it would be a more effectual means to remove Castellane from her thoughts; whose affairs I knew would not permit him to leave Salerno.—Alas! could I have foreseen what miseries this would plunge me into, I would not have laid the foundation for a change in that fickle heart, whose inconstancy has occasioned me so much torment.

This then was the cause of her separation from Castellane; he was not enough in love to marry without the hopes of advancing his fortune: and as Faustina's depended entirely on her father, the mercenary lover could not venture on entering into any engagements. Faustina, on the other hand, wishing to secure his fidelity till some change might happen in her condition, was profuse in her vows of constancy. She took a tender farewell of him the evening before our departure; and spent the whole night in tears, which she did not even dry up in some days after our arrival at Naples. The first thing she did was to write to her dear Castellane. Her letter was the most passionate one I ever saw. She reiterated her assurance of eternal love; and begged to hear from him often, as the only consolation she could hope for during so cruel an absence!

I have troubled you with more particulars of Faustina's history than were, perhaps, necessary to its connexion with mine; but, having a mind to shew you her perfidy and ingratitude in its full extent, I traced her story back to the beginning.

My father now, in hopes of reinstating himself in that right which his opponent was violently tearing from him, had prepared a memorial,[22] with which he intended to wait on the Viceroy, when, unluckily, a severe fit of the gout (of which he had but just recovered when he left Salerno) returned on him with so much violence, that it obliged him to take to his bed. He was extremely vexed at so great a disappointment; telling me that he knew that memorials were oftener thrown aside than read or attended to, unless some person, interested in their success, presented them, and endeavoured to engage the Minister's protection. I told him that, as I had the honour of being known to the Viceroy's lady, I thought myself obliged to pay my duty to her; and would, if he approved of it, wait on her with the memorial, which I was sure she would put in her Lord's hands, and interest him in our favour. My father, approving of this, told me there was no time to be lost; wherefore, dressing myself immediately, I prevailed on Faustina to accompany me to the Viceroy's palace.

When we arrived there, I enquired for the Duchess D'Ossuna;[23] but was informed that she was a little before set out for a country-seat, some leagues from Naples, where she proposed staying a few days. I was mortified at this disappointment; but reflecting that my father might be greatly injured by delay, I was resolved not to go back without making some progress in the business he had entrusted me with. It was a gentleman belonging to the Duchess that informed me she was absent: I desired to know if I might be admitted to the Duke himself: he said he would enquire, and inform me presently.—We were now in a kind of antichamber, in which were above a dozen gentlemen; most of them were walking backwards and forwards, with a restless unsatisfied air, except two or three of the youngest of the company, who had got together at a window, and were entertaining themselves with looking at my cousin and me; and even whispering and laughing, with so little politeness, that it threw us into a sort of confusion. We thought every moment an age, till the Duchess's gentleman brought us an answer; when, after making us suffer a full half-hour, under the ill-breeding of these loitering gallants, he at last vouchsafed to send one of the Viceroy's pages, to tell us (which he did in very bad Italian; for he was a little Spanish boy, whom the Duke was fond of) that the Viceroy was not to be spoke with; but that we might communicate our business to his Secretary. Chagrined to the last degree at this information, I thought of returning home, without acquitting myself of my errand; when, recollecting how much my father had set his heart on the success of my little embassy, or rather urged on by my fate, I resolved to see this Secretary at all events.

I begged the page to conduct me to him. He desired us to follow him; which we did through several apartments. He was all along, as he went, playing and jumping:—at last, bringing us into a sort of lobby, he burst out a laughing, and ran away; leaving us to make out the rest by ourselves.

Faustina and I looked at one another, with much embarrassment:—we were in a vast large house, that we did not know which way to turn ourselves in; nor do I believe we could have found our way out again,—the little mischievous page had led us through so many rooms. I was quite ashamed, and at a loss how to behave; when I saw a door open at the end of the lobby, and two elderly gentlemen came out. I asked one of them, could he direct me to the Secretary? He told me I should find him in the office just before us; and, at the same time, observing that my cousin and I were in some little confusion, he, with great civility, said, if I pleased, he would acquaint him that there were ladies who desired to speak with him. I thanked the gentleman for this piece of service, which I gladly accepted of. He went in again; and, returning in a minute, shewed us into the office within the first, where the Secretary waited for us, as it was less public than the outer one.

He was standing facing us, with his back to the fire, as we entered the room; by which means I had at once a full view of his person:—but never, Eugenia, never did I behold one so striking!—He had something so inexpressibly charming in his countenance, that, at the first glance, you would imagine nature never formed any thing so complete! He seemed to be about thirty years of age; but then, he had a bloom in his face, that would have adorned the most youthful cheek; his eyes were black, and had a mixture of sweetness and dignity in them. In short, his countenance and person (which was of the tallest) conspired at once to form the most graceful object possible! In a word, I was struck at first sight; and, I believe, never delivered myself so aukwardly, or with so much hesitation, as I did to the Chevalier de Ponces.[24]

I told him, in as few words as my confusion would let me, the occasion of my applying to him; and, at the same time, delivered him the memorial; which I begged of him, with all convenient speed, to lay before the Viceroy.—He just ran his eyes over it, with the utmost complaisancy; when, laying it down on a bureau that stood by him, and addressing himself to me, with a smile;—You, Madam, said he, are, I suppose, the Baron's daughter.—I told him I was.—And that lady (looking at Faustina) is your sister, I presume.—No, Sir, was all I answered, a little surprised at his curiosity; and adding immediately, I hope, Sir, you will take the first opportunity of acquainting the Viceroy with my father's business, I rose up to be gone.—You may depend upon it, Madam, said he; and if you will let me know where I may wait on the Baron, I hope I shall have a satisfactory answer to give him to-morrow:—but, perhaps, said he, seeming to recollect himself, his Excellency may be at leisure in half an hour, if you can stay so long; and that may do better; for you can, probably, inform him of some circumstances that may be of weight; and with which I am unacquainted.

I had risen, as I told you, to go away; but sat down quickly again; desirous, as he imagined, of a conference with the Viceroy:—but, alas, it was the person with whom I was already talking that engaged my stay.

He now and then applied to Faustina; but most part of his discourse was addressed to me: and indeed his conversation had such a charm in it, that, instead of half an hour, I stayed above a full one; when, recollecting that I kept him from affairs of more consequence, though I well saw he was pleased with our company, I rose a second time to take my leave: the Chevalier got up at the same time.—I am afraid, Madam, said he, I have detained you too long; and I am the more concerned at it, as I see no likelihood of our getting an audience of his Excellency this morning:—some important dispatches, which he has received from Spain, engage him thus long; but you may depend on my care, added he, obligingly; for I am determined not to sleep till I get an answer that will be every way agreeable to your most sanguine wishes.

Though I could not help having a firm reliance on the Chevalier's word, I was, however, a little mortified at having made no greater progress in the business entrusted to me.—I told him at parting, my father would send to him the next morning. He insisted on waiting on the Baron with the Viceroy's answer: but as my father was then confined to his bed, I thought a visit might not be so acceptable to him from a stranger; and therefore declined it.—He, very unwillingly, acquiesced, telling me I must be obey'd: and we left him.

When I returned home I gave my father an account of my negociation.—I found he was not satisfied that the memorial was left in the Secretary's keeping.—He may neglect, said my father, to present it in time to the Viceroy; or, if he should keep his word with you, the Duke may, for want of being properly reminded, throw it in the heap of undistinguished and neglected papers, that are every day preferred to his hand.—Grieved and mortified at what my father said, I told him that, though I could not, without shewing the highest distrust of the Secretary's integrity, recall the memorial, after the promises he had made; yet, as I would never forgive myself if, through my inadvertence, our cause should suffer, I was willing to try my fortune again; and, for that purpose would, with his Lordship's permission, endeavour to get an audience of the Viceroy next morning. My father, who, as I already told you, had his heart much set on the success of this suit, approved of this; and I pleased with the hopes that I should probably see the object of my new-kindled love, retired with Faustina to my chamber.

The conversation immediately turned on the amiable Ponces.—Well, cousin, said I, what do you think of this gentleman? Is your Castellane to be compared to him?—They are different kinds of men quite, said she: Castellane is certainly very handsome; but, yet I think—that Ponces is handsomer, said I, interrupting her:—allow but that, and I will even forgive you for admiring Castellane. Alas! her heart was but too conscious of this truth: the poison was already received, which afterwards produced the most fatal effects.—She answered me, carelessly, that she had not noticed him enough to give her opinion; but that, upon the whole, he appeared to be very agreeable. This was all that I could get out of her. She avoided talking of him the rest of the day, and appeared more thoughtful than usual: but this I attributed to nothing but her absence from Don Ambrosia; whom I always believed uppermost in her mind.

The next morning I prepared to wait on the Viceroy. Faustina accompanied me; and, as I was determined not to return without having first been admitted to an audience with the Duke, I yet thought it previously necessary to enquire after the fate of the memorial; and, in case the Chevalier had not presented it, I was determined to put it myself into the Viceroy's own hands.—You will smile, Eugenia, and think I was glad of the pretence for seeing Ponces. I own it.—I ordered my coach to stop at the Secretary's lodgings. We were shown into a handsome drawing-room; and the Chevalier, on hearing my name, immediately appeared. Though it was yet early, he was dressed with great elegance.—Oh! I could break in on my narration every minute, to expatiate on his graceful manner and appearance! But what is that now to me? He accosted us with a polite and pleasing air.—This unexpected honour, Madam said he, has saved me from committing a crime this morning; for I was going to disobey you; and, notwithstanding your injunctions, had resolved to wait on you with the news of my success. The Viceroy, added he, is enraged at the injustice which has been done to my Lord, your father; and has already given orders to oblige Osorio to withdraw his claim.—I endeavoured at making some aukward acknowledgments for the trouble he had taken; but he stopped me, by saying, in a softened tone of voice,—If the Baron will allow me the honour of congratulating him, it will more than recompense me for my solicitude on this occasion.—I blushed at this request. There was something in his looks that expressed a great deal more than his words.—I told him that I would venture to assure him, on the part of my father, that he would be proud to thank him for the favour he had done him, whenever he would give him that opportunity. His eyes sparkled with pleasure;—and he said he would, as soon as the Baron was able to sit up, make use of the privilege I had allowed him.

We took our leaves; and, I know not whether the warmth with which the Chevalier seemed to interest himself in our affairs, did not give me at least as much pleasure as his success.

I had occasion to call at the house of a friend, on my return home, where Faustina was engaged to pass the day. I sat about an hour with this lady; who was one of the most sensible and polite persons in Naples. Having told her the business we had been about, she rallied me on my visit to the Secretary; for whom she said all the ladies of the court were dying. He is indeed, added she, worthy of being beloved; for his mind is as amiable as his person: he is, besides, of a noble family; and few men can boast more accomplishments than Don Enenique de Ponces.—This short sketch of his character delighted me the more, as coming from one of such understanding and veracity. It served to strengthen my love; and his praises were so grateful to my ears, that I could have thanked the person who uttered them.

Having left Faustina with our friend, I returned home alone; and, on the coach's stopping at the door of our own house, I observed a footman walking backwards and forwards; and examining the windows, with great curiosity, as if he waited in expectation of seeing somebody whom he wanted. I immediately recollected his livery to be the same which I had seen but a little before, at the Chevalier's lodgings; and, looking in the man's face, I knew him to be one whom I had seen in the hall as I passed through it. He came up to the coach as I stepped out of it; and, slipping a paper, with a great deal of dexterity, into my hand, he walked away, without waiting for my asking him any questions.

As I knew him to be one of the Secretary's footmen, I would have imagined that the letter which he brought concerned only my father's business: but the caution which the fellow observed in watching the door; his privacy in the execution of his errand; and his precipitate departure afterwards, made me suspect that the billet contained something of another nature.

I made these reflections whilst I was going to my father's apartment;—putting, therefore, the paper (which I found heavier than ordinary) into my pocket, I acquainted my father with what the Chevalier had done! and, at the same time, commanding his diligence, I told him that De Ponces purposed waiting on him, to wish him joy, when he would permit him that favour.

I made haste to my chamber, to examine the packet which I had just received. I found, indeed, that it was a billet from the Chevalier de Ponces: and folded up in it there was a little ivory tablet, on the leaves of which were written, with a pencil, these words in Spanish:—"I burn in flames more pure, more bright, more fierce, than those which consume the phœnix. But, alas! my fate is far more unhappy: the phœnix endures his pains but for a while;—mine may outlive the object who creates them!"—I understand so little Spanish, that I could scarce pick out the sense of these lines; and was surprised that the Chevalier should make choice of a language to express his gallantry, in which, though it was his own native tongue, he might have imagined I, possibly, did not understand. I had not yet read his letter; but that soon explained this seeming impropriety. It was wrote in Italian: but I will shew it you, that it may not lose by my repetition.'—Here Adelaide read as follows:—'"I don't know whether I ought to bless the tablets for furnishing me with a pretence for writing to you, or accuse them for possessing my heart with jealousy:—but in the very same moment, I discovered it was filled with love.—Jealousy, which to others serves only to allay an excess of happiness, torments me before I have experienced any joy, but barely that of loving you. The words written in the tablet convince me that your heart is given away. Oh! how much to be envied is his felicity, who is master of such a treasure!—how much to be pitied, the man who must never hope to possess it!"

Nobody, my dear Eugenia, can better judge than yourself, of the pleasure that this letter gave me. To be loved by Don Enenique, was to me a happiness so transcendant, that were I left to chuse a supreme good from all the blessings and bounties which the most indulgent stars ever showered down on a mortal, this only would I have desired to have been my lot. How delighted, then!—how transported was I, to find myself possessed of what I so ardently wished. Gracious God, make me always worthy of his love; and, if an innocent creature, who reveres thy laws, has any right to thy favour, I ask no other recompense on earth but this man's constancy!—I spoke this with my hands joined fervently, and my eyes lifted up to Heaven; but my prayers were not heard.

The tablet which the Chevalier inclosed in his letter I had never seen before; therefore, at first I imagined that he had in reality only made that a handle for writing to me, under pretence that he had found it; and believing it to be mine, restored it to me. Such devices in love are very common; however, observing that the lines on the tablet were wrote in a hand which I thought I had seen before, I examined them again; and soon recollected it to be Faustina's writing. I knew she spoke Spanish perfectly; and concluded that her love for Don Ambrosia had forced those romantic compliments from her pencil.

I waited with some impatience till she should come home, in order to restore her tablets; the loss of which I was sure would vex her. She did not return till late in the evening, when she immediately shut herself up in her own apartment.

I went up to her chamber, and was not a little surprised at the situation in which I found her:—she was lying on her bed, with her face bathed in tears; a letter lay open on a chair by her, which, by the character, I perceived came from Castellane; and I made no doubt but something relative to him was the occasion of her grief.

I approached her with great concern:—Dear cousin, what is it that afflicts you? Is Don Ambrosia sick, or has he committed any crime against you?—Nothing new, replied she (without looking at me); but I begin to reproach myself for having ever loved a man that, I am now convinced, was unworthy of my regard.—Oh Faustina, said I, had you thought thus before you engaged yourself so far, what an infinite deal of pain would it have saved you!—That is true, said she; but we are not always so happy as to be governed by our reason. Look at that letter (pointing to that which lay on the chair) and tell me if you think that love had any share in the dictating of it.—As Faustina seldom indulged me with a sight of any of her lover's letters, I was surprised at this unwonted favour: I read it, and found it contained a great many compliments, and some slight assurances of affection.—This is, said I, returning it to her, an exact copy of Don Ambrosia's mind: and I will not flatter you so far as to say I believe you mistress of his heart.—Can you then blame me said she, interrupting me, if I strive to banish him from mine? Would not you even assist me in a design which you yourself so often wished to see accomplished?—Oh certainly, cried I (rejoiced to hear her talk thus); and, from the disposition you seem to be in, I fancy there will be less difficulty in the task than we imagined. You need only resolve to like somebody better than Don Ambrosia, which I think you can't fail of doing in a city like Naples, where you may have your choice of the handsomest and most accomplished gentlemen in Italy.—Suppose my choice was already fixed, replied Faustina, smiling; I believe I shall have your voice for its being a good one, when I tell you that the Chevalier de Ponces has pleased me, and that, by encouraging an inclination for him, I hope, in a little time, to blot Castellane entirely from my memory.

If Faustina had named any one else, I should have congratulated her on the change which I already saw was wrought in her heart; but, at the mention of the Chevalier, I was seized with such an impulse of indignation, that I could scarce forbear reproaching her with her weakness and inconstancy.

My cheeks kindled up like fire. However, a moment's reflection checked me; and I had so much command over myself as to reply, You should take care, cousin, how you give way to a new passion, before you are sure that it will be more successful than your old one. I am sensible of the Chevalier's merit; but perhaps you may find his heart entertains an affection for some one else. Suppose I should be the object of his love, would you persist in nourishing a flame which, instead of working a cure on your sick mind, might serve only to plunge you into new difficulties and misfortune?—Just so, said Faustina, scornfully, you would have opposed my inclination for Castellane, because you were but too well pleased with him yourself; and from the same motive, I make no doubt, you would stifle my growing love for Don Enenique. But know, Adelaide, that it already has taken root in my breast; and that I cherish this new fire more than ever I did that which I felt for Castellane.—See then, said I (provoked at this declaration) what return you are to expect from the Chevalier. With this I put the tablets and the letter which inclosed them into her hands.

She now, in her turn, felt her cheeks glowing with blushes she could not hide; and I perceived in her countenance, as she read, a mixture of indignation, pride, and disappointment. I was in some pain to think what effect these violent agitations might produce; when, all of a sudden, and enraged, she was going to satisfy part of the transport of her soul by tearing the letter, if I had not directly snatched it from her.—He might have spared, said she, those fulsome compliments, or else bestowed them in the right place.—Why, cousin, said I, he thought, without doubt, the tablets were mine:—and, for the rest, you well know there is so much caprice in love, that you can't blame the Chevalier for liking me, though you may be a thousand times more amiable. I confess I am as much touched with his merit as you are; but I swear to you, that had you been the object of his love, I should have crushed my tenderness for him in its birth for your sake, as well as my own: and it is for your peace only that I would conjure you to use the same precaution.

I did not perceive while I was speaking, that her tears began to flow again. I had no sooner left off, than she burst into the bitterest exclamations against the cruelty of her fate; and presented to me, in a few minutes, a picture of a weak heart torn by a multitude of different passions. I saw rage, grief, jealousy, pride, and love possess her alternately; and, to complete this hurry and tumult in her breast, she had not one resource in the midst of so much distraction: the natural strength and violence of her passions not permitting her even to endeavour to curb them, or so much as once to call reason to her assistance. This belief I am the more willing to entertain, because I would rather attribute her crime to a frail nature than a corrupt heart. Be that as it will, I was so much affected with her tears, that I believe I should have done any thing but resign the Chevalier, to have restored her to her peace; but this was too great a sacrifice. However, the tenderness of my nature would not suffer me to aggravate her pain, by discovering the least joy at the conquest I had obtained over a heart, which I was persuaded she as well as I thought inestimable. On the contrary, I assumed the utmost moderation; and, affecting to speak of the Chevalier's passion for me with some indifference, I conjured Faustina to calm her transports; and endeavoured, by the most tender expressions, to assuage the pangs I saw her suffer. Nevertheless, I so well knew to what excesses the violence of her nature inclined her, that I was very cautious what words I made use of in trying to soothe her; and took care to avoid letting drop any hint that might encourage her in her unwarrantable love; for I was convinced by experience, that, were she even possessed but with the smallest prospect of success, she would have gone any lengths to accomplish her wishes; I attempted, therefore, chiefly by my caresses, to bring her mind to its former tranquillity; and flattered myself I had in some measure effected this before I left her.

Ponces, I have already told you, had begged to make my father a visit; he did not fail sending to inquire after his health regularly; and in a few days, my father, being so well recovered as to sit up, sent the Chevalier word he should think himself favoured by a visit from him. You may be sure he did not need a second invitation. My father had ordered himself to be carried into his study, where Faustina and I were sitting at work, when Don Enenique came to wait on him.

My father received him with all the marks of distinction that were due to his merit, as well as to a person to whom we were obliged. If the Baron's presence was some constraint on the Chevalier, Faustina's was a thousand times more so on me. She watched both our looks so strictly, that I am sure one glance of Ponces's did not escape her. I believe they were most of them directed to me. However, I kept so rigid a guard over my eyes that I seldom turned them towards him; but when I did, I could easily perceive what pain this seeming coldness of mine gave him.

He did not stay long with us; and took his leave without having an opportunity of saying a single word to me in particular; but, to make amends, my father was so delighted with his company, that he insisted, in a free manner, on his coming frequently to see him during his stay at Naples; which he now resolved should be for the whole winter.

Whatever joy I conceived at this, it was not unmixed with the bitterest pain. I saw but too plainly that the unhappy Faustina pined away with love for the Chevalier; and, far from being sensible of her error, she had only banished Castellane from her trifling heart, in order to make room for a man from whom she could expect nothing but indifference. What did I not resolve to say and do, to prevent, if possible, the growth of this malady? The most solid remonstrances, the softest persuasions, I knew, to a temper like hers were equally vain; and I gave over all hopes of reasoning her into a sense of her folly. I once more designed to write secretly to her mother, to get her, on some pretence or other, recalled to Salerno; but I rejected this thought almost as soon as I had formed it. It would indeed, said I, remove her from the Chevalier; and thereby rid both him and me from the uneasiness which her presence must shortly give us, if she persists in her unseasonable love; and, though I have all the reason in the world to believe that absence will work a speedy cure on a mind so weak and inconstant as hers; yet, shall I not have cause to reproach myself if Faustina should, by returning to Salerno, again see Castellane, and reassume her former affection for him (which perhaps may be easily revived by her presence); and by this means plunge herself into misfortunes that may be the utter ruin of her, and afflict her parents to the last degree. I might indeed have advised her mother to be watchful over her conduct, which might have prevented the evil I dreaded; but then, I thought I should be guilty of a piece of cruelty, in not only removing her from Naples, which I knew must be a sensible affliction to her, but even debar her of the liberty and happiness she might enjoy in Salerno, by inspiring her friends with suspicions which must awaken all their vigilance.—Upon the whole, I dropped this thought; and even accused myself for entertaining it a moment. No; let me never owe my peace to any thing that is either ungenerous or insincere; I will rather confess my love for the Chevalier to Faustina (she already knows of his for me) and will conjure her, by the friendship that is between us, not to disturb an affection which I flattered myself my father might be brought to approve of, as he was already sensible of Don Enenique's merit, and knew he had a fortune not unsuitable to mine.

I so much applauded myself for this resolution that I immediately went about the execution of it. I opened my whole heart to Faustina, in terms the most moving I could think of; I assured her that the Chevalier had made an impression on my heart before I discovered that I had touched his; but that now convinced of the sincerity of his love, I had endeavoured only to conceal my tenderness for him, in order to spare her the mortification of seeing us mutually dear to each other: I pleaded my right to his heart, and to my cousin's friendship and aid, as she formerly had mine on a like occasion. She heard me with an air rather of melancholy than resentment.—I see but too plainly, said she, what all this tends to: you will marry the Chevalier: Is it not so? Yet I blame you not. You must, you will be happy! 'Tis I only that am marked out to be wretched.—She uttered these words in so mournful a tone, that it redoubled my compassion for her. She thanked me for my tenderness; and assured me that, as she knew her love was quite hopeless, she would not only endeavour to subdue it, but would try to promote the success of mine. I embraced her tenderly: I found my eyes moist with tears. Cherish, my dear Faustina, said I, this noble, this amiable disposition, and you will soon find yourself superior to all the little ills that have afflicted you.

I had behaved hitherto with great reserve to Don Enenique, on my cousin's account, who, I saw, was on a perpetual rack whilst I was in his sight; but having, as I thought, acquitted myself with respect to her, and obtained as it were her permission to avow my love, I grew less constrained, and assumed a behaviour more obliging. De Ponces, who was a welcome as well as a frequent visitor to my father, was too observant of me not to perceive this change; and, resolving to improve a disposition which appeared so favourable, he took the first opportunity of breaking that silence which had been so painful to him.

He came one morning to wait on my father, who happened to be engaged on business; the Chevalier made that the pretence for stepping into the garden, though in reality he had discovered me walking there, from a window in one of the apartments. I was alone, and did not expect such an interview, when I was surprised with the Chevalier's accosting me. The air with which he approached threw me into some confusion, though it was respectful and even timid; however, he had time to explain himself before I could recover from my disorder.

Don Enenique had that kind of address which captivates at once; and one must hear him favourably almost on any subject.—I can't tell, Madam, said he (bowing gracefully as he drew near me) what impression my boldness may have made on you, since, from the time I restored your tablets to you till this hour, I have never been blessed with a minute's conversation with you, but in the presence of the Baron or your cousin. This difficulty forces me to be abrupt. Tell me therefore, I conjure you, have I offended past forgiveness? Or, added he, after a little pause (with a voice and look irresistibly sweet) will you allow me to hope for pardon?—I own to you, Eugenia, I never was so much embarrassed in my life: I was unable to speak: the want of words redoubled my confusion: I cast my eyes to the ground: the emotion of my heart was visible in my face. Ponces, whose delicacy made him suffer for the confusion he occasioned me, endeavoured to give me a little more courage: he withdrew his eyes from my face; and presenting me his hand, led me up some steps into a terrace-walk; for we had both stood from the time of his first accosting me. I easily apprehended he did this in order to give me time to recover myself; for he proceeded in his discourse as we walked:—Speak, amiable Adelaide, said he; I already begin to flatter myself; I know you have a soul too generous to take any pleasure in the painful suspense of one whose happiness depends on you;—Speak therefore, and let the candour of that excellent heart prevail over your timidity.

I raised my eyes to the Chevalier's face; and thought I could read there the very dictates of his heart. In short, his looks inspired me at once with the same unaffected openness.—What must I say to you, Signior, said I; have you not reason to believe that I have the best opinion imaginable of you, and even the highest esteem. If you suppose that I have kinder sentiments for any other person, you are mistaken; for the lines you saw on the tablets, and which indeed seemed to intimate some such thing, were never wrote by me; and this, if I had had an opportunity, I should have informed you of sooner. I thought I had not said too much; but Don Enenique, who I found knew my heart better than I did myself, put so favourable a construction on my answer, that he thanked me in expressions almost rapturous. In a word, he pleaded his love so successfully, as forced me in the end to make some obliging returns to it.

After a conversation like this, you may be sure the Chevalier let no opportunity slip of securing his interest in my heart; and the artful Faustina had gained such a command over her passion, that she never let the least symptom of it break out; insomuch that I began to flatter myself she had entirely vanquished it; but, while I was applauding this perfidious creature for a conquest which I thought so conducive to her peace, she was contriving my ruin.

She was now become so careless with respect to the Chevalier, that we used sometimes to converse on the subject of our love even before her; and, though I did not altogether confide in her, she yet was well enough apprized how matters stood between Ponces and me. In short, his assiduity at last obtained what he so earnestly solicited, my consent to ask me of my father. He did so the same day I granted it. I can't tell you the particulars of what passed at this conference; but I saw the Chevalier leave my father's apartment; and immediately I was called for, before I had time to hear from him what he had to tell me.—Come hither, Adelaide, said he. What is this I hear? The Spanish Secretary has a mind for you, has he? This he said with a severe look; and waited with his eyes fixed upon me for an answer.—I replied, the Chevalier, Sir, has made his addresses to me, which I confess I have listened to; and am not a stranger to his having asked your Lordship's approbation.—Approbation! interrupted my father, in an angry tone; why, he has just now in point blank terms formally demanded you in marriage; and I, in as point blank terms, have refused him; and that for such reasons as you ought to thank me for. Let it suffice for the present to tell you, that a nobleman of worth, and one of the first estates in the kingdom, seeks my alliance. I expect therefore you will acknowledge my tenderness for your welfare, instead of being chagrined at my denial; but no, added he, I think better of your obedience than to believe you can be displeased at any thing that I shall judge proper to chuse for you. However, as I perceive that you are a little disturbed, retire and shake it off.—I obeyed, without speaking a word; for I thought I could never get soon enough out of my father's presence; and indeed I was so shocked and confounded, that, without directing or even being sensible of my own motions, I found myself in the garden, not knowing how I came there.

I walked two or three turns, in the utmost distraction; and was endeavouring to compose my mind, when I entered a little summer-house, where I was sometimes used to entertain the Chevalier. Those thoughts which had possessed me on my first coming into the garden had rather agitated than afflicted me; but now, my ruffled and confused ideas began to give way to the most melancholy reflections. I was seized with an extreme pensiveness at the sight of this little retirement; and sighed the moment I entered it; and, I confess to you, Eugenia, my weakness was such that I could not refrain bursting into tears. Oh, Don Enenique! said I; and are all our hopes, then, come to this? I sighed deeply; my tears flowed faster than before; and I was obliged to lean against the colonade: my eyes were closed; and I can't say but I was altogether in a state of sensibility. I know not how long I should have remained thus, if I had not been roused by the noise of somebody's entering the summer-house. It was the Chevalier himself!—What is it I see, dear Adelaide? said he;—is it possible I should be the occasion of these tears? or rather, is it possible you can weep when Ponces is so near you?—Yes, answered I, drying my eyes; when Ponces and I must part for ever.—How, Madam? said he; are you then as cruel as your father? I could easily support his harsh denial, because I imagined myself secure of your heart, which I believed faithful.—What can I do? said I, interrupting him; my father says I never shall be yours!—And I say you shall be mine, cried the Chevalier, in spite of all the fathers in the world: and I followed you into the garden, to tell you so.—Oh, Enenique! that is impossible! I know my father is inexorable; and will never be prevailed with to give his consent.—How you talk, replied Ponces: why, I never mean to ask the Baron's consent again: but, if you love me as you ought, that need not startle you.—You know I do, replied I; but don't take advantage of that by endeavouring to persuade me to do any thing contrary to the obedience I owe my father.—Go, then, said he; act contrary to honour, to gratitude, and to love: break all the promises you have made me; give yourself to the man your father intends you for; and leave me to misery.—My father's intentions, said I, I was ignorant of till this day; when he equally surprised and shocked me with the news.—Why, answered the Chevalier, don't you know the happy man whom the Baron prefers?—I assured him that many minutes had not passed since my father, for the first time, had mentioned this circumstance to me; but, without naming the person he had in his thoughts. And I conjured Ponces at the same time, to believe me incapable of changing.—You can conceive me of that no way so effectually, said he, as by consenting immediately to give me your hand. I have an estate in Spain, where I will carry you; and then we shall be out of all reach.—I was so far from relishing this proposal, that, on the contrary, it very much shocked me; and it was not till after reiterated intreaties, that I could be prevailed on to listen to the scheme which the Chevalier laid down. However, I insisted on his waiting a while, in hopes of some favourable change in my father's intentions towards me; though, as I knew him steady in his resolutions, I had but little reason to expect this.

Ponces, unwillingly, acquiesced. I know, said he, we can have nothing to hope for from the Baron: the peremptory denial I received from him convinces me he is determined to bestow you on another. Perhaps, if we let slip the present opportunity, you may be torn from me for ever.—I trembled at Don Enenique's presaging this cruel event; but still conjured him to give me a few days, at least, to consider of what he proposed.

We parted: and as his visits were now prohibited by my father, I promised to meet him every evening in the summer-house, in which we then were. For this purpose I gave him a key (which happened to be in my possession) of a private door, that opened from the garden into a by-street; by which he was to let himself in at a certain hour.

I was extremely at a loss to guess whom my father intended for my husband. I knew he had an opinion of Faustina; and often confided in her judgment:—I did not doubt, therefore, but she could give me some light into this business. I told her what had passed between my father and me; and I begged of her to inform me all she knew of his designs in regard to his disposal of me.—She answered, very naturally, that the Baron had not let her into the whole secret; but had informed her that he had thoughts of bestowing me on the Count de la Rosa.—Good God! said I, interrupting her; to Count de la Rosa!—a man who might be my father; and is known to be one of the most avaricious wretches in Italy!—You know, answered Faustina, laughing, the Baron in that has some little resemblance to him; and therefore does not like him the worse for it.—However, I hope he will not press you to so disagreeable a match: you know he loves you too well to force your inclination.

I should have mentioned in the course of my story (pursued Adelaide) that this Count de la Rosa had, before I left Salerno, often seen me at the house of Signior Carassa, Faustina's father. He was pleased with me; and told Signior Carassa that, if he could gain my approbation, he would demand me of my father: and, as a substantial proof of his love, he would settle any dower on me that my father should require. Though my kinsman thought this would be a very advantageous match for me, he would not, however, encourage the Count, nor mention the proposal to my father before he had consulted me. I at first only laughed at the mention of De la Rosa's passion; till Signior Carassa assuring me of his being serious, and at the same time desiring my sentiments. I begged of him to give the Count as polite a refusal as he could; and I entreated my cousin to conceal the affair entirely from my father; whose regard to wealth I was afraid would incline him to listen too favourably to the Count's offer.

Signior Carassa, who had both prudence and good-nature, promised to manage matters so, that I should hear no more of it: and in effect he kept his word. I avoided afterwards going to my kinsman's house, for fear of meeting De la Rosa: and I flattered myself that my old lover had forgot me; especially as I left Salerno without hearing any more of him.

You may suppose therefore I was not a little surprised at Faustina's naming this gentleman as the person my father intended for my husband. I asked her, could she tell me by what means my father came to know of the Count's inclinations for me? She answered, she could not tell with certainty; but she suspected that De la Rosa, not being able to get the better of his love; and having no reliance on any thing but my father's authority over me, had applied directly to the Baron. And she was even of opinion that the Count was then in Naples.—I was terribly alarmed at this suggestion; and feared Don Enenique had but too just grounds for what he had said to me in the summer-house.

Faustina had been informed by my father of the conference that passed between him and Ponces. She condoled with me on the disappointment of my hopes; and, assuring me she had banished Don Enenique from her heart, she added, that she would now with more joy see us united, than formerly it would have given her pain. Deceived with these assurances, and forgetting she had so lately been my rival, I believed her sincere.

She asked me what measures I purposed taking, in case my father urged my marriage with the Count? Though I had no distrust of Faustina's honour, I did not however chuse to let her into the proposal made me by the Chevalier:—I did not know but there might still be some unextinguished sparks that lay smothered in her heart; and that, notwithstanding, all her efforts might blaze out again on the thoughts of the Chevalier's being lost to her for ever; and perhaps occasion some imprudence in her conduct, that would defeat all my designs:—I therefore only told her that, as I hoped my father would not force me to marry against my inclination, so I had as yet come to no resolution at all. But my fate was nearer a crisis than I imagined.

I perceived a coldness in my father's behaviour, that he had never shewn towards me before. He spoke little to me all that day: and the next morning, as Faustina and I sat at breakfast with him, he told us he intended in a few days to depart for Salerno.—If I was quite thunderstruck at this information, Faustina seemed no less concerned! My father observed it in us both.—I see, said he, the news is not pleasing to either of you. It is for your sake, Adelaide, that I remove from a place where I think you have attachments unworthy of you. I have already told you that I have other views for you than those ignoble ones you have for yourself; and which I hope your prudence will teach you to resign without reluctance. And as for you, Faustina, added he, looking at my cousin; I know not what reason you can have to regret leaving Naples, and returning to your friends and parents.—I had made my father no answer; and Faustina said, respectfully, she would gladly attend him back to Salerno.

I was terrified at this unexpected resolution of my father's:—I dreaded being sacrificed to the Count on my return to Salerno; for I concluded by this motion of the Baron's, that De la Rosa was not at Naples, as Faustina had insinuated. This occasioned me to make some new reflections on the unaccountable manner of my father's being made acquainted with the Count's love for me; which I knew was a secret to every body but Signior Carassa and Faustina. However, these thoughts were but transient; and, without giving myself the trouble to dive farther into this mystery, I turned my mind entirely towards the means of avoiding this hated match.

I knew the Chevalier's arms were open to receive me;—the time I had to resolve in was short;—my heart and my vows were already Don Enenique's. Do not blame me then, Eugenia, when I tell you that I at once determined to yield him my hand on the terms proposed.—However, I concealed my thoughts from Faustina:—my father's knowledge of De la Rosa's passion for me had raised some doubts in my mind; and, though she expressed the utmost concern on our going to Salerno, which she said was entirely on my account, I nevertheless did not chuse to confide in her too far. She asked me, would not I see the Chevalier before we set out? and (as she knew our place of rendezvous, and that we often met) I made no scruple of saying I meant to see him that evening. I found she endeavoured to penetrate into my designs; but I evaded her questions, or gave her general answers.

I went at the appointed hour to the summer-house, where I found the Chevalier waiting for me. It was in the dusk of the evening, when my father always spent an hour alone in his oratory; so that I was sure of having that portion of time to myself.—Ponces did not allow me to keep him long in suspense; he immediately renewed the conversation we had had the day before. My fears now, joined to my love, served to strengthen his arguments; and I no longer refused to yield.—We agreed that Don Enenique should the next night, between ten and eleven o'clock, bring his confessor with him, who should join our hands in the little summer-house we were then sitting in, in the presence of my woman, whom I was to take with me; after which, under covert of the night, we were to be conveyed in the Chevalier's carriage (which was to wait at a private door) to the sea-side, where a bark was to be in readiness, to carry us directly to Spain; for it would be by no means expedient for the Chevalier, after such an adventure, to continue in Naples.

Having thus settled our measures, we parted. Don Enenique went to prepare for our expedition; and I returned to the house, to take such other steps as might be necessary to our design.

I would not allow myself to reflect, for fear of receding from my promise: but, putting up my jewels and other things of value, without once daring to consider what I was doing, I called my woman, who had been all along privy to my correspondence with the Chevalier; and having, in a few words, imparted the secret to her, she seemed so rejoiced at the project, that I began to lose part of the fears that were already oppressing me.

I can't say I was sorry for the resolution I had taken, though my mind was far from being easy. However, I got through the remaining part of the evening in making some secret preparations for my intended flight. My woman was very officious, and took upon her the conduct of a great many things; so that, relying entirely on her care and fidelity, I went to bed, in a state of mind which, though not altogether tranquil, was yet free from pain. As I never closed my eyes, the night seemed very tedious; and notwithstanding I did not wish for morning, it however at last appeared, and I arose off my restless bed.

I passed most of the day with Faustina, to avoid giving her any suspicion; and when night came, concluded the Chevalier would rather be before than after the appointed time; I sent my woman into the garden, to prevent his impatience till I could disengage myself from my father, who always expected my company at supper; after which I was my own mistress, as Faustina and me, at that hour, usually retired each to our separate apartments.

My woman had been gone but a few minutes, when she returned again quite out of breath. I felt a sudden shivering at the sight of her.—What, Theresa! said I, is the Chevalier come?—No, Madam, she replied; I have been just now speaking to his valet at the garden-door, whom he sent to acquaint you that the Viceroy has this minute received some unexpected and very important dispatches from Madrid, which must unavoidably detain Don Enenique for half an hour longer than the appointed time: but that at eleven he will not fail. He conjures you to forgive him, and believe that nothing but his being locked up with the Viceroy himself should have delayed him. His valet assures me that his master was obliged to deliver his message hastily to him at the Duke's closet-door.—Theresa spoke this very naturally:—there was nothing unlikely in what she said; and, as I knew Don Enenique's valet was a faithful person, whom his master had often trusted with messages to me, I did not once doubt the truth of this account, but bid my woman wait for the Chevalier till he should come, and then let me know it.

After I had wished my father a good-night I retired to my own apartment. Faustina had complained of a slight indisposition in the evening, and had withdrawn to her chamber much sooner than usual. My father had happened to detain me longer than was his custom; so that it was now near eleven o'clock; and I expected every moment when Theresa would come to acquaint me with the Chevalier's arrival: but after waiting a considerable time without hearing any thing of her, I concluded she had fallen asleep somewhere, and that Ponces might be waiting for me in vain. In this opinion I stole down softly into the garden, and called Theresa;—but no Theresa answered! I searched the little summer-house, and every place wherein she might possibly have concealed herself; but all to no purpose! when, to complete my amazement, I found the garden-door (of which Don Enenique had the key) wide open! The night happened to be exceeding dark, so that I moved along the walks in no small terror of mind;—when, coming under Faustina's apartment, the windows of which looked into the garden, I saw a light in her bed-chamber.—I told you she had complained of not being well when she retired:—I was apprehensive she was now grown worse, and that her woman had been called up. In this belief I ran up stairs; and, entering her chamber, I found every thing in the greatest disorder! The clothes which she had worn that day were thrown on the floor; several of her drawers were lying open, and quite empty; and a letter directed to me lay on her toilet! These were the contents:— "I am sorry, cousin, that, to make myself happy, I must be the occasion of making you wretched; but such is the fatality that hangs over us. Remember, you robbed me of the heart of Castellane. Is it not just then, that I should possess that of Don Enenique? But yet I will do the Chevalier justice:—he is ignorant of the deceit my love has made me practise. I overheard your discourse in the garden-house; and though my first intent in listening to it was only to frustrate your designs by making them known to your father, on hearing the contrivance of your marriage, I resolved boldly to turn it to a more glorious advantage.—I bribed your woman; and my stars have for once been propitious; for by the time this letter comes into your hands I shall be married to Ponces, in your stead, and far away from Naples. But yet, believe me, I do not triumph in your misfortune; but could wish you a less severe lot. However, I know you are mistress of resignation enough to submit to a fate that is not to be controuled.—Adieu for ever."

What effect the reading of this letter had on me is scarce possible to describe! I continued the remaining part of this fatal night in Faustina's chamber. Amazed and stupified at this cruel stroke of fate, I remained rather dead than alive: and day peeped in at the windows when, endeavouring to rouse myself a little from the lethargic state I was in, I arose from the floor on which I had fallen (perhaps in a fainting fit) and continued there. After

I recovered (if I could be said to recover the whole night) I would have persuaded myself what had passed was a frightful dream; when, finding Faustina's shocking epistle still lying by me, I read it over again; and was but too severely convinced of the reality.

I told you I had entirely concealed my intended marriage with the Chevalier from Faustina: compassion for her weakness had for a long time made me conceal even my love. But what did my pity or my caution avail! I found myself betrayed in the cruellest manner. Had I suffered alone, my sorrow would have been less poignant; but, when I considered that Ponces had fallen a victim to the same treachery that ruined me, my pangs were insupportable.

I found that Faustina had taken the perfidious Theresa along with her. Her own woman, who had never been let into any part of this wicked secret, informed me, that her mistress used to have frequent private conversations with that ungrateful creature; and that Faustina had that very evening forbid her to come near her, saying that Theresa should for the future attend her. I gave but little heed to what this woman told me; and only endeavoured to arm myself against the storm which I saw was coming towards me; for I resolved at once to confess the whole truth to my father, and endure the utmost of his resentment rather than suffer Don Enenique to be branded with falshood and ingratitude.

My cousin's flight could not be long a secret. My father was prodigiously alarmed at her woman's not being able to give any account of her; but, if I did not dissipate his fears, I at least put an end to his uncertainty, by throwing myself at his feet, and, with many tears, relating to him the strange circumstances of the preceding night. My father heard me with more temper than I could have expected. He seemed even melted while I spoke; and, raising me,—You were to blame, Adelaide, said he; and I should be angry at your indiscretion, but that I think it mortification enough to you to lose the person you love:—a suitable punishment, I may say, for your undutifulness. I suppose you can now have no reluctance to return to Salerno. Prepare therefore for your journey immediately. But, added he, I am grieved that, in return for Signior Carassa's friendship, I have so mortifying an account to render him of his daughter.—I withdrew, without making any reply: my heart overflowed with gratitude for the tenderness of my father's behaviour to me. I quitted Naples in two days after this sad adventure; and should have departed with some satisfaction, but for the fear of my being pressed to marry at Salerno.

My father and I set out in our coach; and on the journey I assumed a cheerfulness that was very pleasing to him; he even complimented me upon it.—I am charmed with your spirit, Adelaide, said he; I own I was apprehensive that your heart was too much prepossessed in favour of that tall Spaniard, to permit you so soon to recover your former gaiety; but since I find your prudence and good-sense will shortly teach you to overcome a childish and ill-placed passion, I have hopes that the same motives will incline you to believe, that it was your happiness and interest alone that made me reject the Chevalier's suit; and I flatter myself that the husband I have chosen for you, will soon make you forget the husband of your abandoned cousin.—Oh, my Lord, said I, I need not be put in mind, by that epithet, that Don Enenique is for ever lost to me. I will banish him from my memory; and I am not without hopes that I have resolution enough to effect this, without the aid of any new object; therefore, though I can never enough thank you for your indulgence, I conjure you to let me continue as I am. I go with you most willingly to Salerno; but, if you really wish your daughter's happiness, dispense with my accepting this new lover, till a little time and my own reason will better dispose my heart to receive him; mean while I pray you, my Lord, to name the person whom your paternal goodness has thought of for me.—'Tis the Count de la Rosa, answered my father. I find he has loved you long, though it has been kept a secret from me, till your kinsman, Signior Carassa, informed me of it by letter; which I will now show you, as Signior Carassa's doubts have partly explained themselves.—Saying this, my father put the letter into my hands. This was the subject of it:—

"I could not justify it to the friendship I owe you, if I did not inform you of an affair on which I think your daughter's happiness depends. The Count de la Rosa loves her; and would long ago have asked her of you in marriage, if he had not been prevented by me, who was moved to this by Adelaide's reluctance to the match (for she was not acquainted with his passion); but, as I think it too considerable to be rejected, and the Count still retains the same sentiments for my cousin, he has requested me to apply to your Lordship for him. If your answer is favourable, he means to set out directly for Naples. I hope my young kinswoman will have prudence enough to consider her own interest on this occasion: and that she will take care not to compliment her fancy at the expence of her judgment. You need not let Adelaide know of your having received this notice from me. At a proper time I shall explain myself."—

When I had returned this letter to my father, he told me that he had communicated the contents of it to Faustina as soon as he had received it; that she had enlarged upon the Count's passion for me; but had entreated my father not to let me know that either she or Signior Carassa had given him any information on this head; for, said she, my cousin does not like the Count; and she may take our interposing unkindly; and, as that Lord will certainly come to Naples as soon as he hears that you are inclined to favour his suit, the application will then appear to come immediately from himself.

I beseeched my father to let me know what answer he had returned to Signior Carassa? He told me, such a one as he thought the worth of the offer deserved; and that he had in consequence of that, received a letter from the Count de la Rosa himself, full of acknowledgments, and an assurance of waiting on him at Naples in a few days.—I have, added my father, expected the Count for some time past; when I received the disagreeable news of his being ill (from Signior Carassa) which obliged him to defer his intended journey; but I hope by the time we reach Salerno, to find him perfectly recovered.

Though (continued Adelaide) I easily saw that Faustina was at the bottom of this black intrigue, I was yet at a loss to conceive by what means she had engaged her father to interest himself so warmly in an affair which his kindness toward me had formerly made him decline meddling in: this, together with some ambiguous words he had made use of in his letter, convinced me that Faustina had used treachery to engage my kinsman to observe the conduct he had done. I made no reflections however on the matter to my father, knowing that on my arrival at Salerno all would be unravelled.

Signior Carassa was the first to compliment us on our return. My father had not chosen to inform him by letter of his daughter's flight, concluding that an event so shockingly circumstanced would require all the alleviating powers of friendship to interpose, in order to enable the unhappy father to sustain the news. In this my father judged wisely; for, though he endeavoured to relate the story with all the circumstances he could think of to extenuate the wretched Faustina's crime, her incensed father had hardly patience to hear him out; he uttered the bitterest imprecations against his daughter; and, turning towards me,—I am not surprised, Madam, said he, that the ungrateful, treacherous creature should take the pains she did to promote your marriage with the Count de la Rosa; and to engage me, contrary to my promise, to espouse his interest: but I little imagined, that whilst she appeared so solicitous for your honour, she was contriving the means of sacrificing her own. Oh cousin! said he to my father, this vile creature told me that your Adelaide was on the brink of ruin; and that, if I did not interpose, nothing could save her. She wrote me word (forgive me while I relate it) that your daughter had fallen in love with a young man of very mean degree; and that she was apprehensive either of a stolen marriage, or of something still more fatal. She told me, she was afraid to discover the secret to you, dreading the effects of your resentment towards her cousin; and therefore, as the best means to save her from destruction, she conjured me to sound Count de la Rosa's inclinations; and, if I found them still bent towards Adelaide, to give him all the encouragement in my power, and write directly to you; who, she assured me, would listen favourably to such a proposal. I did as she requested. The Count eagerly embraced the motion; and would, long before this, have been at Naples, if a dangerous fit of illness had not attacked him, just as he was preparing to set out. My father here took occasion to inquire very particularly after the Count's state of health, Signior Carassa's distraction about his daughter having prevented him doing it sooner; but he had the mortification to hear from that gentleman, that his illness was so much increased, that the physicians had no hopes of his life. Though my father was much disturbed at this news, you may suppose it gave me little pain; and the poor Count's death, which happened two days after, as it delivered me from my fears of becoming his wife, was the only consolatory circumstance that could, in my situation, have befallen me.'

'I wish,' cried Eugenia, 'I could heal your grief as effectually as I share in it: but alas! my dear, I am as unfortunate as yourself. Have I not lost the man I loved as well as you?—and lost him in a way so unaccountable, as fills me with apprehensions for his life; or, if even that is preserved, I may never see him more.—Is your situation more unhappy?'—'Oh! a thousand times more,' replied Adelaide; 'you may still call Pimenteles yours; and one fortunate day may yet make you amends for all that is past: but, as for me, I can't even think of Don Enenique without a crime: his vows are dedicated to another: he must live for Faustina; and I don't flatter myself even with the smallest hopes; for have I not reason to believe that he is not so dissatisfied with my cruel cousin, since, in so long a time as he has been absent, he has not once found means to let me hear from him? No, no; the cunning Faustina has found the way to his gentle heart; and has perhaps made a merit of her perfidy, by imputing it to an excess of love. Oh Heavens! (continued Adelaide, lifting up her eyes) thou sufferest the treacherous and the deceitful to prosper, while the secure, the credulous, and the innocent are often undone!

But no more of this (added she); your presence, my Eugenia, brings me comfort; and, whilst you are with me, I will, if it be possible, forget every thing that gives me pain. Let us be happy then, whilst you remain here; and, when you return to Milan, I am resolved to ask leave of my father to go with you. This I am sure he will not refuse me, as it will be a means of dispelling that melancholy, which, in spite of my endeavours to hide it from him, he sees preys incessantly on my heart.'—In effect, these two lovely friends assuaged each other's grief by the most tender and soothing expressions. Adelaide endeavoured to persuade Eugenia, that her dear Don Clement would one day be restored to her; whilst she, on the other hand, who had less consolatory hopes to offer her friend, strove only to prevail on the Baron St. Seberina's daughter to believe that the Chevalier de Ponces would perpetually regret his separation from her; and, so far from loving the author of it, would certainly detest and fly her.

The time that Eugenia had allotted to her stay at Salerno, wanted a good deal of being expired, when one day, sitting with Adelaide, a letter was brought to her, which by the character she knew came from the Marquis, her uncle. As it was but a few days since she had heard from him before, this packet was quite unexpected.—'I have no reason,' said she to Adelaide, 'to expect any agreeable change in my fortune; and yet something whispers me that this letter brings most welcome news.' Indeed she had scarce glanced her eyes on the paper, when such an unusual joy diffused itself over her whole countenance that Adelaide easily guessed it contained something in which her friend's heart was nearly interested.—'Come,' said she, 'shew it me; I see Pimenteles writ in every line of your face.'—'Here, read, my friend,' answered Eugenia, 'and participate with me in the extreme joy I am filled with.' These were the terms of the letter:—'Your presence here, my dear niece, is become necessary. Don Clement, whose loss you so much deplore, is now at Milan: he arrived but this day. I am in haste to communicate the news; which I am sure will be very agreeable to you. I had a glimpse of him as he entered a house adjoining mine; where I am informed he is lodged. My joy at seeing him again had almost made me fly to embrace him: however, I checked that emotion on reflecting what I owe myself and you. I pray Heaven Don

Clement may be able to clear up his conduct in such a manner as may make it consistent with your honour and mine, to accomplish the union I have so much at heart! Nevertheless, I shall not solicit any explanation till you return; as in so delicate a point I do not care to proceed without your concurrence.—Your mother is almost out of her wits for joy. I dread the violence of her passions and the weakness of her conduct: hasten therefore on all accounts your departure from Salerno. In the mean time, be assured I shall be as tender of your love as of your fame.'

When Adelaide had read this letter she returned it to her friend.—'I rejoice with you, happy, happy Eugenia,' said she: 'this delightful event fills me with pleasure in the midst of chagrin. Let us go, my dear; let us fly; you to your faithful Don Clement; and I—from Salerno, from the remembrance of my sufferings, and, if possible, from myself.' Eugenia was too impatient to delay her return to Milan; and the Baron St. Seberina having before consented that his daughter should take that journey with her friend, these two ladies set out the following day, having each of them a governante and a suitable number of other attendants.

They arrived safely at Milan; where the Marquis of Pescara welcomed his niece with all the marks of a tender affection; and Adelaide with the tokens of esteem and respect that was due to so charming a guest.

Though Eugenia was very impatient to learn something concerning Don Clement, she yet thought it proper to be silent till the Marquis should mention him first: wherefore, leaving that nobleman to entertain her beautiful friend, she withdrew to pay her duty to her mother, who, as the Marquis told her, had retired, a little indisposed, to her chamber.

Though Eugenia judged (and not without good reason) that her presence would not be very acceptable to Madame Burganeze, she yet thought it an indispensable duty to wait on her immediately, after an absence of some months. She ran to her chamber without the ceremony of having first apprised her of her arrival. She found Madame Burganeze lying on a couch; but so far from having the appearance of a person disordered by pain or sickness, she seemed rather to have renewed her former youth and sprightliness: a loose gown of silver brocade was wrapped carelessly about her; and her hair was adorned with a variety of flowers, in the disposal of which a luxurious and romantic fancy had exerted its utmost skill. Her hair, which when Eugenia left Milan was inclining to grey, was now of the most agreeable brown; and hung in easy ringlets on her neck. To complete the picture, her cheeks bloomed with a freshness as new as it was becoming. Eugenia was not a little surprised at this unexpected metamorphosis. It was night; but by the light of a single wax-taper (Madame Burganeze not caring for too much glare) she had an opportunity of surveying this enamoured dame, as she lay in a reverie, something between slumber and the most agreeable contemplation.

Eugenia, concluding from the gallantry of her mother's dress that she expected a more welcome visitant (which was really the case) was going to withdraw, without disturbing her, when the languishing Madame Burganeze suddenly started up; and the dimness of the light which was in the chamber, together with the like imperfection in her eyes, made her mistake her daughter for another person for whom she waited.

'Good,' said she, in a pretty loud voice, 'how impatient you are! Why, it must want at least an hour of the appointed time.' Eugenia was startled at these words: she concluded that Don Clement was the impatient lover whom her mother meant; and was very much afraid, that, when she should discover her mistake, her rage would be without bounds. She therefore thought it more prudent to dissemble; and seeming not to have marked what her mother said, she approached her couch and, falling on her knees, desired her blessing; but Madame Burganeze, whether thrown into a more than ordinary confusion, or not being thoroughly awake, or blind, or altogether, was so prepossessed with the notion that it was her expected lover who knelt before her, that, holding out one of her hands, she cried, in the softest tone of voice, 'Here, sweet Pimenteles, take my hand; but I conjure you ask no more.' Had Eugenia been less interested in this unlucky scene, she could have laughed at it; but as her mother and her lover were so deeply concerned in it, it had a very different effect on her: she blushed for the weakness of the former, and was seized with mortifying fears on account of the latter. The love-sick dame still held out her stretched hand; but Eugenia, willing to undeceive her (having first kissed it)—'Tis I, Madam; 'tis your daughter; 'tis Eugenia. I should be under the greatest uneasiness,' added she, 'for having broke your rest, but that I fear your sleep was much disturbed; for you just now uttered some broken words, which seemed the effect of a troublesome dream, from which I can't repent having awaked you.' Madame Burganeze, who was by this time perfectly roused from her rapture, was thunderstruck at those words. It was well her daughter had the presence of mind to impute her extravagance to a dream; for Eugenia already saw her mother was beginning to swell with indignation.—'Your company,' said Madame Burganeze, looking disdainfully at her, 'is as unwelcome as it was unexpected. If Don Clement were not at Milan, you would not have been in such haste to return to it; but let me tell you, child, you have no more share in his affections than my chambermaid has, whatever your vanity may suggest to you. His heart, I may venture to say, is devoted to me; and neither your unseasonable presence nor your uncle's policy shall deprive me of it. We don't want you,' added she, with a malicious smile, 'for an internuncio.[25] Don Clement has no farther occasion for proxies.'—'You do me wrong, Madam,' answered Eugenia, 'to suppose that Don Clement is the motive of my return from Salerno; it was in obedience to the Marquis, who recalled me. Besides, you may remember I was not a stranger to Pimenteles's passion for you before my departure from Milan; therefore can't possibly entertain those presumptuous hopes you upbraid me with; and I assure you my sentiments for Don Clement are the very same with those I believe he has for me.'—'So much the better,' answered Madame Burganeze, in a tone less severe than she had spoke in before;—'I should pity you, to love without the hopes of being beloved again; for that would infallibly be the case. You did ill,' said she, after a little pause, 'to come so abruptly upon me; I was not prepared to receive you; and till to-morrow shall dispense with your attendance; for at present I am much more disposed to rest than conversation.' With these words she threw herself again on the couch, and waved her hand to Eugenia to retire.

It happened that Madame Burganeze, in flinging herself carelessly on the couch, had dropped a letter out of her bosom, which Eugenia took up; and, though she was immediately going to restore it, a strong impulse of curiosity prevailed with her to keep it, as she imagined the contents might possibly discover something in which perhaps she had no inconsiderable share. This reason she thought might, in some measure, justify an action, which in its own nature she would have condemned. Having quitted Madame Burganeze's apartment, she hastened to her own to examine the letter. She found it subscribed by Don Clement; and it contained these few words:—'You are the first lady that ever reproached me with indifference: and, if I have been so long in Milan without discovering the least gallantry, it is far from being owing to a want of sensibility in me; on the contrary, you will find no one more tender, or more grateful when I have the happy opportunity of kissing your hand, which I shall not fail to do at the appointed hour.' Though Eugenia thought the character in which this note was written, was not that of Don Clement, yet his name subscribed to it, together with her mother's expressions, and some other concurring circumstances, left her no room to doubt but that it came from him; and, as it seemed altogether an enigma, so she supposed some new mystery had occasioned its not being written in his own hand.

She was impatient to speak to the Marquis on this subject; but, recollecting that he was then engaged in conversation with Adelaide, she returned to the apartment where they were, leaving Madame Burganeze impatiently expecting Don Clement.

And here it will be necessary to relate that part of the old lady's conduct which was the occasion of Eugenia's finding her in so extraordinary a situation.

Madame Burganeze had no sooner heard that Don Clement was returned to Milan than she looked upon herself as possessed of all her wishes. She flattered herself that his being lodged so near the Marquis, was to have the more frequent opportunities of conversing with her: and expected every minute when she should receive a visit from him, his avowed passion for her, and his friendship for the Marquis, her brother, being sufficient motives for him to waive all punctilious forms; and, without ceremony, throw himself into the arms of two persons by whom he knew he was so much beloved:—but, when several days past without her either seeing or hearing from him, she began to be terribly alarmed!—The Marquis, extremely surprised at this slight, spoke of it in terms which gave her room to think he highly resented it. Fearing therefore that a total breach would ensue between her brother and her lover, she resolved at all events to use her endeavours to renew their former intimacy, though she too plainly saw that Don Clement seemed rather inclined to avoid it.

As the Marquis had never let his sister into the secret of Eugenia's adventure with Pimenteles, she could not penetrate into the reason of his resentment against that gentleman; and, believing it proceeded only from the jealousy of his friendship, which could not brook so cold a behaviour in one who had been so dear to him, she hoped (if by any means she could bring them to a meeting) the Marquis would soon forget his anger; and she should by degrees reconcile him to the union she meditated between the youthful Don Clement and herself:—for she still was weak enough to flatter herself that, notwithstanding his distant behaviour, his love for her had brought him back to Milan. Her hopes thus revived, she sent in the Marquis's name to Don Clement, desiring to see him; concluding that he would not refuse the invitation; and that her brother, without knowing that such a compliment had passed, would receive his friend with his usual warmth:—but how was she mortified at the ill-success of her plot! Don Clement received the message with the utmost politeness; but at the same time excused himself from waiting on the Marquis, on account of some perplexing affairs, which he said for the present engrossed all his hours.

Madame Burganeze was half distracted with rage and jealousy at this reply: for she now feared that it was on account of Eugenia's absence that Don Clement's indifference proceeded.

The Marquis (without knowing the lengths his sister had gone to allure Don Clement back again) was of the same opinion; nor did he wish for an *éclaircissement* till his niece should arrive, whose return he now daily expected.—Finding therefore that Pimenteles persisted in his estranged behaviour, he became in his turn as cold and averse to him as he had once been fondly and warmly attached to him; so that Madame Burganeze, despairing of a reconciliation between them, and trembling at the thoughts of losing Don Clement again, and perhaps for ever, resolved to put herself at least out of suspense; on which account, shifting her resentment and composing her ruffled thoughts, she wrote him the following lines, and sent them by her woman:—'You have been eighteen long days in Milan, without seeing me! Unkind, cold Pimenteles! where is all your love? Must I forget that I am a woman, and woo you to your happiness?—Ah! let me chide you for this strange indifference; and if you hope for my pardon, fail not to ask it to-night. The bearer will wait to conduct you to my apartment at ten o'clock; where, if the charming Don Clement repents, the tender Burganeze can forgive.'

To this kind letter Don Clement returned the answer which Eugenia found in her mother's chamber; and with which Madame Burganeze was so well pleased that, without considering how unbecoming and rash her proceedings were, she thought of nothing but how to appear amiable in her lover's eyes. Accordingly she adorned, or rather transformed, herself in the manner already described; and having dismissed her daughter from her presence, who happened to arrive at so unlucky a minute, she disposed herself to receive Don Clement. He was punctual to a minute; for the clock no sooner struck ten than she heard him coming up stairs with La Pointz, who had introduced him the back way.—As he entered the room she would have rose to salute him; but he appeared so very handsome, that the extreme pleasure she took in gazing at him made her forget all ceremonies; and she continued leaning on her couch with her eyes languishingly fixed on him. Don Clement, who, from the posture she was in, could have but an imperfect view of her face, drew nearer to her; and, putting one knee to the ground,—'So unlooked-for a happiness as this,' said he, 'would more than recompense the sufferings of an age:—and I flatter myself that fortune has yet some favours in store for me; since when I least expected it, she has bestowed so great a blessing.'—'How transported I am,' said Madame Burganeze, raising herself up, 'to find you so constant:—but wherefore do you say this blessing was unexpected?—What had you not to hope from a love so ardent and faithful as mine?'

Don Clement, instead of answering this soft language as she expected, started up from his knee; and, falling back two or three paces, seemed to survey her with an air of surprise!—'What ails the trifler?' cried Madame Burganeze;—'what new whim have you taken into your head?—Was it for this I sent for you?' 'Was it you then, Madam,' answered Don Clement, 'who did me the honour to write to me?'—'This is very silly,' answered Madame Burganeze; 'and if you continue these airs, I shall be downright angry with you.'—'I know not,' cried Don Clement, 'whether to be serious or merry on the occasion; but as I think I am more inclined to the former, we will, if you please, let the joke end here:—therefore, Madam, you must allow me to take my leave.' Saying this, he turned towards the door, when Madame Burganeze caught him by the hand. 'Come, come,' said she, 'no more of this foolery. I am displeased with you already; and let me tell you, you have gone too far.'—Don Clement drew his hand gently from hers; and, bowing low at the same time, 'I have been in an error, Madam,' said he; 'and so I believe have you; therefore I beg once more you will not detain me.' With this he took two or three steps towards the door: but Madame Burganeze, now quite enraged, could contain herself no longer.—'What possesses you?' said she; 'Does this behaviour agree with your former protestations of love? nay, with what you but just this moment said?—Am I less amiable now than I was three minutes ago?—or can your heart rebel so soon?—Speak, coxcomb; and don't provoke my anger too far.'—'As for what I just now said,' answered Pimenteles, a little nettled, 'it was not meant for you, Madam: and as to your talking of former protestations, not knowing that I ever had the honour of seeing you before, it makes me rather suspect that it is you who are possessed;—therefore, lady, to avoid disturbing the family, I beg once more that you will permit me to retire.'—Don Clement here again attempted to be gone; but, unluckily for him, La Pointz had locked the chamber-door on the outside; so that he found himself under a necessity of sustaining all Madame Burganeze's fury. 'Ungrateful wretch,' said she, 'have you forgot our mutual love?—Must all the tears which your absence cost me meet with this return?—And have you the insolence, the barbarity, to own your falsehood, and aggravate it in the most presumptuous manner?—Not only deny your having loved me, and confess those raptures were meant for another, but even disown that you ever saw me.—Monster,' added she; 'your unparalleled villany shall not go unpunished: and if Eugenia be the object of your love, she shall be the first victim to my revenge.'

The violent passion which this frantic woman had thrown herself into agitated her whole frame so much, that, happening to lean against a cabinet, on which stood a pyramid of rich china, she unluckily threw down the whole pile; which, rattling on the floor with such noise, greatly alarmed the Marquis with Eugenia and Adelaide, who were not yet risen from supper. As Madame Burganeze's apartment was not far distant from that in which they were sitting, her brother and the ladies made haste to her assistance; as did La Pointz and some more of the female servants who had been frightened at the noise. They all ran in together without ceremony; so that the chamber was filled in an instant.

Though Don Clement was under some confusion, he nevertheless accosted the Marquis with great politeness; and, without giving him time to enquire into the fracas,—'My Lord,' said he, 'I don't at all wonder at the surprise you seem to be in at seeing me here. I confess, nothing can appear in a worse light; but I hope this lady will do me the justice to remove any ill impressions which this accident may have made on you. For my own part, I am so much ashamed of having occasioned all this disorder, that I must for the present beg leave to withdraw; but will at any other time you please, satisfy your Lordship that, if I have committed an offence, it was unknowingly; and that, bold and suspicious as this visit may appear, I had no design to insult any of your house.'

Don Clement had time to make an end of this speech without any interruption. Madame Burganeze was so overwhelmed with confusion, that she could not open her lips nor lift her eyes from off the ruins of the china; where they were fixed immoveably. The women who had ran in, in their first surprise, concluding that a scene of this nature was not so proper for them to be witnesses to, had all stole out of the chamber; so that none but the three ladies and the Marquis remained.—'Stay, Don Clement,' said the latter; 'there are no persons now present but those who are particularly interested in what relates to you; and there can be no time more proper than this for you to make that explanation we would wish to have:—therefore, with my sister's permission, I must beg leave to enquire into the motives of this secret and unseasonable interview between you?'

Don Clement, who was unwilling to mortify Madame Burganeze by mentioning her letter, was somewhat at a loss how to make a reply; when, casting his eyes on that lady, as if to demand her leave to answer the Marquis's question, she (who read his looks) cried out,—'Speak, cruel Pimenteles! my brother is not unacquainted with my weakness for you; nor can any thing you have farther to say make me more miserable.' With this she flung out of the room, and, locking herself in her closet, left Don Clement at liberty to declare himself how he pleased.

'I believe then, my Lord,' said that gentleman, addressing himself to the Marquis (and at the same time giving him the letter he had that day received from Madame Burganeze) 'you would think me a very insensible man if I refused a summons like this: but I own I thought it had come from a fairer hand, or you would not have found me so rude a disturber of your family.'—''Tis my sister's writing,' answered the Marquis; 'and I can't imagine how you should suspect it came from any other person!'—'Nothing more natural,' interrupted Don Clement; 'and if your Lordship and these ladies will have but the patience to hear me, you will be convinced of this yourself.

I had but just received that letter, and was breaking open the seal when a gentleman with whom I had been intimate in Castile, and renewed my acquaintance with since my arrival here, came in to make me a visit:—as there is an unreserved friendship between us, I made no scruple of shewing him the note; and asked him, laughing, how he would advise me to act; for my valet had told me that the woman who had brought it waited for an answer. As my residence in this city has been but short, and my time ever since I have been here so wholly taken up with business, I had few moments for pleasure; of course I have had no opportunity of making any acquaintance amongst the ladies; on which account I imagined that some gay damsel had a mind to divert herself a little. I was not, however, willing to engage in an amour which was to commence so mysteriously, though I confess my curiosity inclined me strongly to pursue it.—While I was making some reflections on the novelty of the thing, my friend was perusing the letter with a good deal of attention.—Are you not acquainted, said he, with the lady from whom this epistle came?—No, replied I; I am a stranger to the name and the hand! and am in doubt whether I shall take any farther notice of it: for perhaps it may only come from some female adventurer, who has a mind to make herself merry at my expence; or, what is worse, to lead me into an unlucky snare: as strangers who appear to be of distinction are sometimes treated. My friend laughed at my fears; telling me I need be under no concern:—for if (said he) this letter comes from the lady whose name is subscribed to it, you are so far from being in the least danger, that you ought rather to look upon yourself as the happiest man in the world—to have inspired Signiora Eugenia Burganeze with an inclination for you! I am surprised, continued he, that you should be a stranger to this young lady, as she lives next door to you, and is niece to the Marquis of Pescara!—I told him that I had, indeed, received a compliment from that Lord; but that I had not the honour of his acquaintance, nor did I ever hear of his having any family but a sister; who is a lady far advanced in years.—Yes, replied that gentleman, Madame Burganeze, the fair Eugenia's mother. I have been absent from Milan, added he, for some months, and know not whether that lady is still with her brother; for when I left this city, she designed retiring into a convent; and even talked of carrying her daughter along with her. Let us not flatter ourselves therefore too far; for perhaps 'tis some other lady of the name who has wrote to you: or possibly some woman who has only assumed the name to engage you the sooner in her toils.—But we have the means to discover this in our own hands, cried I; for the woman who brought the letter waits below:—whereupon I called my valet, with a design to bid him bring the woman to me; when my friend happening to ask him, did he know her?—the man replied that he believed she was one of Madame Burganeze's attendants; for that he had often seen her going in and out of the Marquis of Pescara's hotel.—Oh, 'tis enough, cried my friend, laughing:—we need ask no more questions. Write an answer immediately, continued he: Signiora Eugenia is as virtuous as she is beautiful; and though she may have a mind to amuse herself with an innocent piece of gallantry, yet, depend upon it, she means nothing contrary to the strictest honour: and if you have in reality been so happy as to please her, it is the greatest felicity that could have befallen you.—He added a great many other things, that inspired me with such an ardent desire to see the lovely Eugenia, that I did not hesitate a moment what my reply should be:—and having in a few words answered the billet, which I now no longer doubted came from her, I thought every minute an hour till the appointed time arrived in which I was to be admitted to her presence.—I came, my Lord, full of the idea which my friend had given me of your charming niece. But judge of my surprise and disappointment! when, instead of her, I found myself on my knees before a person fit indeed to inspire me with reverence, but far unlikely to create love!—Ashamed to be thus deceived by my own too flattering hopes, I was ready to excuse myself to the old lady, and to take my leave of her; when she flew into a violent passion; urged former vows and protestations; told me of (I know not what) love that was between us; and had almost raised herself into a phrenzy, when the destruction of the china luckily alarmed her friends!—This, my Lord,' added Don Clement, 'is the truth you desired to be informed of, and which Madame Burganeze herself must acknowledge. I have therefore nothing to say farther in my justification; but to implore the beautiful Eugenia's pardon for my presumption in entertaining, but for a moment, the belief of being honoured with her love.'—Here he bowed low to Eugenia, and remained silent.

I believe my reader is by this time as much surprised at Don Clement's behaviour as the Marquis and the two ladies were; and think him a very audacious and lying Spaniard: but we shall see presently how he came out of this whimsical situation.

'I know not,' said the Marquis, in a grave and resolute tone, 'what has provoked you to frame this unaccountable story; but certain I am, that nothing but my astonishment could have suffered me to let you run on so long. Whatever reasons you may have for playing on my imprudent sister, I think you owe something to my friendship, and more to my niece; who has made me her confidant in an affair which you ungenerously strove to conceal from me, notwithstanding the regard I always treated you with.'—'How, my

Lord?' cried Don Clement, angrily; 'this farce is too long, and must needs end unluckily!'—'I am of your mind,' answered the Marquis, briskly. 'You are at present under my roof; remember that is your only protection:—for know, young Spaniard, that Eugenia's honour is not a toy for such boys as you to sport with.'—'By Heaven, you amaze me,' cried Don Clement; and added, after a short pause, 'I begin to think there must be some strange mystery in this affair, which I tremble to penetrate. But I declare to you, by every thing that is sacred, that it is yet scarce three weeks since I first saw Milan; nor did I ever, during the whole course of my life, till this night, behold Madame Burganeze or her charming daughter.'

Eugenia, who till now had been silent, could contain herself no longer; but turning to Adelaide, who had been a spectatress of this odd scene, 'Such insolence,' said she, 'is not to be borne; but, if it is possible to raise a blush in a face where boldness and deceit are painted, I will produce something which must cover this daring man with confusion.' Saying this, she ran to her apartment; and bringing thence the poniard which Don Clement had dropped in the wood, and which had been carefully preserved by Eugenia ever since, she put it into that gentleman's hands:—'Look there, Signior Pimenteles,' said she; 'and if you can deny that poniard to be yours, on which your name is decyphered, I will allow you to be a master-piece of dissimulation.'—Don Clement looked at the poniard with manifest tokens of amazement; when, turning towards the Marquis, 'I am no longer in doubt, my Lord,' cried he: 'this dagger has unravelled the whole mystery. Alas! we have all been deceived by false appearances. That young stranger, who assumed the name of Don Clement Pimenteles, was a woman, and my unhappy sister.

Hear then, my Lord, and you ladies, that part of my sister's story which gave occasion to this strange event.

We are twins; and owe our birth, as she may possibly have informed you, to Don Manuel Pimenteles, whose house is not accounted the most obscure in Castile. My sister's beauty (for she was allowed to have much) had gained her a great many admirers; but my father would give access to none of them, except Don Gabriel Sahabedras,[26] Count of Castellar, who was possessed of an estate of eighty thousand piastres a year.[27] This nobleman was upwards of fifty years old; of an imperious, haughty temper; and without any thing to recommend him, but his immense fortune. You may be sure my sister looked upon him as a very unequal match. However, in obedience to my father she received his addresses civilly; but with so much coldness and indifference, that he soon perceived how disagreeable he was to her. This did not however discourage him: he had none of those delicate sentiments with which a generous lover is affected; so as he was possessed of the person of my sister, it was all he desired. He used to tell her that the heart of a woman was too great a trifle for a serious man to spend his time in pursuit of; that he knew it was impossible to confine their inclinations for ever to one object, were it the most amiable; that therefore he was indifferent whether he was beloved or not; and that, so as he was but secured of the person of her he admired, he would take care to preserve her virtue from any attacks; and, for the rest, he would leave her to her own humour.

His carriage was answerable to this unfeeling declaration; he took not the least pains to make himself agreeable to my sister; for, having obtained my father's consent to espouse her, he assumed such an air of authority over Clementina (so my sister is called) as rendered him perfectly hateful to her. In vain did she throw herself at my father's feet, and beseech him not to sacrifice her to a man whom she so much disliked. He had engaged his promise to the Count, and was resolved not to break it. Besides, as Clementina was the youngest of three daughters, he thought it was an alliance she ought to be proud of; and told her, in a peremptory manner, that she should marry Castellar, or never see his face again. My poor sister, drove to the last extremity, came to me all in tears:—Dear brother, said she, if you have a mind to preserve my life, endeavour to soften the obdurate heart of my father; for if he persists in the resolution he has taken, of marrying me to Don Gabriel, I assure you, you will lose a sister who loved you tenderly.—I promised her my assistance; and went that moment to my father. I found him in his closet with Sahabedras and a lawyer, who was busied writing at a table. I gave the cause over at this sight; but, resolving to make one effort more on my father's tenderness, I begged of him to step into the next room with me. He knew I was extremely fond of my sister; wherefore, guessing my errand, he told me, in an angry tone, without giving me leave to speak, that if I should interpose in behalf of that obstinate girl, I would incur the height of his displeasure. Besides, added he, 'tis now too late; for every thing is agreed on between the Count and me; therefore, Sir, be pleased to let your sister know that I expect the last proof of her obedience within these eight days.—I went with this unwelcome message to Clementina's apartment. She received it with more calmness than I expected; and told me, that however rigorous her father's commands were, she was resolved to obey them.

She concealed her chagrin so well, that none of us had the least suspicion of her design. On the contrary, we began to imagine that she had reconciled herself to a lot which she found it was impossible to avoid. In short, the preparations for her nuptials were making with great magnificence, when, on the eve of the day appointed for the solemnization of them, Clementina and her waiting-woman disappeared; and, notwithstanding the strictest inquiry, there was not the least trace of them to be discovered. We found she had taken all her jewels with her, and a pretty large sum of money: at the same time I missed this poniard; but I did not suspect that my sister had disguised herself in man's apparel; I only supposed her fondness for me had induced her to carry it with her as a token of remembrance.'

END OF THE FIRST VOLUME.

Volume II

Eugenia and Adelaide

'My father and the Count were so enraged at Clementina's elopement, that for some time they could not tell what resolution to come to. At length Don Gabriel declared that he would search all Spain, nay the whole world, till he had recovered her; and, on his leaving Castile he swore he never would return to it without Clementina.—It was then that I discovered he passionately loved my sister, notwithstanding the indifference he always affected. For my own part, as my honour was as much concerned as his, I resolved not to be behind hand with him in this expedition; so we both set out together, like true knights-errant, uncertain what road to take; for Clementina had concerted her scheme so cunningly, that nobody was privy to her flight but her woman, who was the companion of it.

I shall not trouble your Lordship with the particulars of this fruitless search; let it suffice to tell you, that, after we had traversed most parts of Spain and Portugal to no sort of purpose, we resolved to separate, and take different routes. We have some relations in France, where I designed to steer my course; and Castellar determined, at the same time, to push his inquiries into Italy. What success he has had I don't know; but I had the mortification to leave France without hearing any news of her; and, almost despairing of ever seeing her again, I was returning into Castile, when, by an express I had the news brought me of my father's death. This obliged me for a while to suspend my purpose of returning home, and to pass into Italy, in order to negotiate some business, and receive certain sums of money from a banker in this city. Some unlooked-for perplexing circumstances in my affairs have obliged me to make a longer stay at Milan than I at first proposed: and, as the uncertain fate of my sister gives me unspeakable concern, I must beseech you, my Lord, and you, Madam (addressing himself to Eugenia) to inform me what you know relating to her; for I am well satisfied that her prodigious likeness to me, joined to her having borrowed my name and habit, has occasioned all this strange confusion.'

'It will be an easy matter, Signior, to satisfy you,' replied the Marquis; 'but, as my niece is best acquainted with the particulars of your sister's story, I shall put that task upon her.—Here, Eugenia; give Don Clement an exact account of all that has past concerning Clementina.' But, during her narration, she took so much pains to conceal the passion she had conceived for the counterfeit Don Clement, that the Marquis several times could not forbear smiling. But, notwithstanding all her care, she discovered so great an emotion at the repetition of several passages of her story, that it was no difficult matter for Don Clement to discover that the charms of his sister had made way for him in the heart of Eugenia. He told that lady that he was certain it was no other than Count Castellar who had forced his sister away: and added, that not having heard from him since, he was under terrible apprehensions on that account.—'Don Gabriel,' said he, 'is violent and haughty: and, as my sister is now entirely in his power, I am sure he will not scruple to use her with the greatest severity if she refuses to marry him; and I know Clementina would sooner suffer death than consent to a union so hateful to her.—Ah dear creature,' continued he, 'were I now in Castile, you should soon be delivered from your tyrant, since you have no longer a father, whose harsh commands forced you on the brink of ruin.'—'I join with you,' replied the Marquis, 'in bewailing the fate of so amiable a creature. I own I felt sentiments in my heart for Clementina, for which I was at a loss to find a name: and I can tell you, niece,' proceeded he, laughing, 'that, had I discovered this secret sooner, you would have found in me a more dangerous rival than you did in Madame Burganeze.'

Don Clement seized on this opportunity to assure Eugenia (with a modest ardour) that, though she had lost a feigned lover in the person of Clementina, she had found a real one in that of Don Clement.—Eugenia answered this only by an obliging look:—and the Marquis said, 'I believe my niece will do no great violence to her inclinations in transferring them from the amiable Clementina to the accomplished Don Clement.' Indeed the resemblance was so perfect between this amiable brother and sister, that it could hardly be called a change in Eugenia's heart, which now felt the same sentiments for the true Don Clement that it had at first conceived for the supposed one. As there was no difference in the age of these beautiful twins, so there was none either in their faces or statures; at least it was so very inconsiderable as not to be distinguished when they were asunder. Don Clement was scarce twenty years old; and had not yet lost that delicacy which youth generally retains to that age. The conversation on this extraordinary event lasted till the night was almost spent; when Pimenteles took his leave of the Marquis, with a promise to come and dine with him next day.

Madame Burganeze, who from her closet had not lost a word of their discourse, was so much ashamed of what had past, that she would not appear; so that the Marquis and Don Clement, with the two young ladies, were the only persons at table. Clementina's distress too much engrossed their thoughts for them to talk on any other subject. The Marquis assured Don Clement that he would join with him most heartily for the recovery of his sister.—'I hope,' continued he, 'our dear Clementina will have resolution enough to resist the inhuman Castellar till we can come to her relief. What should hinder us then from immediately setting out for Spain? for thither I suppose Don Gabriel has carried her. I die with impatience to see my ever-loved creature, and free her from the insolent ravisher.' The Marquis spoke this with a warmth which shewed how much his heart was interested. Don Clement, after expressing his thanks for so generous an offer of his friendship, told him he would readily embrace it.—'Though my affairs here,' said he, 'are in so intricate a situation as to require my presence to settle them, yet, where the welfare of so dear a sister is at stake, I must forego every other advantage to fly to her assistance.'—'Let us be gone then,' cried the Marquis; 'we will set out to-morrow.' Accordingly he gave orders for this sudden expedition; and his commands being executed with as much rapidity as they were given, Don Clement and he found themselves in readiness to depart very early the next morning.

The Marquis in taking leave of the ladies told Adelaide, that he hoped to have the happiness of finding her at his house, on his return to Milan. As for Don Clement, short as the time was, he did not leave Eugenia without receiving some marks of her esteem for him.

Their voyage was prosperous: they arrived safely at Valencia;[1] and set out immediately for the kingdom of Castile, where the Count of Castellar's whole estate lay, and where he always resided. They were informed by a gentleman whom they met on the borders of Castile, that the Count was at a castle he had on the banks of the Guadimara,[2] a few leagues from Madrid: but they could not learn whether he had a lady or any stranger with him. However, as they made no doubt but that Clementina was really in his possession, they resolved, without losing time, to set forward for his castle. Accordingly they redoubled their speed, and reached it towards the close of the day. The nearer they approached, the more they were confirmed in their opinion, that this was the prison of the unhappy Clementina. It was an old castle, which formerly had been very stately and magnificent, but was now partly fallen to ruin; and the walls everywhere so overgrown with moss and ivy, that it could at a little distance be hardly distinguished from a thick dark wood, with which it was surrounded.

There was something however so romantic and charming in the situation, that the Marquis and Don Clement could not help stopping to contemplate the awful solitude. Its remoteness from any other dwelling gave it an aspect peculiarly solitary; and it had been so neglected by the Count, who had a great many other fine seats, that it looked more like the remains of an ancient monastery than the mansion-house of a grandee of Spain. The outer court, which was as full of weeds as if no human creature had ever trod on it, was inclosed with a very high wall, and the entrance secured by a strong gate, which was locked and barred on the inside.

The Marquis and Don Clement, who had alighted from their horses and given them to the servants who attended them, advanced towards the gate, and thundered at it with all their might: but, instead of its being opened, they were demanded from within, Who they were, and what they wanted? The Marquis returned no answer, but knocked louder than before; when the same voice cried out, 'You may be as noisy as you please; but till I know your business you shall not be admitted.'

This suspicious answer redoubled the Marquis's impatience.—'Let us force the gate,' said he to Don Clement; 'I find but too plainly that this pernicious solitude is the abode of your lovely sister. Let us not stand to importune a wretch who no doubt has received orders from his guilty master, not to suffer any but himself to enter the castle.'—Saying this, he beckoned to the two footmen to come to his assistance. But Don Clement, who was of a calmer temper, or perhaps was not at that time agitated with emotions so violent as the Marquis, begged of him to desist; telling him such an attempt would be very imprudent, as they had but two servants with them; and perhaps there might be numbers in the castle who would, without doubt, oppose them, should they even succeed in forcing the gate.—'I believe,' added he, 'the Count is not in reality here, by the caution his domestics observe; I will therefore try an expedient that may get us admittance, without committing such outrages.'—He spoke those words so low that nobody but the Marquis could hear him; when, raising his voice, and addressing himself to the person on the inside of the gate, 'Let not Don Gabriel think,' said he, 'to conceal his treasons within these walls. We are certainly informed that he hides himself here; and, if he does not immediately surrender himself, he will compel us to use violence; and whoever you are that thus obstinately refuse us entrance, you may perhaps have your Lord's life to answer for.'

Don Clement had no sooner spoke these words than he heard the fellow on the inside unbarring the gate. The time he took to do it, and the number of bolts and locks they heard him undo, convinced them how difficult it would have been for them to have forced an entrance. The gate was but now half-opened, which a gigantic ill-looking fellow held in his hand, at the same time that he had fastened a strong chain across it on the inside. He looked rudely at the two strangers; and without the least mark of civility, told them that his master was not there, but at Madrid.—'Friend,' answered the Marquis, 'we are but just now come from thence; and had the Count been there, it would have saved us this journey. I therefore once more command you, as you shall answer the contrary at your peril, to give us admission immediately.'

The sharpness with which the Marquis pronounced this, seemed to intimidate the fellow; and, though it did not procure them the least good manners from him, it however somewhat lowered the insolence of his looks; he threw off the chain; and, at the same time flinging open the gate, he told them, with a surly grin, they might search if they pleased; but they would have their labour for their pains.

The Marquis and Don Clement, without regarding the insolence of this fellow, entered the court, and proceeded directly into the castle, which was readily opened to them by a footboy. He seemed startled at seeing two strange cavaliers; when the porter, who had followed them close, said bluntly,—'These gentlemen want my Lord.—I have told them already he is not here; but they won't believe me; so carry them in, and let their own eyes convince them.' The lad appeared in great confusion at this request. He protested the Count was not there:—but the Marquis and Don Clement persisting in their demand of being allowed to search the castle, the lackey was obliged to yield: wherefore, civilly enough, desiring them to walk in, he led them through all the lower apartments of the castle, which, though lofty and pleasant, were nevertheless most of them empty and full of dust.

The two gentlemen who, from all these circumstances, concluded that Clementina was a prisoner here, after having gone through the lower chambers and those in the first floor, without making any discovery, were ascending another stair-case, in hopes of meeting with better success; when they were stopped by an old Moorish[3] woman who was coming down. She catched hold of the Marquis by the arm, and told him hastily, in broken Spanish, that he would only dirty himself if he went up; for that in the upper story there were only lumber and rubbish. This but served to heighten their curiosity:—so, rushing hastily up, they were followed by the Mooress, who seemed to be much frightened.

The first chamber they entered was so dark, that they could not distinguish any object; when, after having thrown open the shutters, they saw lying on an indifferent bed a young man, who seemed to be in a profound sleep. His fine long hair covered half his face.—But how were they filled with a mixture of delight and grief, when, on the youth's starting up (who had awoke with the noise) they discovered *him* to be Clementina!—She no sooner saw her brother and the Marquis than she gave a loud shriek, and fainted away on the bed, from which she had just risen.—The means used to recover her by the Moresco soon brought her to herself.—She opened her eyes; and casting them first on the Marquis and then on her brother, with looks of transport!—she remained gazing on them, without once offering to speak.

Though the Marquis could hardly refrain throwing his arms round her neck, his respect for her with-held him; and he permitted Don Clement first to embrace her; when, in his turn, advancing to do the same, Clementina's face was immediately overspread with blushes: and she cast her eyes on the ground; from whence she seemed unable to raise them.—'Dear sister,' said Don Clement (seeing her embarrassment) 'assume a little more courage. You see yourself in the hands of two persons who love you dearly. The Marquis already knows your whole story; and has undertaken this journey with me into Spain, on purpose to join his aid with mine in delivering you from Don Gabriel.—You should therefore rather return him thanks for his generosity, than thus give yourself up to the confusion which overwhelms you; and for which I am sure your innocence never gave any cause.'

Clementina, a little emboldened at this kindness from her brother, threw herself suddenly at his feet. 'Ah! my dear brother!' said she, 'how your goodness transports me!—I am indeed covered with confusion when I reflect on what is past; and might reasonably expect nothing but reproaches from you; when, instead of these, you receive me with the most extreme tenderness!—I can't,' added she, 'I dare not look at you without blushing:—and for my

Lord Marquis, to whom I owe a thousand obligations, I cannot lift up my eyes to him.'—'Why so, Madam?' cried the Marquis, with an air that spoke his joy (and at the same time raising her up; for she was still embracing her brother's knees) 'why should you not look at me?—If while I thought you the most accomplished and deserving of my own sex, I loved and esteemed you, do you think you will be less dear to me for being in reality the most amiable of women? So far from it, that I declare to you, this discovery will make me the happiest of men.—If I am still possessed of that place in your heart which you have so often assured me I held; nay, I shall insist on the right I have there,' continued he, smiling; 'for I don't see why the changing your habit should make you change your mind; and if I thought it would have that effect, I would rather for ever see you in this dress than endure the loss of your affection.'—'Come, come,' said Don Clement (seeing his sister quite embarrassed) 'the Marquis is in the right in what he says; and I think you can hardly ever make him sufficient amends for the disorder you have created in his family. Madame Burganeze is almost run mad for love of you: and I find that you had even made some progress in the heart of the beautiful Eugenia!'—'In short,' interrupted the Marquis, 'as you have made the whole family sigh for you by turns, I know not of any reparation that can be offered, unless Don Clement will yield you to me, to punish you for the mischiefs you have occasioned.'—'Agreed,' cried Don Clement; 'provided you will consent that Eugenia shall be mine, who owes large amends for the indignity she offered me in mistaking me for my sister.'—The frankness and vivacity with which both the Marquis and Don Clement delivered themselves, recovered Clementina from her confusion, when all of them growing more serious, Don Clement immediately turned the discourse.—'We waste time,' said he, 'and forget, whilst in the company of our restored Clementina, that we are all within the hostile walls of our foe. Let us first go from hence, and then we shall have leisure to enquire what Castellar's behaviour has been to my sister.'

The Marquis, who was just going to make the same proposal, immediately arose and took Clementina under the arm, while Don Clement led the way down stairs with his sword drawn.—The Mooress having alarmed the servants with the danger they were in of losing the young prisoner committed to their care, two lusty attendants of the Count's, who (together with the surly porter) were all the men he had left at the castle, presented themselves before the Marquis and Don Clement, in order to stop their passage; but both protesting that their swords should force their way through them, they thought it most prudent to submit to the necessity they were under of yielding. Clementina, whose heart fluttered like a bird newly escaped from the snares of the fowler, hung upon the arms of her two deliverers. They hastened out of the castle to their two servants, who attended at the gate with their horses.

In this manner they set forward for Madrid, and arrived about midnight at the house of Don Clement, which his two elder sisters still lived in since the death of Don Manuel, their father.—It is impossible to describe the raptures of Donna Clementina on seeing herself thus happily restored to every thing that was dear to her!—Her brother, her sisters, and the Marquis, whom she despaired of ever seeing again, were all at once given back to her wishes!

Late as it was, they none of them thought of rest; for Pimenteles, impatient to know how the Count of Castellar had conducted himself towards his sister, begged of her to relate what had passed since her forced departure from Milan.—'You shall be informed of every particular,' answered Clementina; 'but as there are some circumstances in the beginning of my story which may be necessary to mention, I shall acquaint you with every thing in order.

As the Marquis, as well as yourself and my sisters, already know the motive of my leaving Castile, I need not repeat it:—I shall only say that having resolved to fly, I made nobody acquainted with my design but my woman, whose fidelity I knew might be depended upon:—and here, my dear brother, I must entreat your forgiveness for concealing my purpose from you: for, though you were as averse from my marrying Don Gabriel as I was, yet I knew you would oppose so rash an action. For this reason therefore I departed privately the night before my intended marriage; having first equipped myself and my maid with man's apparel.

I had heard that the Prince of Bassiniano (who you knew was at Madrid) was returning to Italy; and as I had no settled plan for my conduct, I thought of nothing so much as the means of avoiding the hated Sahabedras, I resolved to take this opportunity of getting out of his reach, and at the same time of seeing a charming country, of which I had heard so much. As I could speak Italian tolerably, I was the more encouraged in this resolution. Taking therefore a close chaise, my woman and I set out, and got safe to Barcelona; where we waited for the Prince's coming. We had the satisfaction to see him the day after our arrival, and embarked with him in a vessel for Genoa,[4] which we reached very happily; and passing from thence to Milan, I had an opportunity of seeing part of the finest country in the world.—The Prince of Bassiniano, with whom, brother, you know you had some slight acquaintance at Madrid, treated me with great distinction; as he looked upon me to be the individual Don Clement whom he knew in Spain: and this circumstance in a manner obliged me to assume your name, which I should not, for my own security, otherwise have done: but I now found it was like to be of great service to me; for by this name the Prince introduced me to many persons of the first quality at Milan, and amongst the rest, to the generous Marquis of Pescara; whom I found every way so deserving of my esteem, that I thought myself more obliged to the Prince for procuring me his friendship, than for all the other favours he had conferred on me. How many happy hours, my Lord,' pursued Clementina, addressing herself to the Marquis, 'have we past together, when your ignorance of my sex gave me the liberty of discoursing with you without reserve! How often have you boasted to me of the freedom of your heart; and that you would not exchange the sweets you enjoyed in my friendship for the love of the greatest Princess upon earth! These were indeed most flattering assurances, and filled me with inexpressible delight:—but whatever satisfaction I took in being beloved by one whom I so highly valued, that happiness had like to have been wholly destroyed; and that at a time, too, when you were endeavouring to bind me still more closely to you by the most endearing ties. In short, my Lord, you gave me to understand that you wished to see me united to your niece, the fair and amiable Eugenia.

So unexpected a favour, and at the same time a circumstance so contrary to the whole scope of my designs, threw me into the utmost consternation.—What could I do? The honour was too great to be refused;—and yet the impossibility of accepting it was still greater!—What, said I, must the Marquis, or what must Eugenia think of a denial?—I am their guest, and have received so many marks of their friendship and affection, that I could kill myself for acting so disingenuous a part. Oh! let me rather confess myself at once to be an unfortunate woman who seeks only for shelter, than any longer abuse so much goodness and generosity. I had almost put this purpose into action the same minute, and was ready to discover myself to you, when I was stopped by an impulse of shame. What am I going to do? The Marquis must look upon me as a rash and imprudent creature; and that friendship which he has hitherto indulged towards me, may be turned into contempt and aversion.—This last reflection silenced me effectually, and threw such a damp on my spirits that I was near sinking down on the spot: but though I resolved still to conceal my sex from you, I was yet at a loss what answer to return; for there were two circumstances which embarrassed me to the last degree. The one was that, as in the frequent conversations we had together, you with the greatest freedom opened your heart to me; I in return had more than once assured you that I had brought my freedom into Italy; and that no lady had yet obliged me to resign it:—so that this was an irremediable bar to my pleading a pre-engagement. But what was still more perplexing to me, I had discovered that I was far from being indifferent to Donna Eugenia.

I had reason to imagine she would not refuse me, in case I was proposed to her for a husband. If the Marquis, said I, should communicate his designs to his niece, and find that she already approves of me, into what sad straits shall I be driven?—I must either fly from the presence of persons so dear to me, branded perhaps as an impostor or an ungrateful wretch; or else disclose a secret that must plunge me into the deepest confusion!—The thoughts of this cruel alternative tortured me for some hours. At length I resolved (as my last expedient) before the Marquis should speak to Eugenia, and discover her favourable sentiments towards me, to throw myself at her feet, confess the whole truth of my story to her, and conjure her to keep the secret. Accordingly I entreated Eugenia by a note I conveyed to her, to allow me a private interview; for I must not omit to tell you that (as we women are more quick-sighted than men in discovering the foibles of our own sex) I had observed that Madame Burganeze had cast a favourable eye on me from the first time she saw me; which had made her more than ordinarily watchful of her daughter, whose beauty she was not a little jealous of, insomuch that I could never find an opportunity of speaking to Eugenia but in her mother's presence:—for this reason then it was that I was obliged to act with so much precaution in requesting a secret interview with the young lady.—She granted it; and I was just making the intended discovery to her when we were surprised by Madame Burganeze.

I leave you to judge, my Lord, and you, brother,' proceeded Clementina, 'how vexatious such an interruption was!—Eugenia was still ignorant of my sex; and I thought it a secret of too much importance to trust Madame Burganeze with; especially at a time when the violence of her jealousy had almost robbed her of her reason. You will think perhaps that the best way to cure her of it was to disclose myself to her at once: but I was of a different opinion. Prepossessed as she was with the belief of my being a man, I could not have disabused her without entering abruptly into a detail of circumstances, which I thought of a nature too nice to be committed to the discretion of a person of so violent a temper. Besides, might it not be a disappointment to her, to find she had set her affections on one of her own sex; which would rather serve to exasperate her against me for the deceit, than engage her to befriend me. Added to all this, I had prepared to relate my story to Donna Eugenia with all the interesting circumstances that could induce her to pity me; and I could not think of making all at once a discovery which I thought might, if managed with prudence, secure me in the happiness which I then enjoyed.

My thoughts were thus employed whilst Madame Burganeze was venting her fury against the innocent Eugenia, whose fear and confusion served to increase mine. At length, in the hurry of my reflections an expedient came into my head, which I did not hesitate a moment in practising.—I feigned a violent passion for Madame Burganeze, and had the courage to declare it; and even went so far as to assure her that I came to her daughter on no other account, than to beg her assistance in the prosecution of my love. I added a great deal to strengthen what I asserted; and Madame Burganeze, already infatuated with her passion for me and vanity of her own charms, was so very weak as to give credit to what I said; and even swallowed the bait with a facility which surprised me. She heard me with pleasure; and I had no reason to complain of the cruelty of my mistress.

But though I had the good fortune to extricate both Eugenia and myself out of this dilemma, I had nevertheless the mortification of being obliged to quit the apartment of that lady, without having it in my power to undeceive her in the opinion she might entertain of the odd confession I had just made to her mother, otherwise than by a sign; which however I endeavoured to make as expressive as possible.

You, my Lord,' pursued Clementina, to the Marquis, 'are no doubt apprized of many of these particulars: I have therefore endeavoured to run them over briefly; and have told you what my own sentiments were, in order to account to you for a conduct which must otherwise appear very strange, even though that secret which was the grand spring of my seemingly mysterious actions is now discovered.

Madame Burganeze conjured me to keep our loves concealed till she could dispose of her daughter in marriage, which she said she would endeavour speedily to do; and then hoped to get her brother to consent to our union.—You may be sure I was not backward in approving these measures; but having already taken such a step towards discovering myself to Eugenia, I was impatient to complete my design.

The Marquis must remember the extreme embarrassment which his discourse threw me into, when, in plain terms, he proposed to me the honour of his alliance. I was driven to extremity. I once more begged of Eugenia to give me a meeting. I thought that after having disclosed myself to her, and engaged her in my interest, my heart would be at ease, and I could at leisure find means to extricate myself from my ridiculous amour with Madame Burganeze. It was only the esteem of the Marquis of Pescara and Donna Eugenia which I was in dread of losing. That amiable lady condescended to gratify me a second time. We were surprised in the wood, and I was forced away, in spite of my feeble resistance. I believe I need not inform you that it was the Count of Castellar (accompanied by a Spanish gentleman, who was his friend) that used this violence.

It seems that after having searched for me in several other parts of Italy, he had been at Milan for some time in disguise, where he by chance heard the name of Don Clement Pimenteles.—As he very well knew that my brother was in France, he immediately concluded it could be nobody but myself who had assumed this new character. Trusting therefore for the certainty of his intelligence to no eyes but his own, he watched all my motions, and had frequent opportunities of seeing me at mass; for I avoided all other places of public meeting as much as possible. Being now convinced he had found the prey he sought after, he kept a constant spy on me; who giving him intelligence of my setting out from the Marquis's, attended only by a single servant, that day on which I had feigned a journey to Lodi, in order to meet Eugenia in the wood, he resolved not to let slip this opportunity of seizing me.

These particulars I afterwards learned from himself: and thus that name, which I was in a manner under a necessity of bearing, and which had procured me a various mixture of pleasure and of pain, was now at length the means of betraying me; and, had it not been for my late deliverance, would have been my destruction; for the Count having accomplished his cruel design, forced me into a calash, which an attendant was leading after him for the purpose: and Castellar, seating himself by me, drove with such fury, that in less than three hours we had got above six leagues from Milan.

It was late when we arrived at an ordinary inn, where Don Gabriel told me I was to pass the night. He led me out of the calash with very little ceremony.

We were shewn by the mistress of the house into a chamber which the Count obliged me to enter with himself; when, after having locked the door, he began to load me with the bitterest reproaches: he did not even stop at calling me wanton and abandoned!—I answered him only with tears.—He assured me, that the world should not rescue me out of his hands; and then left me to the repose I stood in need of, having first ordered something to refresh me.

I threw myself on the bed without taking off my clothes, and passed the most dismal night I had ever known in my life. I reflected with horror on my situation.—I am now in the power of my cruel persecutor, said I:—he no doubt will force me back to the presence of a much incensed father, from whom I must expect the most rigorous treatment: he will compel me to marry Don Gabriel, whom I now hate more than ever; and think that too small a punishment for my fault! I bitterly regretted my separation from my amiable friends at Milan, who I knew would be grieved at my absence; and I was in despair of ever seeing them again. Thus I tortured myself till day-break, when the Count knocked at my door, and asked me, if I was up? I arose off the bed, and he immediately entered the chamber, followed by a servant, who brought in chocolate. I had but very little inclination to taste any thing; however I was obliged to accompany him at breakfast.

When we had done, he proposed pursuing our journey; for he told me, he meant to carry me directly back to Spain. I made him no answer; but being again forced to take my seat by him in the calash, which had fresh horses, we travelled at the same rate we had done the evening before, the Count entertaining me with threats, and expressions of resentment.

Nothing could be more dreadful to me than this journey; when having got out of the Milanese territories, we entered the Pope's dominions; and having reached Civita-Vechia,[5] we found there a vessel ready to sail for Alicante.[6]—The Count, without losing time, obliged me to go on board with him.—The voyage was as prosperous as Don Gabriel could have wished. We arrived safely in Spain. But the sight of my native country served only to redouble my grief!—This, said I, this is the fatal place where I am for ever to be consigned to the arms of a man whom I detest; and who will even think he does me a great honour in accepting of me!

We were no sooner got on shore than the haughty Sahabedras put me into a coach, which he had hired to carry me to Madrid; and, without allowing me time to repose myself after the fatigue of the voyage, he set out with me for the kingdom of Castile. My terror increased in proportion as we drew nearer to Madrid; and what with grief and the hurry of my journey, Don Gabriel found me so ill that he thought it adviseable to stop at the castle where you found me. I was carried in in so weak a condition, that it was some days before I could leave my bed. Meanwhile there was no care omitted for my recovery.—The Count's physician attended me; and in a little time assured him that I would be well enough to be removed to Madrid.

But Don Gabriel had now changed his design of carrying me thither:—he began to consider that my father might perhaps have by this time repented his severity toward me; and that, softened by my tears and prayers, he would no longer press me to accept of a husband whom I had run so many hazards to avoid. On the other hand, he knew that I was entirely at his own disposal; none of my family knew of my being in Spain. He therefore thought it most prudent to conceal me from them, and make use of the power he had over my person, to force me to accept of him.

The solitude I was in seemed fit for so black a purpose. Wherefore, having put one or two of the apartments into some tolerable order, he retained such of his domestics as he thought he could depend on; amongst which number was the old Moorish woman, who was always trusted with the care of that castle.

I was now perfectly recovered; and was surprised that the Count had not ordered some change of apparel for me (for I was still in the male habit in which he had found me); when one morning he entered my chamber, and accosted me with his usual haughtiness.—You can now, Madam, said he, no longer refuse me your hand; you know you are mine by mutual agreement between your father and me: and I question whether any person of quality, after your having abandoned your friends and your country, to ramble about in masquerade, would be very fond of fulfilling those engagements. However, I am willing to pass over your irregularities, provided you will submit with a good grace to obey your father's will, in consenting to make me your husband.—He waited for my answer with his eyes fixed severely on me.—If my father, replied I, persists in his cruel resolution of forcing me to accept of you, I can no longer resist his commands: but till I receive those commands from his own mouth, be assured your importunity is in vain.—I will go then this very day to Don Manuel Pimenteles, said he, and acquaint him with your return to Spain. If he continues just to his promise, I will yield you to his authority; but be assured, that if I find him disposed to break his word with me, or to shew the least indulgence to your headstrong humour, I will convoy you to a place where he shall never hear of you; and from whence all the united power of mankind shall not be able to force you.

He left me after this insolent menace; and I heard no more of him till the next evening; when he entered my chamber with a disordered countenance.—I am sorry, Madam, said he, to bring you news that must afflict you; but I am under the necessity of letting you know that your father is dead, and that you have no choice to make, but that of accepting me for your husband. I have not acquainted any of your friends that you are in my possession; therefore, if you entertain hopes of being delivered out of my hands, they are vain; for I am now absolute master of your destiny.—But added, in a softer tone (seeing me dissolved in tears) I shall make no other use of that power than to procure you a happy establishment for life, and make you mistress of a fortune more splendid than you could have even hoped for. Reflect on the situation you are in, the value of the offer I make you, and what mischiefs your refusal must create. I will give you, continued he, three days to consider of it: and I am persuaded you will not be so blind to your own happiness as to continue obstinate.—I was too much taken up with the grief which the melancholy news he had just related filled me with, to be able to make him any reply. He observed it, and retired.

Though I was greatly afflicted at the death of my father, I however drew this consolation from it,—that there was now no authority which could compel me to marry the Count. Were my father still living, said I, it would no longer be in my power to resist his will; but his death having freed me from all obligations of duty, I shall have nothing to combat but the persecutions of a wretch, whose love or hatred I equally contemn.

Don Gabriel did not appear before me till the three days were expired in which he had desired me to consider of his proposal.

I received him with an air that could give him but little encouragement; however he seated himself by me, and assuming an affable countenance,—I come, Madam, said he, to receive a decisive answer to what I proposed to you. You have had time to reflect on it; and I even flatter myself beforehand, that you will no longer oppose what must contribute to your happiness, as well as to mine. Speak, added he, taking one of my hands:—Do you consent to make me yours?—I remained silent for some time; which Don Gabriel interpreted in his favour; for I observed he waited, smiling, for my answer. In reality, I was studying what reply to make; for I thought it best to dissemble a little, in order if possible to obtain my liberty. At last, casting my eyes on him with more mildness than I was accustomed to do,—You take very strange measures, my Lord, said I, to soften my heart towards you.—Do you think that the rigorous confinement you impose on me, and this habit, which I blush still to behold myself in, are not rather motives of disgust, than inducements to listen to your pretensions.—Furnish me at least with apparel proper for my sex: and if you would inspire me with any favourable sentiments for you, restore me to my friends; suffer me to wipe away my tears for the loss of my father; and you may then claim that from my gratitude which you must never hope to extort from my fears.—I pronounced this in a resolute tone, and looked stedfastly in his face. He only laughed at me; and shaking his head,—Ah Donna Clementina! said he, you must forgive me if I doubt a little the sincerity of your intentions:—after the experience I have had, you may imagine I can have but small dependence on your generosity; for if, whilst you are in my power without any resource, you contemn the advantages I propose to you, do you think I can be so silly as to believe, that when you are at your liberty, and amongst your family, who have always opposed me, that you will then accept of them? No, no, added he; were your father still living, I might perhaps consent to what you demand; but since he can no longer oppose his authority in my favour, I shall hardly be so weak as to put you in possession of a freedom that will for ever destroy my hopes. As for your dress, as nobody but myself shall see you, I declare it to you by every thing sacred, that you shall never alter it, unless it be for your wedding-clothes.—Then sooner for my burying-clothes, interrupted I, furiously; and take this as my final answer,—that I would rather throw myself into the arms of death than yours.—And so you shall, cried he, enraged in his turn; and drawing his sword, with distracted looks, he lifted his arm, in order, as I imagined, to plunge it in my breast. I was seized with a sudden terror at this action, which not being able to overcome, I fell in a swoon at the cruel Sahabedras's feet.

I know not what impression this scene made on him; for when I recovered my senses, I found myself in another chamber, laid on the bed, and no one with me but the Moorish woman.—She made haste to inform me, that her Lord, exasperated almost to madness at my refusal, had certainly deprived me of life, if my sudden fainting had not staid his arm.—I yet tremble, added she, at the remembrance of his fury; and I even fear that nothing but your immediate compliance with his wishes will shield you from the terrible effects of his resentment.—Consider, my dear lady, continued she (affecting to interest herself in my happiness) how fatal your obstinacy may prove to you! My Lord is too haughty and passionate to brook a denial, without a revenge the most severe that he can inflict. Alas! who knows what mischiefs he is now meditating? Indeed, pursued she after a short pause, if I might presume to advise you, I would have you endeavour to repair the injury you have offered him, by beginning this very minute to change your behaviour towards him. Suffer me to carry him some obliging expressions of your sorrow for having offended him. I will tell him, said she, rising,—I interrupted her here; and catching her by the arm,—You shall tell him nothing from me, said I, but that I despise him; and would sooner suffer that death which he just now threatened me with (and which I believe him still barbarous enough to inflict on me) than ever consent to be his wife.

The woman, who no doubt had been instructed in every thing she said, expected that the danger I saw myself exposed to, would have inspired me with other sentiments. She seemed confounded at this reply; and left me with a very surly air, and muttering something to herself.

Upon the whole, when I began to reflect a little, I was far from being terrified at Don Gabriel's menaces. On the contrary, believing that he would not be so wicked as to take away my life, I resolved to treat him with so much scorn and aversion, that he must at length lose all hopes, and abandon me to my fate.

This reflection made me pass the day with some little tranquillity. The Moor attended me at supper as usual: she assured me that she had not dared repeat what I had said to her Lord; who was so exasperated against me, that he protested I should remain a prisoner in the chamber I was then in (which was much worse than that which was at first assigned me) till I had altered my mind. However, added she, he has commanded me to attend on you with my accustomed services; which indulgence I question whether he would have granted you, had I told him with what contempt you treated him this morning.—I affected to believe her; but at the same time assured her that I would never swerve from my resolution.—And indeed I spent the greatest part of the night in fortifying myself more strongly in it.

I was but just risen next morning when the Count came into my chamber. I observed a sort of languor in his face, which dissipated some little impressions of fear that his first appearance made on me. I waited till he should begin the conversation; and from the embarrassment I remarked in his looks, I guessed that his love had got the better of his resentment. He walked several times about the room without speaking. At last, stopping short, he said, in a tone gentle enough,—Are you resolved then, Madam, to persist in your cruelty? Or may I yet hope that you will consent to happiness? Speak, added he; you know I love you. Don't abuse the ascendant you have over me, by shewing fresh marks of a scorn which I have endured but too long.—I replied, I was stedfast in the resolution I had taken,—never to hearken to him till he had restored me to my friends; and in the end assured him, that I would set my love at no other price whatever but that of my liberty.

I saw indignation in his eyes at my discourse: he fell again into those transports of rage which had so terrified me the day before. He threatened me in the severest terms with his vengeance; and, accusing himself of madness for having loved a creature so unworthy of his care, he flung out of the room, telling me I should have time enough to repent of my folly and ingratitude.

I gave but little heed to his threats, being glad to be relieved from his presence. It was some weeks before I saw him again; in all which time I was never permitted to stir out of my chamber, nor did I see any one except the Moorish woman, who told me one day, that the Count was resolved to try me once more; but that if he found me continue obstinate, I was to expect the worst treatment.—Don Gabriel accordingly made me a visit a day or two after:—but whether my resolution had staggered him a little or that he still retained some degree of respect for me, he did not offer any outrage; but then he protested he would keep me a prisoner till he had humbled that stubborn heart which refused to be his; and at the same time he declared that he would blaze it everywhere, that he had kept me for some months in his castle, concealed in man's clothes; and we will then see, said he, whether you will have much reason to wish yourself out of my possession.—He left me with this base insult; and, taking horse for Madrid, where his employments oblige him for the most part to reside, I found myself exposed to the cruellest misfortune, with no other consolation than that of my innocence.

'Tis now some days since he departed; and I make no doubt but he has put his menace in execution.—I had already begun to sink under my fears, when Heaven heard my prayer, and sent the only two persons in the world to my assistance whom I most ardently wished for.'

Clementina having finished her relation, her sisters, who many times had been in tears, conjured her to think of taking some rest; wherefore, retiring to her apartment, the Marquis and Don Clement did the like to those which were prepared for them.

It was late next morning before they rose; when Clementina, having reassumed her proper dress, recalled also with it those modest graces which she had before endeavoured to banish; and she now appeared to the Marquis the loveliest of her sex. After the first salutations were over, the conversation immediately turned on the Count of Castellar. Clementina, who was well acquainted with the fierceness of that Lord's temper, trembled to think of the flames which she knew were kindling, and which must inevitably break out. Her apprehensions were not for her brother alone:—the Marquis of Pescara had an equal share in her concern; for I believe it is needless to inform the reader that the passion she had conceived for that accomplished gentleman had governed all her actions, and had enabled her so strenuously to resist Don Gabriel's violence.—She was persuaded that the Marquis, as well as Don Clement, meditated revenge against Castellar, though both of them affected to speak carelessly of him, in order to disguise their real intentions from her, and prevent her from being alarmed; but they had in reality agreed between themselves to go in search of Don Gabriel that very day, and oblige him to atone for the outrage he had offered Clementina.—The Marquis begged that Don Clement would let him have the honour of avenging his mistress. Pimenteles, whose courage was not inferior to his friend's, opposed this, and declared it belonged to himself alone to chastise Don Gabriel for the insults he had thrown upon his sister; alledging that he only was injured, as the Marquis was not supposed by Don Gabriel to have any interest in Clementina's fate. The Marquis was too much in love, and too much provoked at the remembrance of that lady's ill treatment to accede to the reasonableness of this plea.—A friendly contest continued for some time between the brother and the lover, which should take upon him the punishment of the Count; but in the end each was obliged to yield so far to the other, as to agree that Castellar himself should chuse which of the two he would decide the contest with.

Having thus concerted their measures, the better to conceal them they talked of nothing but pleasures, and the joy Eugenia would feel on seeing them all return safe to Italy.—They were discoursing with the ladies in this manner in Clementina's apartment, when a servant came into the room and whispered Don Clement. He rose off his seat, and, telling his sisters he would return in a minute, he left the room with so composed an air, that they did not suppose it was a business of any moment that called him from them. He went directly into a drawing-room, where the servant told him the Count of Castellar waited for him.

Don Gabriel having been informed of what had happened the night before by one of his domestics (whom the Moor had dispatched to Madrid immediately after Clementina had been taken from the castle) was so enraged at the account, that the messenger had nearly fallen the first sacrifice to his fury: he however constrained himself enough to hear the particulars of her escape, and the artifice the two gentlemen had made use of to get admittance. None of the servants knew either the Marquis or Don Clement; but the Count was so fully persuaded that it could be no other than the latter that had freed Clementina from her captivity, he did not hesitate a moment what to do, but, commanding his footman who had brought him this information not to say a word of the affair to any one, he ordered him to go back to the castle; and, forbidding any of his people to follow him, he went directly to Don Clement's house, who lived but a few streets from his own. That gentleman, as I have already said, found the Count in the drawing-room, where he was walking to and fro in a violent manner.—'You have saved me the trouble,' said Don Clement, 'of going to look for you at your house; for be assured that you shall answer for the wrongs you have done my sister.'—'Your insolence,' replied Don Gabriel, 'in presuming to make use of such violence as you have done, can be atoned for with nothing but your life!'—'Come then,' cried Don Clement, 'we have each of us swords; and a few minutes shall end our quarrel.' Saying this, he threw open the chamber-door which led into the garden, and invited the Count to go along with him. They both hastened down a terrace that faced the door, and turning into a grass-plot from whence they could not be discerned from any of the windows, Don Clement stopped, and drawing his sword, the Count did the like; when somebody called out, 'Hold, Don Clement!—remember our agreement:—the honour of this combat may fall to my lot.' The Marquis, who spoke these words with the greatest precipitation as he ran towards them, and having his sword drawn, ran in between them in an instant, and obliged them to suspend their engagement.

It was the same servant who had acquainted Don Clement with the Count's being in the house, who, happening to overhear part of what they said, had the curiosity to listen to the remainder:—he was one of those who had attended his master and the Marquis at the rescue of Clementina; so, apprehending some ill consequences from Don Gabriel's visit, he had the discretion to beckon the Marquis out of the chamber, where he was discoursing with Clementina and her sisters. He followed Don Clement and the Count; wherefore getting to the spot where they were going to engage almost as soon as they, he had time to prevent the execution of their design. If Don Clement was mortified at the unexpected appearance of the Marquis, who he had no mind should interfere in the quarrel, Don Gabriel was fired with the utmost indignation. 'I don't know how seasonable this interruption may be to you, Signior Pimenteles,' said he, scornfully; 'but for my own part, I am so little disposed for delay, that I desire this gentleman may either retire instantly, or resolve to be a passive witness of our contest.'—'I am too much concerned in your quarrel,' said the Marquis, hastily, 'to submit to those terms:—for learn, proud Castellar, that I love Donna Clementina, and hope shortly to become her husband.'—He needed to have said no more to provoke Don Gabriel.—'I am for you then,' cried he; 'not the brother but the lover of Clementina shall be my first victim, since he will have it so.' Saying this, he advanced towards the Marquis with so much fury, that he hardly escaped a thrust which Don Gabriel made at his heart:—however he avoided it, yet not so nimbly but that he received a wound in his arm. The Count, eager to pursue his victory, pressed on with so much warmth and so little conduct, that the Marquis, who had the advantage of a cooler and more deliberate courage, easily defended himself; and at the same time gave his adversary a wound which made him fall motionless to the earth.

Though Don Clement (who was forced to be a spectator of this rencounter) was rejoiced at his friend's success, he was nevertheless greatly alarmed at the condition in which he beheld the Count. He knew his fortune, and the rank he held at the court of Spain; and was apprehensive his death might be attended with very ill consequences to the Marquis, who was a stranger there:—but these fears began to diminish when he perceived that Don Gabriel still breathed.—The Marquis and he took him in their arms, and, carrying him in, laid him gently on a bed, whilst a surgeon was sent for with the utmost speed. The great quantity of blood which the Count had lost threw him into a swoon; wherein he continued till after his wound was dressed, which the surgeon declared was not mortal: nevertheless, the Count was so much weakened that he remained speechless the whole night.—Don Clement never left his bed-side; and even begged of his sister to visit him, which she readily consented to; and, notwithstanding the cruel treatment she had received, she attended to him with as much care and assiduity as if he had been as dear to her as he was really odious; for during six days, in which he continued in a fever, the amiable Clementina seldom left his chamber.

In all this time there had not any enquiries been made after the Count: for since his carrying Clementina to his castle on the banks of the Guadimara, he had been often accustomed to pass from thence to Madrid and back again, without suffering any of his attendants to follow him; fearing lest the secret should be revealed, by his domestics conversing too freely together; for notwithstanding his threats to Clementina, that he would discover her being in his possession, he in reality used all his endeavours to conceal it. But all his caution could not prevent his servants from suspecting that it could be nothing but a mistress which occasioned his making such frequent and private excursions; so that now, far from being alarmed at his absence, they only imagined he was gone to pass a few days with his incognita:—on the other hand, those servants whom he had left at the castle, believing him safe at Madrid, gave themselves no farther trouble about him. So that had the wound which he received from the Marquis proved mortal, his death might have remained a secret at least till the authors of it had time to withdraw:—but it was otherwise ordained; for in ten days the Count's illness was so much abated, that the physicians declared he was out of danger. Don Clement therefore finding him in a condition to bear the conversation with which he intended to entertain him, sat down by his bed-side, when, accosting him with an air of friendship,—'My Lord,' said he, 'it is with infinite satisfaction that I see you restored almost to your former health; nor would I have you believe that this proceeds from any fears I was under on account of your death: for had that misfortune really come to pass, your rencounter with the Marquis and concealment in my house are both such profound secrets, that *that* Lord might have retired into Italy before the affair could possibly be discovered:—or should he stay, the justness of our cause and the greatness of our injuries would have been a sufficient plea for his pardon.'—Don Clement paused here; and finding the Count made no reply, but seemed as if he attended the conclusion of this speech, he proceeded,—'Consider, Don Gabriel, the insults which you have thrown on our family!—'Tis true my father promised to give you Donna Clementina for a wife; and I myself should have thought your alliance an honour to our house, if the unconquerable dislike my sister had to you had not inclined me to wish the marriage might not take place. I made no secret of this to yourself; and you know I conjured my father not to force Clementina's inclinations; but he was obdurate, and the consequence of this was that my sister was compelled to abandon her friends, her country, and even her sex, in order to her concealment and protection against injuries! Was not this sufficient cause for her to hate you?—But this was not all; you followed her indeed, but rather with the arrogance of a master who pursues a fugitive slave, than with the respect of a lover who would conquer the aversion of his mistress!—What right had you to treat a young maiden of quality in the manner you have since done? To make her a prisoner in your house, to conceal her from her friends, to threaten her with death! or what's worse, the ruin of her reputation, if she refused to comply with your desires!—These are truths, my Lord, which, should they appear against you, would redound but little to your honour; and I much doubt whether your high rank would screen you from the punishment I might with so much justice demand on you: but I am satisfied to overlook all these injuries; and even Clementina herself has with the utmost generosity bestowed the tenderest care on you, and is already inclined to forget the hardships you have made her suffer, provided you will promise to trouble her quiet no more, nor make any farther attempts upon her person. She is now in the hands of a brother, from whom you will find it no very easy matter to tear her:—therefore, my Lord, resign with a good grace those pretentions which no force in the world will enable you to make good.'—Here Don Clement stopped, to observe what impression his discourse had made on the Count. He had avoided in the latter part of his speech to make any mention of the Marquis; believing that the name of a rival would only serve to encrease the consternation he began to remark in Don Gabriel's face, who had heard him attentively without once offering to interrupt him.

When the Count found Don Clement had done speaking;—'You have opened my eyes, Signior,' said he, with a sigh, 'which have been but too long blinded by a misplaced, though ardent, passion for your sister:—I am fully sensible of the indignities I have offered to that lady; I am the more ashamed of it when I reflect on her sweetness and generous concern for me in my illness.—Teach me therefore,' said he (grasping one of Don Clement's hands) 'teach me how to make her a reparation; for I swear to you I have no longer any designs upon her but what tend towards her happiness.'—'Oh, my Lord!' said Don Clement, 'I am charmed to see you in this happy temper of mind! Our revenge, though just, has already been too severe:—since it had almost cost you your life, we can demand no farther reparation: and I think, after the declaration you have made, it would be only injurious to suspect you capable of harbouring any sentiments contrary to so generous a change in your heart. You may depend upon it that I shall for ever bury in oblivion all that is past. I entreat your friendship from this moment; and promise you that neither the Marquis nor Clementina shall any longer look upon you as their foe.'

At the name of the Marquis Don Gabriel blushed, and betrayed some inward emotions which he would fain have concealed.—Don Clement observed it; and believing that he still entertained a secret jealousy against him as a rival, or that the remembrance of his being so very lately vanquished by him had occasioned this disorder, was willing to divert so disagreeable a subject: so all at once changing the discourse, 'I believe, my Lord,' said he, 'you will in a day or two be able to leave your chamber. I am impatient to see you well again:—not,' continued he, smiling, 'that I intend you shall leave me so soon, but I long to entertain you as a welcome guest, without the restraint that physicians and surgeons have laid on you: and I have two sisters besides Clementina to whom you owe a compliment, for the fright they have been in on your account ever since your illness.'—'Indeed,' answered the Count, 'I am the most unfortunate man in the world, to be the occasion of so much trouble; but, *à-propos*, where is the gentleman to whose prosperous courage I think you are indebted for my being burthensome to you thus long—the Marquis I have heard you call him:—He told me before that unlucky combat, that he was to marry your sister; I believe him indeed worthy to be her husband. Has he yet obtained that happy title? Tell me, for I am no longer Clementina's lover, and therefore cannot be his rival.'—He spoke this with so open and candid an air, that Don Clement made no doubt of his sincerity.—'They are not yet married, my Lord,' said he; 'you may imagine that we would not make choice of a time in which your life was in danger to celebrate a wedding. The Marquis himself, whose love for my sister might justify a little impatience on this occasion, was too generous even to press me to conclude the matter till he was assured of your recovery, which (as I hope) will be completed in a few days; and we then flatter ourselves that you will honour with your presence a ceremony, which nothing but the condition you have been in should have retarded.'—'I have,' replied Don Gabriel, 'entirely renounced all pretensions to, or even hopes of gaining your sister's favour; and can hear of her being in the arms of another without a sigh: but I must still confess myself so weak that I could not endure to be a witness of it: therefore spare me, Don Clement,—spare me the mortification of this view; and to be truly generous, suspend your sister's marriage till I am in a condition to remove from your house, when I shall leave you all in full possession of your happiness.'

A request so natural, and even delivered in a soft and humble tone of voice, from a man of the Count's haughty temper, could not fail of moving the person to whom it was addressed.—'I shall obey you, my Lord,' answered Don Clement, 'though I assure you I shall regret losing you more than you can imagine!'

After this conversation the Count, Don Clement, and the Marquis (whom the former had desired to see and be reconciled to) lived together in perfect amity. In a few days Don Gabriel found himself in a condition to go abroad:—so, taking leave of Don Clement, with many acknowledgments for his care and tenderness, he told him he had one request to make, which he hoped he would not refuse to grant.—'I am now going,' said he, 'to a seat I have about two leagues from Madrid, where I intend to pass a month or two; I insist on returning the civilities I have received at your hands, by having the Marquis and you, together with your fair sisters, to spend some days with me.'—'Though nothing would be more agreeable to me,' answered Don Clement, 'than to accept this mark of your friendship, yet I cannot take upon me to promise any thing in the name of the Marquis; on the contrary, I know he is impatient to return to Italy; that he is already tired of delays; and, for my own part, I have some reasons to wish myself in that country, which incline me to hasten our departure as much as possible:—I fear therefore we must debar ourselves the happiness you propose to us;—but you may depend upon it we shall not leave Spain without making you a visit at your villa.'—Though the Count was very pressing with Don Clement, he could obtain no more from him than a promise of waiting on him speedily; upon which he took his leave in a very polite manner, and set out immediately for his country-seat.

The Marquis now at liberty to pursue his inclinations, did not fail of putting Don Clement in mind of his promise.—'I shall defer my return into Italy,' said he, 'no longer than till my marriage with Donna Clementina is concluded; I shall therefore judge of your impatience to see Eugenia again by the haste you make in completing my happiness.'—Don Clement did not need to be put in mind of his mistress; for he longed as ardently to return to the Marquis's beautiful niece as that Lord did to see himself united to Clementina:—he soon fixed the day for his sister's nuptials; and gave orders for such preparations as were suitable to the occasion and the quality of the persons concerned.

In this interval of time it was that Don Clement recollected his engagement to the Count of Castellar; and concluding that it would not be so grateful to him to see Clementina and the Marquis after their marriage, he proposed to the latter to pay Don Gabriel a visit the following day, and carry the ladies along with them. The Marquis readily agreed to it; and Clementina, no longer regarding the Count as an enemy, was as willing to be of the party as either of them.

Accordingly the next morning they all set out for the Count's country-seat. The weather was extremely fine, and happened not to be so warm as is usual in Spain;—so that to make this little journey the more agreeable, the Marquis begged to have the honour of driving his mistress in an open chaise, whilst Don Clement with his two sisters went in a coach.—They were received by the Count Castellar with every mark of friendship and respect:—and after an entertainment, which testified the vast magnificence of this Lord, he presented Clementina with a little casket, which contained a diamond necklace, together with a ring, and jewels for her ears, all of very great value; telling her, in a gallant manner, that though he had intended those ornaments as a bridal-present for the Countess of Castellar, yet he thought Fate had destined them much more gloriously for the Marchioness of Pescara.[7]—The Marquis was charmed with so obliging a compliment: and Clementina was even better pleased with it than with the magnificent present which accompanied it; which, however, she accepted with the politest acknowledgements, fearing Don Gabriel would take a refusal very ill.

The day passed over in the most delightful manner; when, Don Clement thinking it time to be gone, the whole company took leave of the Count, and set out on their return to Madrid, in the same manner they had left it, the Marquis insisting on bearing Clementina company in the chaise.

They had now got about half-way home, and were passing through a narrow road, which was cut across a wood, in which it was impossible for two carriages to go abreast. By means of this circumstance Don Clement's coach had got on at some distance before the chaise in which his sister and the Marquis were. The unevenness of the road obliged them to drive slowly; and they were entered into a very interesting conversation, when they were suddenly alarmed at the appearance of several horsemen, who galloped out of the wood, and enclosed them on every side. The Marquis was attended only by two servants, and Don Clement with the like number, besides his coachman; so they found themselves but seven in all, against twelve, which was the number of their enemies.

The shrieks of Donna Clementina alarmed her brother, who immediately got out of the coach and ran to her assistance. The Marquis had by this time leaped out of the chaise; and having no other weapon but a short sword, which would have been of little use, he hastily snatched a pistol from the hand of one of his servants (who had just taken it from his holster) and let fly at a person masked and muffled up in a cloke,[8] who was endeavouring to force Clementina out of the chaise. The miserable Count of Castellar (for it was he) was born to fall by the hand of the brave Marquis. The bullets with which the pistol was loaded, lodged in his breast; and he dropped dead under the horse's feet. His mask falling off at the same time, discovered this treacherous Spaniard, to the amazement of Don Clement and his friend. The persons who had assisted the Count in this villanous expedition, were so terrified at seeing him fall, that they thought it safest to fly. However, one of them had the boldness to discharge his pistol at the Marquis. It missed him; but unfortunately killed one of his servants who stood near him.

Clementina could not behold Don Gabriel without horror. She was put almost breathless with fear into the coach to her sisters; whilst her brother and the Marquis, with the three remaining servants, rode on each side of it. It was dark when they reached Madrid: and Don Clement, believing that the Count's death would soon be published, was afraid that, notwithstanding the manner of it and the greatness of his crimes, the Marquis might be put to some trouble on that occasion, as the deceased was a man of the highest rank, and had relations in the greatest posts about court; he thought it therefore adviseable to be beforehand with his accusers, and to rely on the clemency of Philip the Third (who then reigned)[9] for his friend's pardon. He made the Marquis acquainted with his design; and, though it was now night, they both took coach immediately for the Escurial.[10]

As Don Clement was known and much respected by the principal ministers, he found it no difficult matter to be admitted privately into the royal presence; where, throwing himself at his sovereign's feet, he declared the cause of his presenting himself before his Majesty; and having informed him of the death of the Count of Castellar, he in a few words acquainted him with the injuries he had received from that Lord, and concluded with presenting the Marquis of Pescara to the King. The Monarch had often cast his eyes on him during Don Clement's narration, and found his person and carriage so graceful, that he was already prepossessed in his favour; he received him therefore with the most gracious condescension; and, finding he could speak Spanish perfectly well, he talked to him some minutes; and assured him, that, as Don Clement had represented the matter, Count Castellar had very justly merited the death which he had brought upon himself; adding, that if his friends were discreet, they would chuse not to make a noise about an affair which would be so much to the dishonour of a man of Don Gabriel's years and high station; and concluded with telling him he might rely on his protection.

The Marquis and Don Clement having with the warmest expressions testified their gratitude to the Prince, took their leave, not a little glad they had so easily got rid of an affair which they apprehended would have been attended with unpleasant consequences. But indeed they had less reason for their fears than they imagined; for Don Gabriel's relations being informed of every particular relating to the affair with Clementina, thought it most prudent to hush up the matter; and, having given out that he was attacked and murdered by robbers in the night, on his way to Madrid, they had him privately interred; and there were few, except his own followers, who knew the truth of the story.

Every obstacle being now removed, the marriage of the Marquis with Donna Clementina was no longer delayed. It was solemnised at the house of Don Clement, though with less pomp than was intended, on account of the tragical adventure which had preceded it. The Marquis however thought nothing wanting to his happiness in the possession of his admired Clementina.

Don Clement, having now acquitted himself towards his friend, reminded the Marquis in his turn of his engagements to him; and, the day after his sister's nuptials, proposed their departure from Spain.—'Your impatience to return to Eugenia pleases me,' cried the Marquis; 'and believe me, my dear Pimenteles, I long to tie the bond which unites us still closer, by giving you my niece: I am ready therefore to depart for Italy; for I am sure Clementina will gladly go with us.'—'Let us be gone then,' cried Don Clement; 'I feel my absence from Eugenia becomes more and more insupportable.' In effect, Don Clement ordered every thing with so much diligence, that in three days they were in a condition to set out on their journey; when, after having taken leave of the two sisters of Don Clement (who chose to remain in Spain) they departed from Madrid; and, after a prosperous journey, reached Milan, without meeting the least accident that could for a moment interrupt their happiness.

Don Clement found himself received by Eugenia, with a joy equal to that he felt at seeing her again. She was charmed at the sight of Clementina, and transported at finding she had become the Marquis's wife.

As for Madame Burganeze, she no sooner heard of her brother's arrival, than, unwilling to undergo the confusion which his presence, together with that of his lady and Don Clement must create in her, she shut herself up in her apartment; when, having wrote a letter to the Marquis, in which she acknowledged her indiscretion, and recommended her daughter to his care, she privately withdrew from his house, without bidding any one farewell, and retired to the monastery of St. Bridget, where she spent the rest of her days; and the Marquis, impatient to see his friend as happy as himself, resigned Eugenia to the arms of Don Clement.

It is now time to say something of Adelaide, whom we left at the Marquis of Pescara's, when he went into Spain; and whom at his return he found still with Eugenia. She rejoiced indeed at her friend's happiness; but her own secret discontents left her but little relish for those pleasures which every day took place at the Marquis of Pescara's house: and though Eugenia was now blest in a union from which she promised herself the utmost felicity, she found an alloy to her joy from the constant melancholy which preyed upon her dear Adelaide: that unhappy lady nourished a secret grief which nothing could diminish. The Marchioness, who was charmed with her, strove all in her power to divert her melancholy; but being unacquainted with the cause, her obliging endeavours were only a constraint upon Adelaide, who would often slip from the company, and retire to her chamber, in order to give a loose to her sorrow.

Eugenia, who had often observed this, followed her one day, and surprised her in tears,—'Dear Adelaide,' said she, 'why will you persist in afflicting yourself thus for an ungrateful man (for such at length I am compelled to think him) whose death would not merit one of those tears which you shed in such floods for his inconstancy:—have more regard to your youth and beauty, which have already gained you a thousand admirers; consider your birth and the vast fortune you have in prospect;—Shall the young, the fair, the rich heiress of the Baron St. Seberina sigh away her bloom for a worthless creature, who, had he been ever so faithful, was undeserving of her love?'—She was going on, but Adelaide interrupted her:—'How easy is it, my dear,' said she, 'to counsel others, when our own hearts are at ease! I am as sensible as you can be, of the folly of tormenting myself for an irreparable ill; and I am even ashamed of my weakness in continuing to weep for a man that any other but myself would despise; but, alas! my heart has been too long accustomed to love him; and I even persuade myself at some moments, that he is entirely without blame; and, notwithstanding that he never let me know his fate, I persist in thinking that I am still to accuse nobody but Faustina.'—'You rave,' cried Eugenia; 'don't indulge sentiments so favourable to the Chevalier, unless you would for ever destroy your own peace. I indeed encouraged you in them at first, imagining it would alleviate your grief to think that Don Enenique would ever preserve you in his memory; but what reason have we had since to suppose that he does so? I grant you, that he was deceived by your cousin; but could the deception last? Was he not at least at liberty to lament his fate to you, since all other consolation was cut off? Yes, certainly he was: do not therefore, I conjure you, nourish an opinion that will serve only to feed the flame which devours your heart. I would to Heaven, my dear Adelaide, that Ponces had never known you loved him! you would then have but little reason to regret the losing him. This circumstance was what chiefly consoled me under the loss of Don Clement. I then felt all the pangs that you now suffer; but it was a great satisfaction to me to think that, should he be unfaithful, he would never know the pain it would cost me; and I was so far from flattering myself with vain hopes, that I called every aid in my power to assist me in banishing from my thoughts an object that served only to torment me; and I declare to you, that had I never seen him more, I should have supported such a misfortune without impatience, and would have endeavoured to console myself as much as possible.'—'How you preach!' cried Adelaide (a little piqued at her friend's words); 'have I not been a witness to the tears you so often shed for the absence of Don Clement? and did I not also see the transports of joy which you discovered on his being restored to you?—Transports that nothing but a happiness which you looked upon as supreme, would have inspired you with. Yes, Eugenia; I saw every thing that passed in your heart. I shared your sorrows with you; but, alas! I cannot partake with you in your joys: and I will even confess to you, that the tenderness which you and Don Clement have for each other, is often a matter of mortification to me. Every word, every look of your amiable husband serves only to keep my misfortune fresh in my memory.—Such, said I, would Don Enenique have been to the unfortunate Adelaide, if a treacherous creature had not robbed her of him.'—Here she melted into tears; and Eugenia was so affected, that, far from being able to comfort her, she could only accompany her in her sorrow.

Such was the situation of the disconsolate daughter of Baron St. Seberina, when she received an express from Salerno, which brought her an account of her father's death, who had been carried off so suddenly, that there was not time to give her the least advice of his illness. Her presence was absolutely necessary at home; wherefore, taking a hasty leave of Eugenia, and the rest of her noble friends, she set out for the kingdom of Naples, in a coach with a gentleman of her kindred, who had come on purpose for her.

The Baron's body had been embalmed before she arrived; so that she had time enough to order his funeral with a solemnity suitable to his quality and the affection she bore his memory.

Adelaide now found herself mistress of thirty thousand ducats a year: she was just nineteen, and possessed of many personal charms; yet, with all these advantages, she still retained so deep a melancholy, that she had almost resolved to renounce all commerce with the world, and shut herself up in a nunnery for life; but she was reserved by fate for other things.

Her father had but just time before his death to recommend her to the care of an old friend of his, a gentleman of the strictest honour and integrity. He was called Signior Fernando Deffari; and was married to a Spanish lady of a noble family, whose virtue and politeness made the Baron believe that his daughter would be perfectly happy under her protection. It was to Signior Deffari's house then that Adelaide repaired after her father's death; and that worthy man having settled her fortune in the most convenient and advantageous manner, she found in him and his lady every thing that could conspire to form the most valuable and agreeable friends; that lady had, along with a great deal of prudence, a gaiety in her manner that is not often found amongst persons of her nation; she endeavoured by the most endearing carriage, to soften Adelaide's grief for the loss of her father; to which she wholly imputed the tears which she saw her shed incessantly. But though Adelaide was sincerely afflicted for her father's death; yet she had another source of sorrow which she had hitherto concealed from her friend. Her superior years, and the respect she had for her (now standing in the room of a parent) prevented her from revealing the secret of her heart; but the repeated caresses of Madame Deffari, and the freedom with which she treated her young friend, at length prevailed over her reluctance; and she one day took an opportunity, from the frank behaviour of her protectress, to make her the confidante of her passion for the Chevalier de Ponces, and the unhappy consequences which had attended it.

Madame Deffari condoled with her sincerely; but at the same time bade her have comfort:—'I know the Chevalier,' said she, 'when I was in Spain; he was of the same province with me; I lived in strict intimacy with his mother, who was a lady of one of the best families in Andalusia.[11] The Chevalier, when I saw him (which is almost ten years since) was a young man of great hopes; he had fine parts, improved by a noble education; and he promised to be as worthy as he was amiable. But the account you have given me of him has indeed much surprised me. Yet, if I be not mistaken, Don Enenique thinks himself still more unhappy than you are. I grant you that appearances are against him: but what if you should find that he, after having too late discovered the fatal error he committed in marrying your cousin, so far from continuing with her, has retired from the world, overwhelmed with shame and grief?—Would it not be some consolation to think that the Chevalier, seeing himself for ever deprived of you, had abandoned the perfidious woman who had been the occasion of that misfortune? Yes, certainly it would: and you wrong yourself as well as him, in believing that he would pass his life with Faustina, after having once dedicated it to you. No, my dear; think better of Don Enenique; for I could almost swear that, let him be in what part of the world he will, he is at this moment regretting the loss of you.'

Adelaide heard her friend talk in this manner with unspeakable satisfaction.—'You have filled my mind,' said she, 'with a delightful idea. I confess I feel an infinite pleasure in the reflection that I am still dear to Don Enenique, though I can no longer hope to be his, and probably may never see him more:—but yet, my dear friend, now you have taken upon you to justify that gentleman, how can you reconcile his leaving me, with the unkind silence he has observed ever since our separation, which is now more than a year? Might I not expect to have heard him complain of a destiny which he knows must have made me as wretched as himself?—had his fate appeared so cruel to him, would it not have been some consolation to have acquainted me with his sufferings?—me, who bore so great a share in them!—And though I neither expected nor desired to see him, I was yet within reach of a letter, which might have spared me the uncertainty I have ever since lived in!—Tell me, Madam, I conjure you, what would you have me think of this?'—'I don't pretend,' replied Madame Deffari, 'to account for every part of his conduct; what I have already said is only an opinion founded on my former knowledge of him; and I confess this last circumstance somewhat puzzles me:— however, even with respect to this, we may form conjectures of the cause of your never having heard from him;—perhaps your father might have taken care to intercept any intelligence from him, to prevent a fruitless and improper correspondence:—or maybe Faustina, with the assistance of the unfaithful Theresa, might have been artful enough to prevail on the credulity of Ponces so far, as to make him believe that you yourself were accessary to her flight with him. Might not she, with all the dissimulation she is mistress of, have represented her passion in the most lively colours, and assured him that Adelaide, touched with her grief, and not loving half so well as she did, had yielded him to her wishes, and even assisted her in the accomplishment of them; resolving herself to wed the Count De la Rosa, whose wealth and titles she preferred to the Chevalier's passion. Might not Theresa have backed this by a thousand protestations; and might not Don Enenique, deceived perhaps by oaths, tears, and a million of falsehoods, have his jealousy raised to such a height'—'Forbear,' cried Adelaide, 'for Heaven's sake forbear to finish this cruel picture!—I consent to his marrying Faustina, and myself wed the Count! Sure he could not believe such a monstrous, such an impossible thing!—Alas, he knows my heart too well! But yet, the treacherous, the artful Faustina!' added she (after a pause) 'Oh! Madam, you have awakened a dreadful thought! Why did you not rather encourage me to believe that Ponces had abandoned me ungratefully? I should have endeavoured to despise, and (in time) to forget him:—but if, on the contrary, he accuses me of ingratitude and perfidy,—how do you imagine I can support such a terrible reflection? Oh! if this be the reason of his neglect, I lay nothing to his charge:—I forgive him and acquit him. But I must sink under this weight which oppresses me.'—Her tears stopped her speech, and she sunk down on the arm of Madame Deffari, who sat by her.—That tender friend was afflicted to the last degree, at the condition in which she saw this unfortunate lady. She pressed Adelaide's face to her bosom, and drying up her tears with her handkerchief,—'Forgive me, my dear child,' said she, 'and don't put me to the pain of believing myself the cause of this heavy affliction. Why will you thus torment yourself for what may be only a chimæra?—You know I told you it was a conjecture, merely, which I was going to offer; and one that probably has nothing in it: at least all the foundation which I had for it was that, knowing the Chevalier to be a man of the strictest honour and integrity, I was of opinion that there must have been some foul play to prevent his making explanations to you:—however, I beseech you, don't let what I have just now said make the least impression on you: you know I love you with the tenderness of a mother, and would do any thing to dispel the grief which hangs over you perpetually:—and I don't know,' said she (after a short silence, and seeing Adelaide disposed to listen to her) 'but I have thought of a remedy, which, if it will not quite effect a cure, may at least divert the malady. You must know then, I have long had a design to pay a visit to my native country, and had even prevailed on Signior Deffari to go with me, when your father's death (by consigning you to our hands) put a stop to our intended journey. However, if you are inclined to see Spain, I think this need not retard us any longer; but remember we are not to see the Chevalier,' added she, smiling; 'and you must promise me that you will not make any enquiries after him but through my means.'—'I consent to that most willingly,' answered Adelaide, 'though perhaps your tenderness for me may incline you to conceal the truth from me, if you find his situation to be such as you think the knowledge of it would give me pain.'—'Don't trouble your head about that,' replied Madame Deffari; 'I'll answer for it we shall find better entertainment than a recital of his adventures.'—Adelaide made no reply to this, but begged Madame Deffari to let their departure be as speedy as possible.

Signior Deffari, who tenderly loved his wife, was rejoiced that his ward had consented to take this journey with her; he made haste to prepare every thing for it; and in a few days they were ready to sail in a vessel bound for Cadiz.[12] The voyage was extremely pleasant and agreeable. Signior Deffari wanted nothing in the society of his amiable wife, who, for her part, was charmed with the prospect of seeing her relations and her country, from which she had been absent so long: and Adelaide felt a secret pleasure at the idea of being in a place which she believed contained every thing that was dear to her. Her head was filled with these thoughts when she reached Spain; and Madame Deffari (impatient to see her friends, who, most of them, resided in Andalusia) hastened ashore, and went directly to the house of her brother, who had for a long time been expecting her arrival.

Whatever emotion Adelaide felt at finding herself in the very province where Ponces was born, and where she was sure he must be known; she however resisted the curiosity she had to be informed what was become of him: the promise she had made to Madame Deffari she resolved to observe punctually. That lady however did not fail to enquire privately amongst her friends, whether he was in Andalusia, and what was his situation? But all she could learn was that he had been at an estate he had in Valencia about a year before; and that, having left his affairs in the hands of a particular friend, he had disappeared, and nobody could give any account of him but that friend, who said he had gone abroad, and intended to make a tour through Europe. But she could not discover whether he had a lady in his company, or any other particular relating to him.

This account (believing that Adelaide was impatient to hear something of him) Madame Deffari communicated to her, as there was nothing in it which could augment her trouble. 'I believe,' added she, 'that the Chevalier flies from all the world. Had Faustina been with him I should certainly have heard of it; but I am apt to think that, detesting her for the vile cheat she put on him, he abandons her, and seeks to hide his grief and disappointment in some place where he is not known;—but be that as it may, we must not think of him any more; for it is plain to me that Don Enenique, despairing to possess you from his fatal engagements to your cousin, is studious to avoid every thing which may recall you to his mind. Be satisfied then, dear Adelaide, and follow his example, by endeavouring to forget a man to whom Heaven did not think fit to join you.'—'I submit,' cried Adelaide; 'I submit without murmuring to the decrees of Providence!—but let us talk no more on a subject that has already cost me too dear.'—Madame Deffari, pleased to find her in such a disposition, said all she could to fortify her mind; and Adelaide received great consolation from this very amiable woman.

Amongst the number of friends who came to compliment Madame Deffari on her return to Spain, the Bishop of Seville[13] was one of the first. This Prelate, for whom she had a particular esteem, came one morning to see her; and, after a short visit, was ready to take his leave, telling her he was engaged to pass the day with two young and handsome ladies, who lived at a villa about a league from thence. He added that they were so very amiable, he wished that she and her fair friend were acquainted with them.—'I,' continued he, 'think myself highly honoured by their friendship, as they are not only women of great quality, but of exemplary virtue; and withal endowed with so much wit and judgment, that I often prefer their conversation to that of the most ingenious of the men.'—He had no occasion to say more to excite the curiosity of the ladies to whom he addressed himself. So great an encomium from a person of this good Bishop's character, made them long impatiently for a sight of these two excellent women.—'And do you fancy,' said Madame Deffari, 'that you shall have the charming creatures all to yourself, and not take us along with you?—For my part, I long to embrace them; I am sure Adelaide does the same; and we insist on your letting us have that pleasure this very day.'—'I should have made you an offer of this myself,' replied the Bishop; 'for though these ladies live extremely retired, yet I am sure they will be pleased with your acquaintance, and even thank me for the honour.'—'Come then, my dear,' cried Madame Deffari to Adelaide; 'let us go and see if my Lord Bishop has not enlarged on the perfections of those two unknown fair ones.'—Saying this she led the way down stairs; and finding the Bishop of Seville's coach waiting at the door, they got into it.

During their short journey, the Bishop told them that the persons whom they were going to see, though they lived in the most perfect union, were not sisters, nor any way related; that one of them was called Donna Clara d'Avilas,[14] daughter of the Marquis of Solar; the other, Donna Cynthia Cardonas, niece to the Duke of Segorbe, and allied to the house of Aragon.[15]—'There is something,' added he, 'a little particular in their history, which is the occasion of their retiring at an age when the pleasures of the gay world (in which they were bred) must have appeared very alluring.—I will not relate any part of their story, because you would lose much pleasure by hearing it from any mouth but their own; and I make no doubt but they will entertain you with it when you become a little acquainted with them.'—These words brought them to the gate of the castle of Cardonas,[16] where, being informed that both the ladies were within, the Bishop gave his hand to Madame Deffari while Adelaide followed them into a large handsome parlour, where they found Donna Clara and Donna Cynthia busied in a piece of embroidery.

By the air with which they received the Bishop of Seville, his two companions perceived how welcome a guest this venerable man was to them. They accosted Madame Deffari and Adelaide (whom the Bishop introduced as a young stranger of quality) in a manner that shewed at once their politeness and the sweetness of their dispositions:—they embraced the latter with the freedom of a sister, asking the Bishop what they must give him for making them so happy?—In short, these ladies found one another so very agreeable, that they soon became familiarly acquainted. They thought the day passed too quickly; and these amiable Spaniards would not suffer their two new friends to depart without making them promise to come again in a few days, and spend a week at their castle; which Madame Deffari the more readily consented to, as Signior Deffari was to be absent from her for some time, on business which called him to Seville.

On their return home, the two ladies did not fail to express their admiration of the two young persons they had just been visiting:—they bestowed a thousand praises on them; and protested they were more charming than even the Bishop had represented them, though Madame Deffari said she observed a certain air of melancholy in their faces, especially in that of Donna Clara.—Adelaide was so impatient to see them again, that Signior Deffari was no sooner gone to Seville than she put his lady in mind of her promise; who, as well to gratify Adelaide as her own inclination, went the same day to the castle of Cardonas; where they now purposed to pass some time.

The two amiable friends received their guests with the utmost joy. They told them they must now look upon themselves as at home; and that, laying by all constraint and ceremony, they were each to suppose themselves in their own house.—'I will shew you your apartments,' said Donna Cynthia (to whom the castle belonged) 'and you shall tell me how you like them.' Saying this, she led them into a gallery, from whence there was a door to their lodgings, which consisted of a handsome antichamber, two bedchambers, and three neat closets; two of which were properly furnished for dressing-rooms, and the third for a study.—'There,' said Donna Cynthia, 'are to be your quarters:—you will find some entertainment in that little library, as well as in our park and other improvements.'

Madame Deffari and Adelaide were charmed with their situation!—Every thing was elegant and regular within the castle; and the woods, meadows, and gardens, with which it was surrounded, together with the river Guadelquiver,[17] which washed the walls of it, rendered it one of the most delightful abodes in the world.—They passed the day with all the satisfaction that could possibly result from the conversation of persons highly pleased with each other; and it was late before they parted to betake themselves to rest.—Donna Clara having waited on the two ladies to their apartment, gave Adelaide the keys of a cabinet which stood in the library; and, having called a woman to wait on them, retired.

When Madame Deffari had withdrawn to undress, Adelaide unlocked the cabinet, to lay by some jewels which she had just taken off; when, opening one of the drawers, she saw a little gold box, which seemed by the colour to have lain a long time neglected. She took it up, and, having opened it, she was surprised with the picture of a young man of about five or six-and-twenty years of age, and of an agreeable soft countenance!—The painting was very delicate and lively, and the setting adorned with precious stones; but by the circumstance in which she found this picture, she concluded that it represented some person whom the ladies of the castle either had but little value for, or else had some other reasons for putting it out of their sight!—She remembered that the Bishop had told her there was something particular in their stories; and fancying that this picture might possibly have some relation to them, she resolved to take occasion from thence to lead them into a conversation she so much wished for.—She laid the picture as she found it, and went to bed without saying any thing of the matter to Madame Deffari.—They rose early next morning; and hearing that Donna Clara and Donna Cynthia were both up and gone into the park, they followed them. After the first compliments were over, Madame Deffari seating herself at the foot of a tree, the pensive Donna Clara took her place by her, and both entered into a serious conversation; whilst Adelaide, taking Donna Cynthia under the arm, walked gently on to enjoy the sweets of the morning.

Adelaide, who thought this a good opportunity to engage Donna Cynthia to a recital of her story, which she was impatient to hear, entered immediately on a subject which she thought was most likely to introduce it.—'I am little obliged to Donna Clara,' said she, in a lively way, 'for giving me the keys of her cabinet, where I found the picture of a young man, so very handsome that I could scarce sleep the whole night, for thinking of him!—How pleased should I be,' added she, 'to find that he was one of your family, and that he was to pass the day with us!'—Donna Cynthia sighed; and, shaking her head, answered, 'I should be very sorry if that picture had in reality made any impression on you; because the person for whom it was done is dead! and it has lain a long time where you found it, as we seldom go into that apartment; being unwilling to be too often reminded of the original.'—'A brother?' replied Adelaide.—'No,' cried Donna Cynthia; 'nothing akin to either of us: but he was a man who was once very dear to Clara; and I don't know whether his death (had he been faithful) would not have occasioned hers.'—'Did he then forsake her?' cried Adelaide (who could not help being moved) 'Oh, Heavens!' added she; 'are all mankind perfidious?' 'You would think so,' added Donna Cynthia, 'were I to relate to you the circumstances which have befallen myself and Donna Clara. But why, lovely Adelaide, do you exclaim against the treachery of men? I hope you have never experienced any of their ingratitude.'—Adelaide blushed a little at this. 'I don't know,' said she, 'whether I have any thing to accuse but my own ill stars, for the loss of a person who was engaged to me by the most solemn vows:—but I shall let you into the whole secret, provided, in return, you will relate your story to me, which I am sure must have something interesting in it.'—'That I will readily do,' answered Donna Cynthia; 'but as I must at the same time, acquaint you with some particulars of Donna Clara's life, it is but just that lady should participate with me in the pleasure of hearing your relation.'—Adelaide quickly consented to this; and they agreed to walk into the park after dinner, with Donna Clara, whom they now saw advancing towards them with Madame Deffari.—After their walk they went into the castle:—and Donna Cynthia having told her companion of the promise she had made Adelaide, they were all three impatient for an opportunity of being by themselves. Dinner being over, and Madame Deffari having retired to the study, where she said she would amuse herself with a book for an hour or two, the three ladies hastened to the park; and there, chusing a seat in which the heat of the sun could not molest them, Donna Cynthia, without waiting for the least entreaty, immediately began her tale:—

'The incidents of my life, and those of Donna Clara's, have such a connection that, in relating to you my story, I must necessarily spare my friend the trouble of repeating any of the circumstances of hers. We are both of Madrid; and, entering into an early acquaintance, our friendship increased with our years. It happened that we were both addressed at the same time, by two gentlemen who were considered as highly accomplished. Donna Clara's lover was called Don Raphael de Portia (the same whose picture you saw); and he who called himself my slave, was named Don Izidor de St. Ivorio.[18]

If I was pleased with the agreeable person and sprightly wit of this young man, Clara was no less charmed with the like graces in Don Raphael: there scarce past a day in which we had not some new instance of the gallantry of those two gentlemen (between whom, I must inform you, there was as strict a friendship as that which Donna Clara and I had for each other). It was now about four months that an intercourse had subsisted, as delightful as can be imagined to result from an innocent passion for a deserving object; for such my friend and I believed each of our lovers to be; and we looked upon our affection for them but as a suitable return to their love for us.

Donna Clara was then under the conduct of her father and a stepmother, not the most indulgent, who had a daughter of her own to provide for, before she would suffer Clara to be disposed of:—she was therefore under much greater embarrassments than I was, who had my fortune almost at my own disposal, and had nobody to controul me but an aunt, with whom I had been brought up, and from whose tenderness I might expect every thing that could make me happy.—How much do I envy you, said Donna Clara to me one day! It is in your power to recompense Don Izidor's merit whenever you please; your happiness is in your own hands: but my case is very different; for I dare not make Don Raphael's pretensions known to my father till my sister is first disposed of;—which I believe will be soon, interrupted I; for I know your mother is a lady of too active a temper not to promote her daughter's interests; and I am apt to think she has some design on foot, by the great intimacy she has lately entered into with the old Count de Pulvez, whose son, you know, is one of the finest gentlemen of the province.—Clara was of the same opinion with me, so that we now both imagined that her sister (who was the only obstacle in her way) would soon be removed; and she would then be at liberty to allow Don Raphael to apply to her father. Our loves, said I, began together; and one happy day (I hope) shall tie both the nuptial knots. My aunt already approves my choice; and I only wait till your father has done the same by yours, to give my hand to Izidor.

Clara embraced me for this mark of my tenderness for her. But should Izidor, said she, be acquainted with your intentions, he must needs be jealous of a friendship which so much delays his happiness.

This conversation happened whilst we were walking in the gardens of the Escurial; and we had but just done speaking when we perceived our two lovers coming towards us. They soon joined us; and after a short general conversation, Don Izidor took me by the hand, and, making a gallant compliment to Clara, who had that moment given hers to Don Raphael, he led me towards another walk; leaving our friends at liberty to entertain each other where they thought proper.

We were no sooner alone than Don Izidor, throwing himself on his knees with an air of transport, seized both my hands; and fixing his eyes on mine, with the most passionate looks, he seemed at a loss for words to express the emotions of his soul.—I chid him for so unseasonable a rapture; and made him rise from the posture he was in.—What do you mean, said he, by depriving me of the inexpressible pleasure I just now tasted? Was it not cruel in you to disturb a reverie so transporting? Can these proofs which I give you of my tenderness be displeasing? or have you found out any new method by which you would have me convince you of the excess of my love? Dear Cynthia, continued he, why won't you suffer me to name that long-expected day which is to make you mine for ever? Why these insupportable delays?—I should not (pursued Donna Cynthia) repeat to you a trifling conversation so little worth your attention, but for reasons which you will hear presently explained. The ardent and tender manner in which Don Izidor spoke, made me almost forget the promise I had made to Donna Clara; but, soon recollecting myself, I told him the obligation I had laid myself under to her; and if, added I, you love me as you would have me believe, you will make no difficulty in conforming to my will in this particular.—Ah cruel! cried he, how severe a task you enjoin me! Perhaps it may be a tedious while before Donna Clara will be at liberty to marry Raphael; and I perceive my happiness is wholly to depend on that of another! Ungrateful Cynthia! I see but too plainly how indifferent I am to you!—With this he turned from me with all the marks of violent grief.—Who would not have believed him sincere!—Stay, Don Izidor, said I; and be convinced that Cynthia does not deserve these reproaches. 'Tis true indeed I promised Clara that I would not make you my husband till she should have it in her power to do the same by Don Raphael; but she is too generous to insist on this agreement, if she finds her marriage is not likely to be accomplished in a very short time.—I shall then, said he, after a short pause, be more obliged to Donna Clara than I am to you. I know a heart tender as hers will readily absolve you from a promise so injurious to my love. I will go to her this minute, throw myself at her feet, and beseech her to free you from it.—Hold, hold, said I, seeing him ready to leave me; to what are you going to expose me? Of what weakness would not Donna Clara accuse me, when she should find that one half-hour's conversation with you had made me forget the promise which our long friendship had exacted from me! Be contented, added I; and believe that I shall be as just in fulfilling the engagements to love, as I am to those of a friend; I will desire you to wait but two months (no very important trial of your constancy) and will, at the expiration of that time give you my hand, let the event of Clara's love be what it may. I flatter myself, however, that her sister will in the mean time be espoused by the Count de Pulvez's son; but if the Marchioness her mother should be disappointed in this scheme of hers, I doubt poor Don Raphael's constancy will undergo a severe trial.—Don't mistake the matter, answered Izidor, laughing; if Raphael should lose Donna Clara, I have hopes that he would outlive the misfortune.—How! said I, does he not love her then?—Oh certainly! cried Izidor (in some confusion); but, as he is not without fears of a disappointment, I believe he is armed against it.—This answer was far from satisfying me. I trembled for Donna Clara, and pressed Izidor so earnestly to explain himself, that at last I obtained the hateful discovery to which I urged him.

Don Raphael, said he, does not in reality love your friend; for he is actually engaged to another. His mistress is now in Portugal; and it is only to divert his melancholy till her return, that he pays his court to Donna Clara, whose situation he knows will hinder him from being obliged to come to a sudden *éclaircissement*; for we both know that the Count of Pulvez has other views for his son than the elder sister of Clara. But, dear Cynthia, continued he, you must keep this secret inviolably. For Heaven's sake, suffer Donna Clara to continue in her error till time shall disabuse her.

It is impossible for me (proceeded Donna Cynthia) to describe to you what I felt whilst Izidor was speaking! I was seized with disquiet from the first moment he had dropt those words which led me to foresee part of Clara's misfortune; I even dreaded the explanation which I was pressing him to make; and every word he uttered pierced me like an arrow. I made sad reflections on the baseness of Don Raphael; and could not help turning them all at once on Don Izidor.—What have we not to fear, thought I, from a sex which is capable of so much cruelty and dissimulation; perhaps this very Izidor, this favoured lover, may be as vile as Don Raphael, who was no less lavish in his testimonies of affection to Clara.

I was so struck with this thought, that I listened to Izidor without interrupting him; and even remained silent for some minutes after he had done speaking. He imagined no doubt that some suspicions of himself might naturally enough mix themselves with my reflections on what I had just heard; and to remove those, he told me, with an obliging confidence, that I must not judge of all mankind by Don Raphael.—I own, said he, he has not dealt with that sincerity we could have wished; but I hope my charming Cynthia does not therefore form an opinion injurious to her faithful Izidor.—I don't know what to think, said I, coolly; but, in my mind, a lady of Donna Clara's birth is not a fit person to be trifled with; and, if Don Raphael could not live without an amour till the return of his mistress, he should have made choice of some other object.—Hush, hush, for God's sake! cried Izidor, alarmed at my grave manner of speaking; you forget that I trusted this to you as a secret of the greatest consequence!—And indeed I then believed that Don Izidor's disclosing it was more owing to his warmth than any infidelity to his friend.

The day began now to close, and we parted. I saw Donna Clara alone advancing towards me; but my thoughts were so wholly taken up with what I had just heard, that, without speaking one word to her, I took her under the arm, and we both walked to our coach (which waited for us at the garden-gate) as neither of us chose our lovers should attend us to it.

Clara during our walk had been as silent as I was; and being seated in the carriage, I perceived a pensiveness in her looks, which I had never observed before:—she seemed to be wrapped up in thought; and I could easily see the constraint she put on herself in endeavouring to hide something that troubled her. At last, with a deep sigh (which she tried to suppress) What ails you, Cynthia? said she.—I looked earnestly at her; and saw so much grief in her eyes that I no longer doubted her having discovered the infidelity of her lover.—Ah Clara! replied I, how can you ask me the occasion of my trouble, when I find you are no longer ignorant of the falsehood of that ungrateful man?—How! said she, with some surprise, does Don Izidor make a boast then of his treachery? and has he had the barbarity to insult you?—Don Raphael, you mean, replied I (thinking in her confusion she knew not what she said); God forbid that Izidor should be guilty of so much perfidy!—These words threw her into a perplexity from which I saw she could scarce recover herself; she remained in suspense for a minute, and then told me that she did not mistake that Don Izidor de St. Ivorio was the basest of all mankind; and added, that it was on my account she appeared so dejected; assuring me at the same time, that she imagined, by my melancholy and the answer I made her, when she asked me the occasion of it, that I had penetrated into her thoughts.—These words left me no room to doubt that I was betrayed as well as she. However, I begged of her to explain herself.—She told me that after Izidor and I had left them, Don Raphael and she had taken several turns in the walks, and that at length, being tired, they seated themselves on the brink of a canal; the flowers which painted the banks of it, the smooth transparency of the water, and the thick spreading trees which shaded it, formed so delightful a scene, that it seemed to inspire Don Raphael with a thousand new and agreeable thoughts.—"This place, said he, is certainly inhabited by the Muses. I feel their inspiration; or rather, one of them has just now whispered something in my ear, sacred to the beautiful Clara.—Give me leave, said he, to commit the precious lines to paper, before they escape my memory.—With this he took a pencil out of his pocket, and at the same time a handful of papers; but with so little care, that he dropt one of them without observing it.

He fell immediately to writing with so much attention, that he gave as little heed to my taking up the paper as he had done to his letting it fall. It was folded so carelessly that, seeing it addressed 'To the beautiful Donna Violante,'[19] I with a jealous curiosity proceeded directly to the contents; and, though I made no doubt of its being wrote by Don Raphael, yet, casting my eyes first at the bottom, judge of my surprise, to see it subscribed by Don Izidor!—Believe me, my dear love," continued Donna Clara, "this sight grieved me as much as if I had seen Don Raphael's name to the detested paper. I read it twice over. These were the words:

'The more I struggle with my chains, the stronger they hold me;—doubtless a punishment imposed on me by Love, for endeavouring to free myself from a captivity so delightful; which, in spite of your coldness, most beautiful and obdurate Violante, I am determined to submit to whilst I live.'

Don Raphael, having finished his verses, presented them to me to read; but I was too much disturbed to give any attention to them; I returned him the note, and begged of him to tell me who this dangerous beauty was, of whose cruelty Don Izidor complained?—Don Raphael could not conceal the chagrin that this unexpected question gave him. I saw vexation in his face; but, affecting an air of raillery, he told me, that in reality Don Izidor had no great reason to complain of the severity of Violante, as she was a lady of a temper not apt to throw her lovers into despair.—In short, said he, Don Izidor has a mind to divert himself with a piece of gallantry, in which (were you to know the character of the lady he addresses) you would be convinced there is nothing serious.—I told him that neither the sense nor the language of that letter seemed to be adapted to a loose woman, as he would insinuate; nor was it possible for him to persuade me into a belief that Izidor would address a person of that character in the style of a respectful lover.

Notwithstanding the gaiety which he had assumed, this speech quite confounded him: he blushed; and, casting his eyes on the ground, seemed to study for an answer. I took advantage of his perplexity; and tapping him gently on the shoulder,—Come, come, Don Raphael, said I; I know you are vexed at the discovery I have made. It is in vain to dissemble with me; and since I am obliged to chance for letting me into part of this secret, make me indebted to your sincerity for the remainder.—You can't call it an infidelity to your friend, continued I, finding him still silent, since it was without your participation that I got my first light into this intrigue; and I can assure you, you will leave me under much worse impressions of him, if you don't explain the matter truly to me.—What will you have me explain? answered Don Raphael, looking fearfully at me Would it not vex you on Donna Cynthia's account, if I should tell you that Izidor loves another?—No, replied I (affecting indifference); I know not how far he is engaged with Donna Cynthia; and we can none of us dispose of our hearts.—These words seemed to revive his confidence; and begging my care of the secret he was going to repose in me, he told me, that he had done Donna Violante the greatest injustice in painting her in such false colours; for that she was in reality a virtuous and beautiful widow; and possessed of a fortune so brilliant, that Izidor would be the happiest man in the world if he could obtain her. 'Tis about a month, added Raphael, since he first saw her; and, dazzled with her charms, or rather with her riches, he formed a design on her; and began by writing to her in a manner as animated as if by a real passion. He would trust no one but me to be the bearer of this letter, lest (by means of his servants, who knew of his attachment to Donna Cynthia) the secret should be betrayed. I put the letter into Donna Violante's hands, as she returned one day from prayers. She received it without hesitation; and, having just cast her eyes on me, continued her walk.

I drew no ill presage from this beginning; and went directly to Izidor, who waited for me, to declare my success. In talking of the merit of Violante, I took occasion to ask Izidor what had encouraged him to address her; and on what foundation he built his hopes of success.—He told me that, on Violante's part he had yet met with little encouragement, his acquaintance with her having scarce gone farther than a bare salute; but, added he, I am not without good hopes from the vivacity of a young widow, who, I am sure, can't be proof against the spirit with which I mean to pursue her.—I stopped him short, and asked him,—had he forgot Donna Cynthia?—No, he replied; I should prefer her to any woman living; but, as my principal end in the choice of a wife is a commodious fortune, Violante has in this point the advantage of her; and, if I succeed in that quarter, I fancy I must make a little free with my fidelity to Donna Cynthia, whom, however, I will not lose sight of till I am secure of the widow; but if I fail there, I shall assume the marriage-chain with Cynthia with the credit of as constant a swain as ever sighed. I need not in the mean time, added he, be afraid of pressing her to come to a conclusion; for I find by some hints she has dropped, that her romantic attachment to her friend Clara is likely to keep her single till that lady is at liberty to give you her hand; for it seems she can't be happy herself till her friend is so. In short, pursued Don Raphael, Violante's reception of his letter filled Izidor with the gayest expectations imaginable; he had begged for an answer; which he requested a servant of mine might call for, on account of the reasons I mentioned. I was with him when the footman returned with a letter in his hand. Izidor, who flattered himself that the letter was as favourable as his heart could wish, broke it open with eagerness; but his joy was suddenly damped when he found that it was his own letter which Violante had sent back, with no other ceremony than that of putting it in a cover.

I confess I could not help laughing at the consternation of my poor friend; he looked sometimes at me, and sometimes at the letter he held in his hand, and seemed quite confounded at this behaviour of Violante.—What is become of your hopes now Izidor? said I; you see the conquest is not so easy as you imagined.—I don't give it up yet, answered he (a little recovered from his surprise); it is a peevish trick of Violante's I must own; but I am not so young a lover as to take the first repulse.—Upon the whole, he was so far from being disheartened, that he wrote to Donna Violante again the next day, in terms more passionate than before. She did not indeed treat this letter with the same contempt she had done the other, by sending it back; but then her answer was such as I thought would have discouraged Izidor from any farther attempts.—She sent him word by her woman, that it was in vain for him to hope that he could ever make the least impression on her heart, which was not at all disposed to love: that she indeed pitied him; but that she could not afford him even that sentiment, if he continued to persecute her with letters: and in conclusion, desired him to think no more of her.—This answer, forbidding as it was, did not however incline Izidor to despair. He drew no unfavourable omen from Violante's keeping his last letter, and condescending so far as to send her woman to him with a message. He therefore resolved to make use of this lucky opportunity of gaining over to his interest one whom he found was in Violante's confidence. He slipped a purse of pistoles into her hand, telling her at the same time, in a melancholy tone, that he would endeavour to obey the cruel orders of her lady, as far as it was in his power: but for her last injunctions,—that he should think no more of her,—if she expected to be obeyed in that, she should at once have commanded him to die.—Biancha (that was the maid's name)[20] was on a sudden become so fast a friend to Don Izidor, that she could not resolve to leave him, after executing such rigorous commands, without affording him some comfort. She told him that she wondered the hardness of Violante's heart could be so very insensible to so much merit and generosity! She owned indeed that her mistress had never appeared much affected with his passion; but added, she did not think his case so desperate, since Violante did not seem to prefer any other to him. I have executed her orders faithfully, continued she; and now if

I give you a word or two of advice from myself, I think it will not be amiss. I know, pursued she, that Donna Violante's heart is tender and susceptible of soft impressions; but then I know too that she loves to make trial of the constancy of her admirers.—Not, said she (hastily interrupting herself) that I would have you think I would by this insinuate that she is less serious in the sentiments I just now delivered from her; but you know, Signior, that perseverance is what a lady can easily forgive in a lover: same time it must be managed with address. I advise you therefore to let this matter rest for a few days, as if in compliance to Donna Violante's will (as well as to prevent her having any mistrust of my aiding you in your design) and then, the violence of your passion getting the better of your resolution, and not permitting you to be silent any longer, you must renew the attack. You understand me, added she, with a significant look; and if my interest in Donna Violante can be of any service to you, I am more yours than my lady's.—Don Izidor relished the advice of the cunning Biancha so well, that he could not forbear embracing her; and promising to follow it to a tittle,[21] dismissed her.

I was present, pursued Don Raphael, at this conversation, and could not help observing to Don Izidor that the promises of this mercenary girl had elated him as much as if he had received the kindest message from his mistress. He told me the work was half done; and that he was impatient to have a few days over, that he might put Biancha's idea in practice; the success of which he said he did not doubt. I knew it would be in vain for me to represent to him the injustice he did Donna Cynthia: Izidor is of a temper not to be contradicted; and I was convinced of the impossibility of dissuading him from what he had once resolved on.

It is now five days, added Don Raphael, since he last wrote to Donna Violante;—and thinking that long enough for a man so much in love to impose silence on himself, he this day sent those lines which I so unluckily dropped. I am to wait on the fair widow with them to-night; and am to add every thing which I can think of to soften her heart, in favour of my friend. Such are the particulars," continued Donna Clara, "which I learned from Don Raphael. I parted from him without making any remarks on Don Izidor's conduct, which he, by reiterated intreaties, conjured me to conceal from you."

I could not help admiring the singularity of these incidents (pursued Donna Cynthia): and however ill-natured our stars were in condemning us to love such hypocrites, I thought we yet owed them some thanks, for the discoveries we had made of their falsehood.—I did not hesitate a moment to acquaint Donna Clara with the perfidy of Don Raphael.—You see, said I, we are equally abused: our injuries, like our loves, are the same:—but let us at least be just to ourselves, and abandon these traitors before they have time to add to our vexation.—Agreed, answered Donna Clara; and may Don Raphael's mistress (whoever she be) repay his love with ingratitude.—Yes, cried I; and let Violante be the ruin of the faithless Izidor!—These words, (continued Cynthia) though they seemed to be nothing more than the first sallies of anger in a disappointed woman, were afterwards but too fatally verified. We made a resolution on the spot, never to see our two lovers again, nor to vouchsafe them any reasons for the conduct we intended to observe towards them.

We had an opportunity the next day to try the strength of these resolutions.—Don Izidor came as usual to make me a visit; but I refused absolutely to see him:—Donna Clara observed the same behaviour with regard to Don Raphael. They each of them wrote to us; but we sent back their letters unopened; at the same time forbidding the messengers to bring us any more, on pain of being ill-treated.—As for our two lovers, though such a conduct might probably pique their pride, yet, certain I am, it was so far from giving them any disgust, that I rather believe they were glad of such an opportunity to break with us; for they were so punctual in obeying our orders, that neither Clara nor I heard any more from them!

I could not however resist a curiosity (hardly to be excused) to know how Izidor succeeded with Donna Violante. I was some time at a loss to know who to employ to get me the intelligence I wanted:—at last I fixed on a proper person. There was a young man who had formerly been a valet de chambre to my father, to whom (on account of his good services) he had at his death left a pretty annuity, which enabled him to live independently.—This fellow had, together with a good person, some agreeable qualifications, which I knew would be of use to my design:—in short, my project was that he should endeavour to insinuate himself into the good graces of Biancha (Donna Violante's woman); and by that means make himself master of her lady's actions.—I proposed it to him; and he readily embraced an opportunity of obliging me. There was no great difficulty in getting an access to this damsel:—Roderigo (that was my agent's name) in a few days got acquainted with her; and soon found the way to her heart, insomuch, that in a short time after I had enjoined him his task, he had gained so far upon her confidence as to enable him to give me the account I am going to relate.

Don Raphael, said he, according to the promise he had made his friend, went that very evening (after he had parted from Donna Clara) to wait on the fair widow, fully resolved to use all his art in giving her a favourable impression of Don Izidor. Violante no sooner heard his name pronounced by Biancha, than she desired him to be admitted.—Raphael, charmed at this happy beginning of his negociation, was in a moment in her dressing-room, whither she had thought proper to withdraw on purpose to receive him: and my friend Biancha, out of a curiosity natural to her station, posted herself where she could not lose a word of their discourse.

After the first compliments were over, Don Raphael, being seated near Violante, conjured her to hear him patiently on a subject, on which he said he would not dare to entertain her, without being first assured of her pardon.—Violante answering this preliminary with a gracious nod, encouraged him to proceed.—Suffer me then, Madame, said he, to solicit you in behalf of Don Izidor; the most deserving and the most unfortunate of men! I don't come to represent him as an obstinate and importuning lover, who is resolved to tire you with his passion: on the contrary, I would have you look on him as an unhappy generous man, who submits, without murmuring, to the fate your scorn has condemned him to; and I am only now come to lay at your feet the last efforts of a passion which his reason, in obedience to your will, has in vain attempted to subdue. Behold, added he, putting one knee on the ground, and presenting Don Izidor's letter to her,—behold the dictates of a heart pierced with your cruelties! and which nothing but death or the adorable Violante can restore to peace!—Here he paused to observe what impression this fine preamble made on the lady.

He discovered indeed, that she listened to him with a sort of pleasure, which encouraged him to proceed in the same strain; for having taken the letter out of his hand, she remained with her eyes fixed on his face, as if in expectation that he had something more to say.—Don Raphael, who rightly enough guessed that Violante was of a romantic turn of mind, resolved to treat her in that style.—Permit me then, said he, to breathe Don Izidor's sighs, to speak all his pains, and to pour out a torrent of vows at your feet.—He ended his rhapsody by throwing himself prostrate on the floor, and protesting he would not rise till she had expressed some pity towards his friend.—You are a skilful advocate, Don Raphael, added she; and Izidor is much obliged to you. If any thing could win me, 'tis his way of making love by proxy: it has something whimsical in it, which suits my humour:—prithee let us carry on this scene. I will suppose you to be your friend Don Izidor; and let me see how you would go about to woo an obdurate mistress.—Oh, Madam! answered Don Raphael, if you would suffer the real Don Izidor to speak his sentiments before you, you would find them much fuller of tenderness and delicacy than I shall be able to express.—Psha, cried Violante, you must be a very insensible Cavalier indeed, if the sight of a fine woman can't inspire you with nothing that is pretty.—Oh! pardon me, Madame! answered Don Raphael, I was only doing justice to my friend: but if you will have me to personate him, permit me then to tell you, relentless Violante, that I can no longer support your cruelty:—you know that I have loved, or rather, adored you, from the first moment I saw you; and no words can express the anguish, the anxiety, the unsupportable torment, which your scorn has, since that fatal time, condemned me to! Cease then at length, your frowns, most amiable creature; or prepare to see the heart which idolizes you bleed before your eyes!

Don Raphael accompanied these words with an air and tone of despair; and, clapping his hand with the most passionate gesture on his sword, he had drawn it half-way from the scabbard, when Violante, either quite forgetting herself or alarmed for the poor gentleman's life, threw her arms suddenly about his neck (as he kneeled before her) and, embracing him ardently,—You shall not die, my dear Chevalier, said she; Violante is not insensible to your merit; and loves you with a passion equal to that which you express for her.—Though Don Raphael thought this was carrying the jest a little too far, he was not however remiss in point of gallantry; but, returning Violante's caresses, he told her that he thought Don Izidor, from being the most wretched, was become the happiest of men! and that he hoped his friend had nothing now to do, but to come and receive those marks of favour in person, which she had vouchsafed him as his representative. How! cried Violante, starting; would you so easily forego the right I have given you to my heart, and yield up that love to another which I have just now lavished upon you?—Impossible! I can't entertain so mean an opinion of you; and I promise myself you will be as willing to return my tenderness as Don Izidor would.—Don Raphael, who did not expect this, was struck almost speechless. She perceived his embarrassment.—Don't be surprised, said she; you see my weakness; and after what I have said, I shall no longer endeavour to conceal it:—I liked you the first moment I saw you, and had even the curiosity to enquire who you were. I flattered myself that the billet which you presented to me as I came from church, contained your own sentiments:—judge then, how I was chagrined at the disappointment, when I found it came from Don Izidor! I determined never to see him; nor could I endure to hear his name pronounced by any mouth but yours. Consider then, Don Raphael, whether you will prefer his friendship to the love I offer you? Don't mistake my meaning, said she (seeing him thoughtful); I have no design upon your liberty, nor do I intend ever to give up my own again;—but you see I am young and rich: and I am vain enough to think that nothing but the regard you have for Izidor, could hinder you from improving the kindness I have for you.

Don Raphael laid hold on these last words, which he was resolved to turn to his own justification.—You judge right, Madam, said he; nothing but the inviolable friendship which subsists between Don Izidor and me, could make me hesitate a moment; I am but too sensible of the value of these favours you would bestow on me, but must own I am not worthy of the honour you do me:—for, alas! charming Violante, I can repay you nothing but my utmost gratitude!—Don Izidor suffers enough already from the scorn of an adored mistress, without receiving a fresh wound from the treachery of a beloved friend! Recall your heart then; and if you are determined not to bestow it on the unhappy Don Izidor, reserve it at least for one more worthy of it than Don Raphael.—He pronounced these words in so grave, yet persuasive, a tone, that any female but Violante would have retreated: but she was not so easily to be put off; she was a woman of impenetrable cunning; was extremely insinuating, and had all her life been used to intrigue. She found she had mistaken Don Raphael's temper (which was not the most forward); and apprehended, very justly, that the strange advances she had made had shocked him. She resolved, if possible, to retrieve this wrong step; and, seeming to be moved at what he said, she bent her eyes dejectedly to the ground; and then, as if it were stealing a bashful look at Don Raphael, she let fall some tears, which she could always command, and begged him to leave her to repent a weakness she was not then able to conquer. This piece of dissimulation had the desired effect. The artful tears of this cunning creature entirely subdued the weak inconstant heart of Don Raphael, and washed away all his scruples of honour. He threw himself at her feet, implored her pardon, and swore he would sacrifice every thing to her.—Don Izidor's friendship and the confidence he had in him, were no longer remembered!

The artful Violante dried her eyes; and finding that Don Raphael had fallen into her snare, they from that time commenced an amour, from which they promised themselves great felicity.

Don Raphael told her it would be best to flatter Izidor with some hopes, that he himself might continue his visits under pretence of negociating for his friend, till his intimacy in Violante's family should intitle him to visit her on his own account. Violante approved of this; and Don Raphael took his leave.

These were the particulars (continued Donna Cynthia) which Roderigo told me past at their first meeting: he added, that Don Raphael had often waited on the widow since, under the notion of a friend and confidant to Don Izidor; that he had even prevailed on her once to see Izidor, the better to amuse and blind him, as well as to prevent him from prying too curiously into Raphael's conduct;—which he was so far from suspecting, that he thought himself obliged to his good offices for this mark of the lady's favour.

Roderigo, who knew how Clara and I stood with respect to those two base men, took the liberty to say we had no great loss of them as lovers; and made so many keen reflections on this new piece of treachery in Don Raphael, that I could not help blushing at finding a more lively sense of honour in a poor fellow of his education, than in two men who might boast of their birth and breeding! I did not chide him for this freedom; but bid him continue the part he had acted, and inform me if Izidor should come to discover his friend's kindness to him.

I communicated this news to Donna Clara; and told her that as Violante was become as much, or more, her rival than mine, she had an equal right with me to be informed of what past between her and Don Raphael. We could neither of us forbear laughing at this whimsical turn:—and as we already looked upon our two lovers with a good deal of contempt, we imagined that the farther accounts which we expected from Roderigo, would serve to confirm it:—and we proposed some diverson at the figure Don Izidor would make when he should come to know how much he had been fooled by Don Raphael.

It was almost a month before we heard any more of the adventure; when, one morning, before Donna Clara (who had past the night at my house) or I were up, my woman came in and told me that Roderigo desired to speak with me. We both dressed ourselves hastily; and concluding something extraordinary had brought him at so early an hour, we desired that he might be admitted. He no sooner appeared at my chamber-door than I observed such an unusual concern in his looks, that I could not forbear crying out,—What's the matter, Roderigo? What news?—Ah! Madam, cried he, looking at Donna Clara, the worst that can be imagined!—And it relates to Don

Raphael, cried Donna Clara: you may speak without disguise; for he is so indifferent to me, that nothing concerning him can give me the least pain.—She spoke these words without well knowing what she said: they seemed to drop from her tongue without being guided by her reason; and I believe they were uttered through a sort of confusion, which Roderigo's expression had thrown her into: for the first thought which rushed into her mind was, that Raphael was married to Violante (which, considering that woman's character, would have been mortification enough to Clara, had she in reality hated Raphael)—Roderigo still looked at her with concern in his face.—God be praised, Madam! said he; I wish you may always continue indifferent towards ungrateful men!—Why, Roderigo? said Clara, affecting to smile, pray is Don Raphael married, or dead?—He is dead, answered Roderigo;—the unfortunate Don Raphael has paid the price of his folly with his life!

I desired Roderigo to repeat the particulars of this melancholy event.—You may remember, Madam, said he, "that I told you Don Raphael paid several visits to Violante, under colour of serving Don Izidor; but that gentleman growing at length a little impatient at the coquetry of Violante, or perhaps suspecting part of the truth (by Biancha's means, who was always his friend) he resolved to watch Raphael at his next interview with the lady. He gave him a letter to deliver to her; and, without appearing in the least to suspect his fidelity, he prayed him to carry it to her; which the other readily undertook to do. Last night was the time appointed for this purpose, or rather was the fatal period marked out by Heaven to end Don Raphael's life! The jealous Izidor, by the help of a few pistoles, prevailed on Biancha to conceal him in her mistress's closet; first engaging him by a solemn promise, that he would take care not to discover himself. He appeared so calm, that Biancha did not apprehend any evil consequences from this compliance. Don Izidor, impatient to have his suspicions either banished or confirmed, was looking through a casement in the closet door, which was covered by a silk curtain, when Don Raphael entered the chamber where Violante was waiting to receive him. Her dress was negligent, but elegant at the same time. He saw her receive Don Raphael with a freedom which convinced him they were on very good terms: and making him sit by her on a sopha, they entered into a conversation which left him no reason to doubt his friend's treachery. He could scarce contain himself at what he heard:—but this was not all; he saw Don Raphael take the letter he had given him for Violante out of his pocket, and presenting it to her, with an ironical smile,—I had almost forgot, said he, to deliver you this letter from one of the most passionate of your lovers, the unfortunate Don Izidor, who languishes under your frowns.—Prithee read it, said Violante; it will divert us a little.—Don Raphael broke open the seal, and read it with a loud voice; accompanying every word with so ridiculous a tone and gesture, that Violante was ready to die with laughing.—The enraged Don Izidor could bear no more;—he burst open the closet-door, and, throwing himself on the two lovers, he buried his dagger in the unhappy Raphael's bosom, who instantly expired! Violante had only time to give a loud shriek, and then fell motionless on the sopha! Don Izidor, satisfied with the sacrifice he had made to his revenge, left the house directly; Biancha (who had been a witness to this scene from another closet, where she had hid herself at my request) not having power to stop him or give the alarm to the family. These (continued Roderigo) are the particulars which I learned from Biancha this morning. Violante, who has been the occasion of this miserable disaster, is in the most deplorable state imaginable; and all the friends of Don Raphael are now in pursuit of his murderer!"

Whatever my concern was at this dreadful account, Donna Clara's was infinitely greater: for now it was that she found how dear Don Raphael had been to her. She reproached herself for it; and would fain have believed that she rejoiced at his death as a punishment due to his crime. She accused him of treachery and ingratitude, and of having occasioned her a thousand torments! for which she ought to detest his memory, and to congratulate Izidor on having at once both revenged himself and her! Thus for a while she pleased herself, with thinking that her just anger had got the better of her love:—but, alas! I soon found she deceived herself!—this was but a vain resource, which her resentment at first offered to console her under a misfortune, that she was in reality scarcely able to support! Whilst Raphael lived and courted another, a just pride stifled, and she flattered herself had entirely subdued her passion for him; but in that her heart betrayed her: for now the scene changed in a moment, and represented this faithless lover to her imagination in the most amiable light in which partial love could place him. She condemned herself for having deserted him, without being sure that what Don Izidor had said of him was true:—she blamed Violante alone for his unhappy fate; and accused that wretched woman, Don Izidor, and herself, by turns. She lamented Don Raphael with floods of tears; and I found that it was a sort of decorum she kept up with herself, which prevented her giving a loose to them at first; for when she had, as it were, mitigated his crime, she gave herself leave to weep without restraint. I knew the softness as well as the generosity of her nature, required this tribute to the memory of a man whom she had once loved so well. I therefore gave way to her grief; considering that time and her own good sense, would administer more comfort than I was capable of affording her.

Don Raphael's friends used the utmost diligence to find out Don Izidor; but he had the good fortune to escape their pursuit. His flight however was so precipitate, that it was found he had taken nothing with him but a small sum of money; and his whole estate, which was considerable, was confiscated to the crown. As this affair made a great noise, and was little to the credit of Donna Violante, she soon after disappeared; and I believe has never been since in Madrid.

As for Donna Clara and myself, we could no longer relish a place which had been the scene of such a disaster.—My aunt, who loved me too well to oppose my inclination, at last yielded to my desire of retiring to this castle, which is on my own estate. Donna Clara's father dying about the same time, left her entirely mistress of herself; and I had no difficulty in persuading her to accompany me. Here my friend and I pass our time in an agreeable though melancholy solitude; for we converse with few besides the good Bishop of Seville, who now and then honours us with his company. 'Tis now three years since we lived here; and we are so well satisfied with the pleasures of our retirement, that we have not the most distant thought of ever changing it.'

Here Donna Cynthia ended her narrative; and, perceiving that night had insensibly stole upon them, she proposed to the ladies to return home, telling Adelaide she would claim her promise the next evening, when they would with pleasure take the opportunity of adjourning to the same place.

They were surprised at their return into the castle, to find the Bishop of Seville sitting with Madame Deffari, who told them, that *that* prelate having just alighted from his carriage, she was going to send for them into the park; saying, she believed they had met with some enchanted palace, or fairy abode, which had so much prolonged their walk. Donna Cynthia excused herself and her companions; and changing the discourse, addressed herself to the Bishop, asking him to what mighty good chance they owed the honour of seeing him at that unusual hour (for that gentleman living some miles from the Castle of Cardonas, never came to visit them so late, but when he intended to pass the night there; and of this he always sent them notice)? so that Donna Cynthia concluded it was something materially particular which had been the occasion of his coming at almost nine o'clock at night.

'You may be surprised indeed, daughter' answered the Bishop, 'at seeing me here at such an hour, without first acquainting you with my design:—but an accident brought me into your neighbourhood this evening, and detained me in it longer than I expected; and, as I know my chamber is always ready for me, I make no scruple of throwing myself on you as a guest to-night.'—'You do us honour,' replied Donna Cynthia, 'but, if it be no secret, will you let us know what that accident was, to which we are so much obliged?'—'I will tell you,' answered the Bishop; 'you know Father Theodore, whom you surnamed the Solitary, and have had such a curiosity to see from the description I have given you of him. The person we are speaking of (added he, directing his speech to Madame Deffari) lives about a quarter of a league from this castle; and it was mere chance which led me first into his acquaintance. A violent storm of wind and rain obliged me once, as I happened to ride this way, to turn into his little lodge for shelter. He received me with great civility and good-nature; and upon my inquiring into his circumstances (as I saw him in a poor habitation) he told me he was an Italian monk, of the order of St. Hyronimo,[22] who, having raised himself some enemies on a point of religious controversy, was obliged to fly from their persecution. I found him a man of so much humanity and good-sense, that I have since that time frequently called at his house in my way thither, to have the pleasure of half an hour's conversation with him; but he is so complete a recluse, that these ladies, though he has for a long time lived so very near them, never once had a sight of him. But indeed it is no wonder; for he assures me he has never stirred farther than his little garden. You must know then, that this poor solitary is now at the point of death; and, having sent a peasant to me this morning, I made all the haste I could to him, the countryman telling me he was dangerously ill, having got a violent cold (by sleeping late on the grass) which had thrown him into a fever.

I found him in reality very ill, and weak. Having begged me to sit down by him, and first thanked me for affording him my presence, he told me he had something to communicate to me, which, amongst his other sins, would not suffer him to die in peace.

Know then, said he, that I have deceived you in my profession, my name, and my country: for the former of which in particular I must intreat your pardon and absolution. You know, continued he, that I have always made you believe that I was an Italian priest, who fled from the persecution of my enemies; but this is far from the truth; for I only put on the religious habit for my better security and convenience, as I believed the monk's cowl would not only render my person more inviolable, but would make people less curious to pry into the method of life I purposed to lead.

Are you not an ecclesiastic? cried I, amazed at what I heard him say.—No, my Lord, no, answered he; I am the most unfortunate man living.—But pray hear me out.—He then proceeded to tell me his real name and country, which I find to be our own; for he is actually a Spaniard; but having gone into Italy in quality of Secretary to the Viceroy of Naples, he there got acquainted with a young woman of quality, whom he married unknown to her friends; and embarking with her in a vessel for Spain, he had the misfortune to lose her.

This disaster so much embittered his life, that, resolving to renounce the world, he, on his arrival in Spain, sold his estate in Valencia, and retired to this province, where it seems he was born; and where,' added the Bishop, 'I am afraid he will soon end his days; for, after having exhausted his spirits in relating to me all the circumstances of his unhappy story, he had scarce strength enough to go through with his confession, and to repeat some prayers after me, which he begged I would offer up for his sins.

I stayed so late with him,' pursued he, 'that I thought it would be in vain for me to attempt going home to-night. Besides, as I have sent to Cadiz for a physician, I would chuse to be in the way when he visits him.'

Adelaide, who listened attentively to the good bishop's discourse, had laid the most violent constraint upon herself to hide the tumult in her bosom which this relation had occasioned. She concluded that the supposed Father Theodore could be no other than her lover, the Chevalier de Ponces. She asked the Bishop of Seville, with a trembling voice,—Whether the sick person had desired his name to be concealed?—'No,' replied the Bishop; 'he is called Don Enenique de Ponces.'—At that dear name Adelaide could no longer contain herself:—she fetched a deep groan, and fainted away on the neck of Madame Deffari, who sat by her. All the company were startled and surprised, except that lady, who well knew the cause. Adelaide was soon brought to herself by the remedies which were applied; and the Bishop of Seville, with Donna Cynthia and Donna Clara, having altogether, with great earnestness, demanded the occasion of her so sudden illness, Madame Deffari, with Adelaide's permission, acquainted them in a few words with the whole of her friend's story.

The good Bishop seemed quite astonished with this new discovery; and, addressing himself to Adelaide (whom he now saw easing her swoln heart with tears) 'Be comforted, Madam,' said he; 'your husband is indeed dangerously ill; but the hopes of seeing you again may work miracles; and perhaps restore him to health,—you whom he believes dead, and whose loss I have heard him so bitterly deplore.'—'Alas, my Lord,' answered Adelaide, 'it is not me whom he deplores; you know my friend informed you that it was my cousin whom he married and took away with him (believing her indeed to be me) but he must certainly have soon been undeceived; therefore it is to Faustina's memory that he dedicates all his sorrow.'—'You are mistaken,' cried the Bishop, 'and wrong the Chevalier; for he lost his wife without ever being undeceived in his belief of its being you whom he married; and, if you be that Adelaide, the daughter of the Baron St. Seberina, Don Enenique never was unfaithful, nor ceased one moment to love you.'—'Explain this, my Lord,' cried Madame Deffari. 'I am overjoyed at what you tell us.'—To this the Bishop replied:—'I shall give you the information you desire in the Chevalier's own words:—

"I have informed you, my Lord, of the opposition my passion met from my Adelaide's father.—With difficulty I prevailed on her to yield to my entreaties; and obtained at length an almost reluctant promise to meet me the following evening, after dark, in a summer-house in the garden; where a priest, whose service I had secured, had engaged to unite us in indissoluble bonds. She was faithful to her appointment; but appeared under such extraordinary agitation, that, fearing a return of her former scruples, I hastened the ceremony that secured her mine; and, putting her and her attendant into my chaise, I mounted my horse; and in a short time we reached the sea-side; where, still favoured by the obscurity of the night, we got on board a brigantine[23] I had hired for the purpose; and we set sail immediately.

Adelaide instantly retired to her cabin; and I was preparing to follow her, when Theresa stopped me, saying, her mistress had requested to be left a short time to her own thoughts.—Though grieved and disappointed at this proposal, I replied, Her will should be obeyed, however painful to my heart; and, desiring Theresa to return to her mistress, I remained buried in reflection on a conduct which might have been construed into indifference, had she not that very night given such undoubted proofs of the most sincere attachment.

In a few minutes Theresa delivered me a short note from my dear Adelaide: the hand was scarcely legible, so greatly were her spirits affected. As nearly as I can remember (and often have they come across my thoughts) these were the words:—

'Your ready compliance with a request so apparently unkind, has obliged me greatly. You cannot, my dearest Ponces, doubt of my love; but you must own the sacrifice I have made of filial affection, duty, and all those ties I have hitherto most revered, require the tribute of sorrow I cannot deny them.— A few hours, I trust, will compose my spirits; and I shall meet you in the morning in a frame of mind better suited to that union on which my future happiness must depend.'

I reiterated my assurances of compliance to her maid; and even admired this sensibility of mind in my Adelaide.—I retired to the captain's cabin for the remainder of the night. In a few hours we fell in with a little fleet, which the Viceroy of Naples was then sending on a grand expedition. We had scarcely joined them (which we would rather have avoided, and should have done so, had the weather been clear) when we were, most unfortunately met by some pirates of Barbary,[24] who instantly attacked us.—The Spaniards fought bravely, though under much disadvantage, the brigantines being so crowded with men that they had not room to defend themselves regularly. It was now peep of day,[25] and I had mingled in the fight, not daring to trust myself with a sight of Adelaide in such an alarming moment; but the precious charge animated me with uncommon fire; so that, after a fierce engagement which lasted near an hour, I leapt in the enemy's ship which had grappled my brigantine, and advancing with my sword drawn towards the captain (who had more than once attempted to board me) we began a very sharp and long encounter.—Most of my men followed my example, and engaged with the Turks; who defended themselves with great bravery. For my own part, I was received by the infidel with uncommon intrepidity; when, after exchanging several blows, I fortunately laid him dead at my feet.

But oh! how dear did this victory cost me! During the engagement between the two vessels, my brigantine had started a plank, which the crew in the confusion they were in, had not discovered, and most of them having followed when I boarded the Turk, there remained but few hands to assist her behind. The ships had by this time got clear of each other; and, to complete our distress, the wind had risen so high, that it was impossible for the sailors who were with me to get to the relief of their comrades. How dreadful was my situation when I saw the brigantine which contained the treasure of my soul just ready to be swallowed up by the waves; for the water had by this time almost filled it. The storm had severed our vessels so, that it was only possible to distinguish my dear Adelaide running distractedly on the deck, followed by her woman, who was wringing her hands. But what were my agonies, when, after a fruitless endeavour to get to their succour, I saw the fatal brigantine sink to the bottom!—I beheld every thing dear to me perish before my eyes in one dreadful moment, and was at this sight so little master of myself, that I was going to plunge in after her, if some of the people about me, who saw my despair, had not held me. I was carried to the cabin, where my servant had followed me, rather to prevent me from committing any violence on myself than to offer me any consolation; which he knew at that time would be a vain attempt.

In the mean time the two fleets were dispersed, as well the Turkish as Spanish; which without doubt was providential; for it not only saved a great many lives that must have been lost, had the engagement continued, but also retarded that black enterprise the Neapolitan ships were going on; and which God has since been pleased so happily to defeat.—Your Lordship can't be ignorant that I mean that execrable design against the Republic of Venice.[26]

We tossed about the remainder of that day and the whole ensuing night, when the following morning the storm abated. As we had made ourselves masters of the Turkish ship, I ordered them to pursue our melancholy course to Spain, where we arrived without meeting any farther molestation.

Of all the money and jewels I had carried with me from Italy I had nothing left, having lost all in the vessel; but this would have given me little concern, had the waves spared my beloved wife. The master of the brigantine which was sunk, lost nothing in the exchange he had made; for the Turkish ship proved to be very rich; so that most of his crew were well rewarded for the hazard they had run.

I now found myself the most forlorn wretch in the world. In one moment I took a review of all my calamities.—In what a condition, said I, am I returned to my native country! I left it, possessed of a considerable employment, and flushed with a thousand flattering hopes: but where are they now? I have abused the Duke d'Ossuna's favour by absenting myself from my post without his knowledge; and that at a most critical time.—I have stole away from Naples like a criminal; and such indeed I am; for, after having engaged a virtuous, young, and beautiful maid to forsake her friends and her country to follow my fortunes, I have seen her perish before my eyes! I accuse myself of her death; for it was her love for me which occasioned it.—Yes, cried I, had Adelaide never beheld the wretched Enenique, she had still lived, still been happy.

Thus I reflected that I had lost the best part of my fortune, my hopes, and my wife. I made no doubt but the Baron St. Seberina, her father, would make the most diligent inquiry after her; and that, assisted by the Viceroy, who must also be provoked at my flight, I should inevitably be discovered; and though, had Adelaide lived, I was not without hopes of appeasing the Baron, yet I had every thing to apprehend from the fury of an incensed father, who, having lost an only child, would not fail to look upon me as the author of her death. These reflections made me form a resolution at once what course to take. I repaired with the utmost privacy to Valencia, where I have an estate.—I put it into the hands of a friend, who was to remit a small sum to me yearly, making him acquainted with my design; and at the same time desired him to give out that I was gone to travel. I changed my name to that of Father Theodore; and disguising myself in a monk's habit, I resolved to pass the rest of my days in mourning the loss of Adelaide; and to live as solitarily as if I had really been a holy man.—The many years I have been absent from Andalusia, together with the alteration in my person, made me so little known there, that I concluded it would be no hard matter to conceal myself under a borrowed name.

I chose Andalusia for my residence for two reasons; the one, that being the place of my nativity, and at the same time one of the most delightful parts of Spain, I had a particular attachment to it; the other, that I imagined, should there be any search for me, my enemies would least suspect me to be in the very province whither I knew it was most likely they would direct their first inquiries. I bought this little dwelling from a poor man who had lived here many years; and I only wish to exist, in order to make an atonement for a life which (though not blameless) has yet been fuller of misfortunes than crimes."

I could not (proceeded the Bishop) hear this unhappy young man conclude his sad story without shedding tears. I have already told you how much he had impaired his strength by talking so long. However, after having past some hours at his bed-side, which were spent as well in affording him consolation as in hearing a detail of his adventures, I left him in a tranquil state of mind; but so weak in body, that I am not without fears of losing him:—therefore, good daughter,' added he, addressing Adelaide, 'though you have again found your lover, and found him such as you would wish him to be; yet have a care in giving a loose to the emotions of your heart! He is indeed most worthy of your love; and I wish Heaven may spare him to make you happy:—but I conjure you not to build your happiness on a life, of which we must be so uncertain.'—'Oh, my Lord!' cried Adelaide (her face bathed in tears) 'assist me with your counsel; and teach me, if possible, to bear these cruel strokes of fate without murmuring.'—'Don't talk of murmuring,' interrupted the Bishop, gravely; 'God forbid, child, that you should presume to repine at the decrees of Providence. You ought rather to fall on your knees, and adore its wise and merciful dispensations, which have preserved you in a most wonderful manner, at the same time that it permitted the destruction of that miserable woman who betrayed you!—Consider that, had you been in her place, you must have perished; and the Chevalier would, in reality, have had the loss of that wife to lament, whose life seems to have been the care of Heaven! Let this consideration fill you with the utmost gratitude.—You are to believe that, if God is pleased to take Don Enenique to himself, it is not in order to afflict you; but, on the contrary, to work some special end of his own; perhaps to give you a farther opportunity of exercising that admirable patience and submission, which he has already blest you with; and to teach you not to put too great a value on the transitory enjoyments of this life.—We ought therefore, without laying schemes of happiness for whole years, which an accident of one minute may destroy, to content ourselves to live (as we all are) poor dependants on the mercies which are hourly vouchsafed us!'

Whilst the good prelate was thus endeavouring to comfort his fair pupil, she strove as much as possible to stifle her sighs.—Whatever submission she shewed to this venerable man's advice, her thoughts were too much agitated at this time, to be easily calmed.—She thanked him, however, in the most respectful terms, for the zeal he expressed for her happiness and peace of mind.—It was now pretty late; and the messenger whom the Bishop had sent to Rios[27] for the physician, was returned with him, and came to acquaint his Lord that he had left him at the house of the sick man.—Adelaide was afraid to shew too great an impatience to know what was the state of the Chevalier; but Madame Deffari, who guessed at what past in her mind, entreated the Bishop to send for the physician, that he might give them an account of his patient's state of health. Accordingly the Bishop dispatched one of his servants for him; the Chevalier's little habitation being only two or three fields length from the castle.

When the physician arrived, he assured them that the Chevalier was still in a high fever; and that he had little hopes but from his youth and strength. He added, that his patient was delirious, and could not be prevailed on to take a cordial which he had brought with him to procure sleep.—The whole company were alarmed at this account! The Bishop was deeply moved at Adelaide's sorrow, as well as at the Chevalier's danger.—He assured her there should be nothing omitted that could tend towards his relief:—and, rising up, he let the physician know that he would go with him to his patient, to try if his presence would have any salutary effect.—Accordingly they both departed from the castle:—and Donna Cynthia, perceiving that it was now almost midnight, entreated her guests to think of taking some repose.

Adelaide went indeed to bed; but those persons must never have felt a pain like hers who imagine that she slept.—Ponces, the amiable Ponces, still faithful and constant as ever, was a thought which transported her beyond expression:—but then, that same Ponces, amiable and constant as he is, is at the point of death!—This cruel reflection quite distracted her; and she rose before day, to learn, if possible, what she was to expect.

Madame Deffari was still asleep; and finding all the house in a profound silence, she waited in her antichamber, walking backwards and forwards with the utmost anxiety, till she should hear some of the family stirring. But the Bishop of Seville, who judged of her inquietude, did not leave her long in suspense. That good man, who had (together with the physician) sat up all night, no sooner saw day-light than he hastened to the castle of Cardonas; and, going directly to Adelaide's apartment, he met that lady in the gallery; who, on hearing him come up stairs, was advancing to receive him in the utmost agitation.—'The Chevalier is still alive,' said he (without waiting for her asking him) 'and though not out of danger, yet, from having rested a little, his fever is somewhat abated.—I found him,' added the Bishop, 'light-headed, as the physician told us; and I remained almost two hours by his bed-side before his reason returned, when I prevailed on him to take the dose which was prepared to make him sleep; and which I almost began to suspect he had refused from the physician, less out of want of recollection than a disinclination to live; for it was with some difficulty that I persuaded him to take it; and not till after I had represented to him the heinousness of his endeavouring to hasten his own death, by not only the neglecting, but absolutely refusing all means of preservation. But I found he had quite different notions from mine:—for, shaking his head, he told me that, after having made his peace with God, he hoped it would not be imputed to him as a crime, if he pressed forward on his journey to a better world, in order to leave one which was hateful to him:—however, at my request he said he would no longer refuse the aids which I had so generously procured him. In effect, the cordial which he accepted from my hands so composed him, that he slept for near three hours; and on his awakening seemed much refreshed.'—'Oh, my Lord!' cried Adelaide, 'how infinitely good are you! Sure Heaven sent you to be a comforter and preserver to me, as well as to the unhappy Chevalier, who, without your charitable assistance, had by this time been no more!'—'Give God the praise,' (answered the Bishop) 'who has pleased to make me instrumental in this good work. But moderate your joy; for I have already told you that, though Don Enenique is much better, he is nevertheless not out of danger.'—'If he knew I was alive, and so near him,' replied Adelaide, blushing, 'I am sure it would help him to recover.'—'On the contrary,' answered the Bishop, 'it might only serve to irritate his disorder; for sudden impulses of joy and surprise have often produced effects as fatal as those of grief. However, you may be sure I shall, when his strength permits, take an opportunity of making the discovery to him in such a manner as he will be best able to bear. In the mean time I must chide you for your impatience: for I well perceive by your eyes, that you slept but little last night.'—Adelaide was something abashed at this gentle reprimand: however, relying entirely on the goodness of the Bishop, she conjured him to continue his kind offices to the Chevalier, and to indulge her so far as to let her know from time to time how he did.—'And I leave it to you, my Lord,' added she, turning her face away, 'to inform him that Adelaide still lives, and lives only for him.'

Madame Deffari, with Donna Cynthia and Donna Clara, were by this time up; and, longing to enquire after the Chevalier's health, they were rejoiced at the hopes the Bishop gave them by his account: and indeed they so much interested themselves in Adelaide's happiness, that one would have thought it was the particular concern of each of them.—Donna Cynthia invited the physician to breakfast with them; and they had the satisfaction to hear from him that the Chevalier's disorder was so much abated, that he began to entertain the best hopes imaginable of him:—in effect he recovered his strength so well in a few days, that the Bishop of Seville, believing that the knowledge of Adelaide being alive would much contribute towards restoring him to perfect health, he resolved no longer to defer a discovery on which the happiness of two such virtuous and amiable persons depended. He intended to prepare the Chevalier by degrees for the joyful news he had to disclose to him: wherefore going to make him a visit, as was his daily custom, he found him reclining on his bed, with a book before him, on which he seemed very attentive. He laid it by when he perceived the Bishop at his bed-side; and, accosting that reverend man with a cheerful air,—'I would prefer nothing on earth but your Lordship's company,' said he, 'to the author I have been just now reading, whose sentiments I am the more delighted with as they serve to confirm me in a resolution I had taken (in case it pleased God to restore me to health) to assume that holy weed in reality, which I have so long presumed to wear only as a disguise. This I think the smallest atonement I can make for my profanation of the sacred habit.'—'I am pleased,' answered the Bishop, 'to find you entertained in so edifying, as well as agreeable a manner; and wish you would bestow more of your time in an employment which would take off your thoughts from the melancholy subjects which so often engage them. You are now but just recovered from a dangerous fit of sickness, which had almost brought you to the brink of the grave! summon up therefore all your spirits; banish the gloom which has so long hung over you; and prepare your mind to taste the sweets of peace. You have disburthened your soul of a weight which had a long time oppressed it;—you have made me the confidant of your sorrows, as well as of your sins.—I have absolved you from the one, and hope I have administered some consolation to the other. In such a frame of mind as I flatter myself you are now in, I must approve the resolution you have taken, effectually to bid the world and its vanities adieu. You will in this solitude have leisure to discover the charms of piety and true devotion:—charms which the world are but little acquainted with; where they are so obscured with avarice and hypocrisy, that their splendor is altogether lost! Here you must look upon yourself as just entered into a new world. You must forget that you were ever any other than what you now are:—that you ever had a name, a fortune, or a wife. Let all the vanities of your youth be forgotten; and let the memory of nothing but your faults dwell with you. A little use will make all these things easy; and every day will advance your happiness and repose. You must learn to fix your eyes on the supreme Author of all good; and to look upon him as the end of all your wishes and desires:—this will put you in a state to be envied by kings.—Your life will be always sweetened with hopes the most ravishing that can touch a human heart, without any mixture of those fears which render the mortal condition so miserable:—you will no longer regret the seeing your treasure swallowed up by the waves, nor sigh for having the object of your love torn from you. Such blessings are those which you may promise yourself from a religious life: I would wish you therefore, my son, to have a relish for such a life before you enter upon it. 'Tis true, the longer you are acquainted with it, the more amiable it will grow (an attribute, I think, which piety has peculiar to itself); but then, I would by no means encourage you to bind yourself by vows before you are well apprized of your own strength of mind, and are sure that no motives would be powerful enough to tempt you back into the world, which you renounce. 'Tis necessary therefore before you proceed too far, to weigh nicely the importance, and be fully convinced of the steadiness of your resolution.'

'Oh, my Lord!' replied the Chevalier, 'that task is long ago performed. I have searched into the innermost recesses of my soul; and I can boldly declare that if all the riches, titles, and honours in the universe were laid at my feet, they would not shake my settled purpose, nor once tempt me to renounce this poor covering. No, my reverend friend; you have inspired me with a holiness, and raised my hopes to such a degree, that it is not in the power of any thing to make me forego them.'—'Ask your heart one question more,' replied the Bishop, 'and then I have done. Suppose your Adelaide, that Adelaide whom you so much loved, were to be restored to your wishes, are you proof against a temptation so full of charms?'—'Ah! why do you rip up a wound,' replied the Chevalier, 'into which you have but just poured a balm? Alas! I fear were such a miracle to be wrought, I should too soon forget all my pious resolves!—Yes, my Lord, I own myself so frail a wretch, that Adelaide could even force me from the altar!'—'How weak is man!' replied the good pastor, lifting up his eyes to heaven. 'Oh, my God! what wretches are we! to be thus enslaved by our passions!—Indeed, young man, I pity you,' added he. 'Alas! you are deceived in imagining that you have acquired that victory over yourself, which is necessary for the holy life you purpose to lead. I well perceive that you despise riches and pomp not out of a Christian humility, but because another object engrosses all your affections!'—'Don't reproach me thus cruelly,' answered the Chevalier, 'with a weakness which I have made no scruple to confess to you. 'Tis true, my love for Adelaide was beyond all description; but I own this without blushing. She was my wife; amiable and virtuous as ever man was blest with; and if it be in the power of nothing but that dear wife (who now lies buried in the deep) to make me swerve from my duty, don't, I conjure you, let the thoughts of an impossibility debar me from that happiness, for which you have made me long so ardently.'

The worthy prelate fixed his eyes gravely on the Chevalier. The secret he had to disclose to him was of so uncommon and very affecting a nature, as obliged the Bishop to pause for some time, in order to collect himself, so as to be able to make the important discovery in such a manner as would least surprise and discompose the mind of his friend. The Chevalier observed his countenance, which seemed expressive of something more than common; and, bending respectfully towards him, 'I fear,' said he, 'you think me incapable of discharging those severe duties which the profession I am ready to embrace will exact from me; and that you judge it expedient perhaps that I should undergo a longer probation than ordinary. If these be your sentiments, speak, my Lord; for I attend with the utmost submission to hear your final sentence on me.'—'Hear me then, my son,' answered the Bishop; 'for I am going to speak, though not on the subject you expect yet on one; which, next to your eternal welfare, concerns you most nearly. Prepare yourself then for astonishment; prepare your heart for joy; but above all, prepare, with gratitude and humility, to adore that Providence who in so wonderful a manner preserved and now restores to you—your wife! For know, Don Enenique, your Adelaide lives! To her then, who has the best right to your vows, be they all dedicated; whilst I, highly content with being instrumental in promoting the happy union, will join with you in admiring the various ways which Heaven takes to bring about its purposes.'

The Chevalier, who was fully possessed with a belief of Adelaide's death, looked upon this as the effect of a delirium; and, fearing that he was again fallen into his former state of raving, conjured the Bishop to tell him, whether he was awake, and in his senses; and if all he had heard was real?—The Bishop then proceeded to relate every particular as he had it from Adelaide's own mouth.—But Don Enenique, still doubting of his own happiness, asked,—might he not be permitted to see Adelaide?—The Bishop answered, she was not far off; and that if he thought the sight of her would not agitate his spirits so as to endanger his health, he himself would conduct her to him directly. Don Enenique grasped his benefactor's hand, and, pressing it eagerly, conjured him by no means to delay his felicity.

The Prelate arose, and kindly bidding him endeavour to govern the impetuosity of his wishes, he left him to go to the Castle of Cardonas, where he informed the ladies of what had passed. But he had scarce time to finish what he had to say, when the overjoyed Adelaide flew to the Chevalier's habitation; the Bishop and Madame Deffari (who had a desire to be witnesses of their meeting) followed. Adelaide had stopped at his chamber-door a little, to recover her agitated spirits; and, notwithstanding her impatience to behold her beloved Don Enenique, she had not the courage to enter the room, till the Bishop, laying hold of her hand, and begging her to compose herself, led her directly to the Chevalier.

An ecstasy of joy overpowered him so, that (though he endeavoured) he was not able to rise; and the equally transported Adelaide could only throw herself on his bosom, where, hiding her face, she gave vent to her tears.—She wept indeed; but sure they were not tears of sorrow which she shed on the breast of Don Enenique, but such as flow from transports too strong for the poor expression of words! However, having recovered herself a little, she raised her head, and the Chevalier and she gazed at each other in silence so long, that the Bishop, fearing such tumultuous joy might overcome Don Enenique's hardly recovered strength, thought proper to correct those raptures, which seemed so wholly to possess their faculties as almost to deprive them of their proper powers.

'Chevalier,' said he, 'gently tapping him on the shoulder, you see that without a miracle your wife (for such I suppose she will shortly be) is restored to you, beyond your hopes. Let the future part of your life therefore (since your temporal engagements must necessarily prevent those spiritual ones you proposed) be spent so, as to render you worthy this distinguished mark of favour from Heaven; and though the first steps you took to gain this lady were not quite blameless, yet you have I think fully atoned for them; and I know of no reward so suited to your fidelity as that which is now bestowed on you.—May you live many days to participate of such an unlooked-for enjoyment, and may your gratitude and future conduct in life be such as will justly entitle you to merit so divine a favour;—for so I think I may justly pronounce it!'

Adelaide during this interval of the Bishop, had not yet thoroughly recovered herself from the unspeakable transport of joy which the sight of her dear Enenique had occasioned. But when the good man had finished his congratulations to her lover, she attempted in broken accents to utter some expressions in return for the Bishop's kind wishes; however, the worthy prelate observing that she was not yet properly composed to deliver herself, kindly interrupted her; and taking her by the hand, addressed her as follows:

'Pardon me, my dear Adelaide, for being so abrupt as to interpose whilst you are speaking: but as I've said thus much to my worthy friend Don Enenique, suffer me also the indulgence of a word or two to you.—As for your part, Madam,' added he, with a most affable air, 'I well perceive that it is needless for me to tell you that you are fully recompensed for all you have suffered, by being in the possession of this virtuous and valuable man; and, as you have also expiated the fault of your disobedience (when you meditated your former flight with your lover) so I hope you will pass the remainder of your days in that uninterrupted state of felicity which in my opinion you both are so highly deserving of.'

This grave address of the Bishop recalled (as it was intended) the two lovers from their mutual transport; they both at once, as if informed by the same mind, threw themselves at the venerable man's feet, and embracing his knees, began to pour out the warmest acknowledgments that hearts overflowing with love and gratitude could suggest.—He raised them both up, and, presenting Madame Deffari (whom till now in the hurry of their joy they had overlooked) to the Chevalier, he quickly recollected her; and, being told it was to her he was indebted for seeing his Adelaide in Spain, he broke into fresh exclamations of praise, thanking Madame Deffari, and calling her his good angel. In short, Don Enenique having once given a loose to the transports of his heart, almost exhausted his strength in endeavouring to give them utterance.

Donna Cynthia had desired the Bishop of Seville to make a compliment on her part to the Chevalier, and to invite him to her castle; where he would find every thing more for his convenience than he could at his own house.—Don Enenique was easily prevailed on to accept of this offer; wherefore, finding himself now able to perform so short a journey, he was put in the Bishop of Seville's coach, who, with Madame Deffari and Adelaide, accompanied him to the Castle.

That amiable lady, Donna Cynthia, received him with all the tokens of complaisance and affection which a sincere and generous heart could dictate:—it was done in such a manner as convinced the Chevalier that she interested herself in his happiness; so that now being accommodated with every thing necessary to his present state, and, above all, blest with the company of his ever-dear Adelaide, he in a short space of time recovered his former health and spirits.

No obstacle now remaining to the joining the hands of this truly happy pair, the preparations for this ceremony were short, and without that pomp so much affected by the great, and so little essential to happiness. The Chevalier Ponces received his Adelaide from the hands of Signior Deffari, who came to the Castle of Cardonas for the purpose of being present on this happy occasion; and the good Bishop of Seville (who was so much delighted at their union) tied the nuptial knot of this amiable couple.

Donna Cynthia entertained her noble guests for several days at the Castle; where they spent the time in the greatest harmony and conviviality: and it was her wish and expectation to have had the happiness of their agreeable company for a considerable while, without the least interruption; but unluckily Signior Deffari received a packet, which informed him that his affairs immediately required his presence in Italy. As he was therefore under the necessity of taking his leave, he politely apologised to Donna Cynthia and the new-married couple, at the same time expressing an uneasiness at being obliged to withdraw himself earlier than he designed. Adelaide in her own mind was not displeased at this event, and gladly laid hold of the opportunity of returning home. She took however an unwilling leave of her valued friend, the Bishop of Seville: nor could she bid adieu to Cynthia and Clara without shedding tears,—the unhoped-for happiness she had found at the Castle of Cardonas, had endeared that spot to her so much; and though she carried thence the blessing it had put her in possession of, she could not take her leave of it without a considerable degree of regret. Donna Cynthia and Clara were equally affected at parting with so amiable and endearing a friend.

They all embarked together for Italy; where, being safely arrived, the first thing Adelaide did was to repair to Milan, to pay a visit to her old and dear friend Eugenia, whom she found in perfect contentment with the accomplished Don Clement; that gentleman having been prevailed on by his lady to remain still in Italy. Don Enenique and Adelaide stayed some time with the Marquis and Marchioness of Pescara, and then returned to Salerno (whither Signior Deffari and his lady had gone before); where they lived in the enjoyment of as perfect happiness as this life can afford.

THE END.

Explanatory Notes

Volume I

1. *Salerno . . . Naples*: located on the coast, Salerno is historically significant as the location of Europe's first medical school developed in the eleventh century. Prior to the novel's setting, the much-contested kingdom of Naples had been under Sicilian and, briefly, French rule but was governed by Spain from 1504 until the War of the Spanish succession (1701–1714).
2. *Seberina*: a variation of Santa Severina, a town in the region of Calabria in southern Italy, situated west of Crotone and northeast of Belcastro.
3. *Sulmona*: the birthplace of Ovid, Sulmona is located in the region of Abruzzo in southern Italy.
4. *Marquis of Pescara*: also a character in John Webster's *The Duchess of Malfi* resurrected, along with many others from that play, in Lewis Theobald's *The Fatal Secret: A Tragedy*. A Dublin edition was published in 1736 three years after *The Fatal Secret* was first performed at Covent Garden. Though of questionable originality, Madame d'Aulnoy's *Ingenious and Diverting Letters of a Lady's Travels into Spain,* first published in Paris in 1691, gives an account of Spanish nobles and lists the Marquis of Pescara as in possession of estates in Naples in the late seventeenth century. The book was popular throughout the first half of the eighteenth century. See, for example [Marie-Catherine Le Jumele de Barneville] Madame d'Aulnoy, *Ingenious and Diverting Letters of a Lady's Travels into Spain. Describing the Devotions, Nunneries, Humour, Customs, Laws, Militia, Trade, Diet, and Recreations of that People. Intermix't with Great Variety of Modern Adventures, and Surprising Accidents: Being the Truest and Best Remarks Extant, on that Court and Country,* 5th ed. (London: Printed for Samuel Crouch, 1703).
5. *Pimenteles . . . House of Telbes*: the name Pimenteles is possibly derived from that of the ambitious and formidable Fernando Álvarez de Toledo y Pimentel, third duke of Alba (1507–1582), who was made Viceroy of Naples by Philip II in 1556. Pimentel achieved distinction as a Castilian statesman but also notoriety in his role as governor-general of the Netherlands (1567–1573), during which time he established the Council of Troubles. Primarily designed to identify rebellious aristocrats, and sanction their execution, it was also known as the Council of Blood. The name Teles, if not Telbes, is significant in Castilian-Portuguese history. The fourteenth-century monarch, Ferdinand I, married Leonor Teles (1350–1386) who, upon her husband's death, acted as regent for their daughter, Beatriz. As a girl, Beatriz was married to John I of Castile and the stipulation that any male issue would inherit the throne of Portugal was the occasion of a significant dynastic crisis.

6. *Castile*: extensive region of peninsular Spain and its political and administrative centre since the early sixteenth century. At the time of the novel's setting the kingdom of Castile was one of the most densely populated areas of the Iberian Peninsula.
7. *Bassiniano*: possibly a reference to Bassiano, an area southeast of Rome which also lends its name to Portia's suitor in *The Merchant of Venice*.
8. *La Pointz*: possibly an allusion to Poins, the childhood companion of Prince Hal, with whom he shares a joke at Falstaff's expense in *Henry IV Parts 1* and 2. Variations in spelling, including to Poinz, in early play texts have led to the conjecture that Shakespeare 'intended him for a cadet of the family of Poyntz, one of high antiquity, found in *Doomsday Book,* under Gloucestershire.' See George Russell French, *Shakspeareana Genealogica Part I. Identification of the Dramatis Personae in Shakspeare's Historical Plays from K. John to K. Henry VIII* (London and Cambridge: Macmillan, 1869), 68.
9. *Lodi*: a town in Lombardy, northern Italy, southeast of Milan.
10. *Aurora*: perhaps a knowing literary allusion to Alain-René Lesage's picaresque novel, *Gil Blas* (1715–1735), in which the eponymous hero thinks himself promised an assignation in the garden at midnight with Aurora—the object of his passion—by her 'duenna' Dame Ortiz. In fact, it is Ortiz who appears in order to lead him to Aurora's apartment. Aurora explains she has summoned him to ask for his help in finding out more about the man upon whom she has set her sights.
11. *duenna*: 'in Spanish and Portuguese contexts: a (typically elderly) woman employed as a governess and companion to the young women or girls of a family' (*OED*). Richard Brinsley Sheridan's comic opera, *The Duenna*, was first staged on 21 November 1775 at Covent Garden.
12. *Ursina*: an earlier literary Ursina is the protagonist of one of several cautionary tales included in John Reynolds's *The Triumphs of God's Revenge against the Crying and Execrable Sin of Wilful and Premeditated Murther. With His Miraculous Discoveries, and Severe Punishment Thereof. In Thirty Several Tragical Histories; Digested into Six Books, Committed in Divers Countries beyond the Seas*. Reynolds was the author of stories ostensibly translated from originals written in France, Italy, Spain, Sweden, Portugal, and Germany, and further to publication of the first book in 1621, collected editions proved popular until the late 1770s. Disguise is to the fore in Ursina's Italian history of revenge upon her lover, Sanctifore, who is the father of her unborn child. When he abandons her to marry another woman, Ursina adopts a Friar's habit, kills him with a pistol and is executed for her crime.
13. *calash*: 'a kind of light carriage with low wheels, having a removable folding hood or top' (*OED*).
14. *governante*: a word derived from the Dutch and French, to mean in this instance governess or one entrusted with the supervision of young women.
15. *Carassa*: the name has noble but negative connotations in the figure of the Neopolitan Cardinal Oliviero Carafa who was elected Pope in 1555. An ally of France, he was violently opposed to the Habsburg dynasty and provoked hostilities with the Holy Roman Emperor Charles V and King Philip II of Spain. He was succeeded as pope by his nephew, Gian Pietro Carafa, who also persevered in anti-Spanish policy.
16. *Faustina*: Faustina the Younger was the wife of the second-century Roman Emperor Marcus Aurelius, but the choice of name is more likely an allusion to the Venetian mezzo-soprano Faustina Bordoni (*c.* 1700–1781), whose rivalry with Francesca Cuzzoni, a leading soprano, was a matter of public spectacle. Referred to only by her first name, Faustina had made her debut in Carlo Francesco Pollarolo's *Ariodante* in 1716, three years prior to the establishment of the Royal Academy of Music for the

purpose of encouraging operas. An accomplished actress and acknowledged beauty, Faustina made her London stage debut in 1726 in Handel's *Alessandro*, performing alongside Cuzzoni in a role which saw her triumph over her adversary to win the heart of the eponymous hero, played by another celebrity, the castrato Sensino. Handel composed for both women, though when Cuzzoni refused to sing an air he had written for her, he reputedly thought her possessed with 'the spirit of a devil' and threatened to throw her out of a window. Encouraged in their opposition by the rivalry which was also intensifying between their supporters, Faustina and Cuzzoni fought on stage during a performance of Bononcini's *Astianatte* in June 1727, and their antics are traced in the rivalry between Polly and Lucy in John Gay's *The Beggar's Opera* (1728). See Bryan Loughrey and T. O. Treadwell (eds), 'Introduction,' in John Gay, *The Beggar's Opera* (London: Penguin, 1986); William Coxe, *Anecdotes of George Frederick Handel, and John Christopher Smith* (London: Cadell and Davies, E. Harding, Birchall, and J. Eaton, 1799), 18.

17. *breviary*: 'in the Roman Catholic Church, the book containing the "Divine Office" for each day, which those who are in orders are bound to recite' (*OED*).
18. *Signior Ambrosia de Castellane . . . Sardinia*: Castellane is a small town situated on the banks of the Verdon river in the French Alps. The kingdom of Sardinia became part of Spanish territory with the accession of Charles I of Spain in 1516.
19. *home*: direct, to the point.
20. *Osorio*: the name is possibly borrowed from the eminent Portuguese prelate, theologian, scholar, and courtier Jerónimo Osório (1506–1580), who had originally studied civil law.
21. *Viceroy of Naples*: Naples became a Spanish territory in 1504 and for the next two centuries was ruled by Spanish government officials.
22. *memorial*: 'a statement of facts forming the basis of or expressed in the form of a petition or remonstrance to a person in authority, a government, etc.' (*OED*).
23. *Duchess D'Ossuna*: Osuna is a town in the province of Seville, in Andalusia, southwestern Spain. Don Pedro Téllez-Girón, 5th Count of Ureña, was created first duke of Osuna by King Philip II of Spain in 1562. His first wife, Leonor Ana de Guzmán, was kinswoman to the seventh duke of Medina-Sidonia, commander of the Spanish Armada in 1588.
24. *Chevalier de Ponces*: a Spanish connection to the name is Juan Ponce de León, an explorer who may have set sail with Columbus on his second expedition to the New World in 1493, and who is credited as the founder of the first European settlement in Puerto Rico.
25. *internuncio*: a borrowing from the Italian meaning go-between or intermediary.
26. *Sahabedras*: the house of Sahabedras was in the early sixteenth century presided over by the Earl of Castellar in Seuil, in the Ardennes region of northern France.
27. *piastres*: small silver coins of principal though not exclusive use in Spain and across the Spanish Empire and current from the late fifteenth-century to the French Revolution.

Volume II

1. *Valencia*: situated on the Mediterranean coast of Spain, Valencia was an autonomous dominion of James I of Aragon until 1479 when, further to the marriage of the Castilian heiress Isabella, to Ferdinand II of Aragon, it was united with the kingdom of Castile. Under their sovereignty, Valencia enjoyed economic and cultural prosperity.

2. *Guadimara*: silently corrected from Euadimara—reference to Guadimara is made again in Volume 2—this is likely in each instance a distorted reference to the Guadarrama, a tributary of the Iberian peninsula's longest river, the Tagus, which flows westwards across Spain to Lisbon, Portugal.
3. *Moorish*: in the late fifteenth century the Moors in Spain were threatened with exile unless they agreed to a Christian baptism, and by the 1520s, it was an offence to practise the Islamic faith. However, suspicion of these Christian converts, or Moriscos as they were called, prevailed and, after decades of antagonism and resistance on both sides, a royal decree in 1609 forced a five-year exodus.
4. *Genoa*: situated in the Liguria region of northwest Italy, the city of Genoa enjoyed relative economic prosperity in the sixteenth and seventeenth centuries. It is located approximately seventy-five miles from Clementina's next destination, Milan.
5. *Civita-Vechia*: founded in the second century (and meaning 'old city'), Civitavechia is situated on the coastline referred to as Centumcellae and has since become central Italy's principal port.
6. *Alicante*: an important port city in Valencia, southeast Spain and site of Santa Bárbara Castle, a large medieval fortress extensively developed during the reign of Philip II. In the early eighteenth century, during the War of the Spanish Succession, the city and the castle were briefly under English command before being surrendered to the French in 1709.
7. *Countess . . . Marchioness*: the wife of a marquis is more senior in rank than a countess, whose status is equivalent to that of an earl's wife in the British system of peerage.
8. *cloke*: French from which cloak is derived, and an acceptable, if rare alternative spelling.
9. *Philip the Third*: King of Spain and of Portugal (as Philip II) from 1598 to 1621. Though considered to have delegated responsibility for governance to a succession of favoured statesmen, Philip presided over a country which enjoyed peaceable relations with much of western Europe. Although Spain's principal antagonists continued to be the Turks and the Venetians, the King's treatment of its Moorish communities was the most contentious conflict of his reign.
10. *Escurial*: comprising a palace, monastery, and college, and under construction for much of the first half of the former King Philip II's forty-two-year reign, the Escorial is sited at the foothills of the Sierra de Gaudarrama and takes its name from its location in San Lorenzo de El Escorial, northwest of Madrid.
11. *Andalusia*: the southernmost region of Spain, and later setting for John O' Keeffe's comic opera *The Castle of Andalusia* (1782). An autonomous territory, Andalusia presently comprises eight provinces, which include Seville, Cadiz, and Jaén.
12. *Cadiz*: Cádiz is a seaport in Andalusia situated on a narrow peninsula which extends into the Atlantic at the Gulf of Cádiz. In the sixteenth century it was vulnerable to attack, principally from Barbary pirates or corsairs. See note 24.
13. *Bishop of Seville*: Seville is a province and capital city in Andalusia, which experienced the nadir and zenith of economic prosperity in the sixteenth century.
14. *Donna Clara d'Avilas*: the name possibly alludes to Saint Teresa of Ávila (1515–1582), the renowned daughter of the medieval city and province of Ávila de los Caballeros, situated in the Castile-León of Spain, some seventy miles northwest of Madrid. Canonised in 1622, she had established a convent in Ávila in 1562 for the purposes of advancing her reform of the Carmelite order to which she belonged. Her emphasis upon a more strict observance of the Carmelite's commitment to austerity and contemplation led to the creation of a new order of the Discalced Carmelite nuns and influenced the reform of monasteries.

15. *Cardonas . . . Aragon*: the duchy of Cardona incorporated estates in Castile, Andalusia, Catalonia, and Valencia, where, at least by the late seventeenth century, the duke of Segorbe also had land. See Madame d'Aulnoy's *Ingenious and Diverting Letters of a Lady's Travels into Spain*. Aragon, an historical region of northeastern Spain, is the origin of a dynasty of rulers who, from the medieval period until the fifteenth century, presided over territories which made for the Kingdom of Aragon.
16. *castle of Cardonas*: established in the ninth century by the Count of Barcelona, also known as Wilfred 'the Hairy,' the castle of Cardona is an impressive fortress in Catalonia, northern Spain which, during the fourteenth and fifteen centuries, belonged to the powerful dukes of Cardona. At the fall of Barcelona on 11 September 1714 in the War of the Spanish succession, the castle surrendered to the French and Castilian armies fighting for Philip V of Spain.
17. *Guadelquiver*: one of the longest rivers in Spain extending more than four hundred miles from its origin in the mountains of Jaén province to its mouth at the eastern end of the Gulf of Cádiz.
18. *St Ivorio*: the name is shared with F. Aliso de St. Ivorio, Secretary of the Holy Inquisition in Bologna, whose letter detailing the capture of Signor Gaudentio di Lucca prefaces the latter's equally fictitious *Memoirs*, published in 1737. Attributed until almost the end of the century to Bishop Berkeley, this popular romantic tale of intrigue and adventure, which sees the eponymous di Lucca settle for several years in the central African utopia, Mezzarannia, was written by Simon Berington. See Lee Monroe Ellison, 'Gaudentio di Luicca: A Forgotten Utopia,' *PMLA* 50, no. 2 (June 1935), 494–509. Clara Reeve imputed it to 'the pen of a master,' comparing it most favourably with *Robinson Crusoe* as a strikingly original narrative which 'may safely be put into the hands of youth.—Such books cannot be too strongly recommended, as under the disguise of fiction, warm the heart with the love of virtue, and by that means, excite the reader to the practice of it.' See *The Progress of Romance*, vol. 1 (Dublin: Printed for Price, Exshaw, White, Cash, Colbert, Marchbank and Porter, 1785), 124–5.
19. *Violante*: a name previously used for both scheming and saintly characters in such as John Beaumont's comedy, *The Spanish Curate* (1622), a possible collaboration with Philip Massinger, and *Wonder! A Woman Keeps a Secret*, Susan Centlivre's witty exploration of female ingenuity. *The Spanish Curate* was revived in the Restoration and early eighteenth century, and Centlivre's play, set in Lisbon at the close of the War of the Spanish Succession, was performed and first published in 1714.
20. *Biancha*: also the name of the lover of Cassio whose jealously is instrumental to Desdemona's downfall in Shakespeare's *Othello*.
21. *to a tittle*: 'with minute exactness, to the smallest particular, to a T' (*OED*).
22. *St. Hyronimo*: an order influenced by Eusebius Hieronymus, St Jerome, who founded a monastery in Bethlehem in the fourth century.
23. *brigantine*: 'a small vessel equipped both for sailing and rowing, swifter and more easily manœuvred than larger ships, and hence employed for purposes of piracy, espionage, reconnoitring' (*OED*).
24. *pirates of Barbary*: at their most formidable during the seventeenth century, these Muslim pirates operated from well-equipped vessels off the North African coast. The ships' captains in particular hailed from the Barbary strongholds of Algiers and Tunis, regions which had a long and contested history with the Turkish or Ottoman Empire.
25. *peep of day*: dawn.

26. *design against the Republic of Venice*: the volatile relationship between the Turks and the Spaniards in the first decades of the seventeenth century was frequently played out in the Adriatic or so-called Venetian Gulf. In 1618, a group of mostly French men resident in Venice were considered architects of a rumoured and unauthorised conspiracy to bring about the fall of the republic, and summarily executed. The origins and verity of the movement are as ambiguous as the part played in it by Pedro Telléz Girón, third duke of Osuna. Viceroy of the Spanish kingdom of Naples between 1616 and 1620, he has been both accused and acquitted of having given his assent to any such design.
27. *Rios.* Coto-Ríos is a small village in the remote mountainous Andalusian province of Jaén.

Silent Corrections

Volume I
Page Number

2 journies> journeys [stages]
5 sawand> saw and
5 ever yday> every day
6 appartment> apartment
11 oldwoman> old woman
12 feel> fell
12 bye-road> by-road
12 turnd> turned
15 own, “proceeded the Marquis,”> own (proceeded the Marquis)
16 this, “proceeded the Marquis,”> this (proceeded the Marquis)
16 had, “continued the Marquis,”> had (continued the Marquis)
16 conversation, “continued the Marquis,”> conversation (continued the Marquis)
17 is it> Is it
19 Abbe> Abbé
25 falshood> falsehood
25 was> were
26 atempt> attempt
29 engages> engage
30 inadvertance> inadvertence
38 in so much> insomuch
39 bye street> by-street
40 certainly> certainty
43 rouze> rouse
44 suffer ed> suffered
44 falshood> falsehood
47 this, “added she;”> (added she)
47 myfriend> my friend
49 Pimenteles’> Pimenteles’s
50 wave> waive
51 *ecclaircissement*> *éclaircissement*
53 villainy> villany
56 a-year> a year

Volume II
Page Number

61 Euadimara> Guadimara
64 vivicity> vivacity
66 st raits> straits
69 o> on
69 Alicant> Alicante
71 before hand> beforehand
72 Sahabedras'> Sahabedras's
74 know> knew
74 fi rst> first
76 attend-him> attended to
79 pagination 68> 86
80 gallopped> galloped
80 horses feet> horse's feet
80 villanous> villainous
84 a-year> a year
85 puzzles me: — [o?]ut however> puzzles me: — however
86 extremly> extremely
86 resoved> resolved
87 recal> recall
88 Arragon> Aragon
90 a-kin> akin
91 at the old> with the old
92 should not, pursued Donna Cynthia> should not (pursued Donna Cynthia)
92 *ecclaircissement*> *éclaircissement*
92 Pelvez> Pulvez
93 me, proceeded Donna Cynthia,> me (proceeded Donna Cynthia)
95 explain,> explain?
95 at me?> at me.
96 [as you imagined> as you imagined
97 incidents, pursued Donna Cynthia:'> incidents (pursued Donna Cynthia)
98 in so much> insomuch
98 whether> whither
101 particulars, continued Donna Cynthia,'> particulars (continued Donna Cynthia)
101 chamber-door> chamber door
103 These, continued Roderigo,> These (continued Roderigo)
104 changin> changing
105 bishop's> Bishop's
109 could not, "proceeded the Bishop,"> could not (proceeded the Bishop)
111 absolutelyrefusing> absolutely refusing
111 bedside> bed-side
114 extasy> ecstasy

For Product Safety Concerns and Information please contact our EU representative GPSR@taylorandfrancis.com
Taylor & Francis Verlag GmbH, Kaufingerstraße 24, 80331 München, Germany

www.ingramcontent.com/pod-product-compliance
Lightning Source LLC
Chambersburg PA
CBHW071525100726
47908CB00004B/1293

* 9 7 8 1 0 3 2 0 9 2 2 3 2 *